Secret Agenda

Secret *Agenda*

ROCHELLE
ALERS

NATIONAL BESTSELLING AUTHOR

ARABESQUE®

Recycling programs
for this product may
not exist in your area.

SECRET AGENDA

ISBN-13: 978-0-373-83135-7
ISBN-10:   0-373-83135-8

www.kimanipress.com

Printed in U.S.A.

Dear Reader,

Many of you have asked about the extended family and friends of the Coles, who were first introduced in *Hideaway*. My response is *Secret Agenda*. This latest novel continues the ongoing Hideaway Legacy series, with Diego Cole-Thomas taking center stage in this romance.

Stranger in My Arms provided a glimpse of Diego when he assumed control of ColeDiz International, Ltd. But as CEO of a privately held conglomerate, he takes the company in a new direction with its first stateside venture. However, when his business commitments conflict with his many social obligations, he hires recently widowed Vivienne Neal as his personal assistant. He is awed by her sensual beauty, intelligence and social grace, and Vivienne becomes his stand-in date and constant companion.

But when Vivienne finds herself doing double duty as a personal secretary and social escort to the CEO, who is well-known for his brusque manner and intimidating reputation, she doesn't realize until it's almost too late that she needs him to do more than just satisfy her long-denied sexual passion. Pursued by an assassin who will stop at nothing to retrieve her late husband's little black book, Vivienne must rely on the only man who can protect her from harm and restore her faith in love.

I invite you to join Diego and Vivienne on their journey of passion and intrigue, an adventure that will test their willingness to risk it all.

Yours in romance,

Rochelle Alers

HIDEAWAY SERIES

Everett Kirkland • Teresa Maldanado* • Samuel Cole • Marguerite Diaz[11]

Oscar Spencer• Regina Cole • Aaron Spencer
- Clayborne
- Eden

Martin Cole •Parris Simmons[1]

Tyler Cole • Dana Nichols[5]
- Martin, II
- Samuel II

Arianna

Nancy Cole • Noah Thomas

Timothy Cole-Thomas • Vivienne Neal[13]
- Diego Cole-Thomas
- Celia

Nichola Bennett
- Nicholas

Ynez
Grace
Malinda

Josephine Cole • Ivan Wilson
- Gisela
- Esther
- Joseph
- Felipe
- Ashley

David Cole • Serena Morris[

Gabriel Cole • Summer Montgomery[10]
- Imanuel
- Anthony
- Imani

Alexandra Cole • Merrick Grayslake[12]
- Victoria
- Cordero

Jason/Anna (twins)

Matthew Sterling • Eve Blackwell[4]

Christopher Delgado • Alejandro Delgado[2]
- Alejandro

Joshua Kirkland* • Vanessa Blanchard[7]
- Esperanza
- Matteo

Sara Sterling • Selem Lassiter[4]
- Isaiah
- Eve/Nora (twins)

Emily Kirkland[7]

Michael Kirkland • Jolene Walker[8]
- Teresa
- Joshua-Michael
- Merrick

LEGEND
* - Illegitimate Birth
1 - Hideaway
2 - Hidden Agenda
3 - Vows
4 - Heaven Sent
5 - Harvest Moon
6 - Just Before Dawn
7 - Private Passions
8 - No Compromise
9 - Homecoming
10 - Renegade
11 - Best Kept Secrets
12 - Stranger In My Arms
13 - Secret Agenda

PART ONE
Diego Cole-Thomas
ColeDiz International Ltd.

Prologue

James McGhie turned the key in the ignition of the stolen car, and put the heat on its highest setting. Despite wearing a pair of his mama's hand-knit woolen gloves, his fingers were beginning to stiffen up from the cold. He knew sitting in a car with the engine running was certain to draw attention, but he wasn't going to risk the freezing weather, because then he would have to explain to Mrs. McGhie why her precious baby boy—as she referred to him—had frostbite. There were some things he told Mama but many more things he didn't. James realized there were hazards to his job, but losing a digit or two was not in his game plan.

He'd sat patiently waiting for his target to reappear, but the frigid D.C. temperature made his wait very uncomfortable. He took a quick glance at his watch. Forty minutes had passed since U.S. Representative Sean Gregory entered the bank across the street from where he sat in an old black sedan.

He sat up straighter, one hand going to the earpiece. "I just spotted him."

"Where is he, Jimmy?" asked the gravelly voice in his ear.

"He just came out of the bank near the Dupont Circle Metro."

"Stay with him."

The man who'd been trained by the country's best intelligence agency peered through a pair of binoculars, his gaze fixed on his target. He'd spent days waiting for the brash young politician to leave his Georgetown town house. The day before, McGhie had gone to the town house but Gregory's housekeeper had told him her employer wasn't feeling well and wasn't receiving visitors. But from the looks of the nattily dressed man sauntering down the street, he appeared to be the picture of health. Everything about him—his cashmere topcoat and expensive, tailored dark suit—reeked of arrogance, and that included his walk.

"He just got into his car," James whispered into the microphone under his jacket lapel.

"Follow him for a couple of blocks, and then we'll take over."

He followed the late-model Lexus sedan until a black Ford Crown Victoria smoothly maneuvered in front of his bumper several yards ahead. He'd done what he'd been instructed to do and now the rest was up to the men in the Crown Vic. Personally, he liked the Connecticut congressman. But he couldn't afford to let his personal feelings interfere with completing his assignment.

He'd been instructed to follow Congressman Gregory and report back when he was alone. If the men who were hired to take out Sean Gregory didn't find what they were looking for on him, then it was up to McGhie to break into the congressman's home and search for the little book that could become a huge political scandal.

James sat in a well-worn recliner watching CNN, while enjoying his second beer after several helpings of his mother's delicious lamb stew. He'd stopped off to have dinner with her, leaving with enough plastic containers filled with leftovers to last him for several days, before retreating to his sanctuary—a furnished studio apartment in a middle-class D.C. neighborhood.

He turned up the volume on the remote when the program he had been watching was interrupted for a breaking news story. An obviously grief-stricken Speaker of the House announced that Connecticut Congressman Sean Gregory had succumbed to injuries he'd sustained in a hit-and-run earlier that morning as he'd stepped out of his car only yards from his Georgetown residence.

The camera shifted to a scene outside the town house where the media, police, the crime scene unit and a crowd of onlookers had gathered. The television reporter announced that the late congressman's wife, who'd flown in from Stamford, Connecticut to attend a fund-raiser, was unaware that her husband had been fatally injured until she arrived at their home. A spokesperson for the Gregory family reported Vivienne Gregory was too distraught to talk to the press.

Cursing under his breath, James pressed a button on the remote and turned off the television. Vivienne Gregory's decision to make a visit to D.C. had changed everything. His cell phone rang seconds later and he answered it before the third ring.

"Yeah," he drawled, dispensing with any pretense of

being polite. While he detested the man who'd paid him to do his dirty work, it was his voice that he hated even more.

"He didn't have the book on him, and with the little wife in town it means that you have to figure out another way to get into—"

"I know it changes everything," he said testily, interrupting the caller on the other line. The man who he took his orders from had messed up—big-time! In his attempt to eliminate the popular congressman they'd forgotten about his wife. They were lucky *if* Gregory took what he knew to his grave. If not, then whatever Gregory had uncovered was certain to rock Capitol Hill to its venerable core.

The young woman who'd befriended Gregory's chief-of-staff had told James that the congressman carried a small leather-bound notebook at all times—a notebook James's boss suspected contained the names of other congressional members who'd received kickbacks on government contracts in their districts. Another source at the Justice Department revealed that Gregory had requested and had been given immunity *if* he informed on those *"on the take."*

The well-orchestrated hit-and-run had eliminated Sean Gregory, but finding the snitch's little black book was now a priority for James McGhie. After the police completed their investigation, he would have to break into the town house, look for the book and then leave without a trace.

Chapter 1

Six months later...

"**Y**ou'd be perfect for the position as Diego Cole-Thomas's personal assistant, Viv."

Vivienne Neal stared intently at her old college roommate, her expression impassive. Alicia Cooney was the only person she let call her Viv. To everyone else she was Vivienne. Suddenly a smile began to curl around Vivienne's mouth, her lips parting and displaying a set of perfectly aligned white teeth. "That's what you said about my last interview, which I'm embarrassed to say was a miserable failure."

Alicia's eyebrows lifted in surprise. She could count on one hand the number of times she'd seen her friend smile in the two months since Vivienne had moved to Florida. Vivienne's expression softened, revealing her delicate features, cinnamon-brown complexion, a round face with high cheekbones, a delicate chin, sensual mouth and tawny-colored eyes that had a slightly startled look.

"It wasn't because you weren't qualified. The wife of your potential employer saw you as a threat. The difference here is Diego Cole-Thomas doesn't have a wife."

Vivienne's smiled vanished quickly. "I am not a home wrecker. And if that had been my intent, I certainly wouldn't have been with a man who's more than twice my age."

"Charles Willingham isn't your average run-of-the-mill, thrice-married, sixty-nine-year-old letch. I heard somewhere that he likes to pinch his female employees' behinds. He gets away with it because if they complain, he either pays them off or he marries them. It helps that he's one of the wealthiest men on Florida's Gold Coast."

Vivienne waved a hand. "I didn't let him get close enough to touch me and I could care less about his money."

Alicia rolled her vivid emerald-green eyes upward. "That's because you never had to concern yourself with money, unlike me who grew up dirt-poor. If I hadn't been blessed with brains and this face and body," she drawled while waving her hand in front of her chest, "I'd still be slinging hash in a diner like my sisters, mother and grandmother. Luckily, I learned early on how to capitalize on my assets," Alicia continued, so matter-of-factly that Vivienne knew it wasn't a boast.

She smiled again. Alicia had used her brains and her physical assets to her advantage when she attended college on full scholarship and succeeded in marrying a first-round NBA draft pick. Petite, blond, green-eyed Alicia Cooney had caught the eye of Rhames Tyson during freshman orientation, and dated him exclusively throughout college much to the consternation of many of the African-American coeds.

A week before graduation, Rhames signed a multimillion-dollar contract with a California pro basketball team, when Alicia informed him that she was pregnant with his child.

Vivienne was Alicia's maid of honor in a wedding that became a media spectacle. But Alicia's Cinderella marriage ended when her husband insisted on driving—although his blood alcohol level exceeded the legal limit—totaling his six-figure import. He also shattered both knees, which ended his pro ball career. Alicia lost the baby and Vivienne invited her friend to stay with her and recuperate from the physical and emotional injuries. Less than a year after exchanging vows, Alicia filed for divorce, moved to Florida and set up an executive staffing agency.

Now, their situations were reversed. After losing Sean, Vivienne decided to list their mausoleum of a house in an exclusive, upscale gated community in Stamford, Connecticut with a real estate agent. She put the contents of the house in storage and moved to West Palm Beach, Florida, to stay with Alicia until she figured out what she wanted to do with her life. Her parents had wanted her to move in with them, but at thirty-one she didn't want to be treated like a child again. She'd fought too hard for her independence to now relinquish it to her overbearing mother.

She ran a hand over her straightened dark-brown hair with reddish highlights. It was longer than it had been in years. Sean had been dead six months and she had to pull herself out of her funk.

"Tell me about Diego Cole-Thomas before I agree to an interview."

Alicia crossed her bare feet at the ankles as she lay back on the cushioned chaise on the lanai. "I happen to know him better than most of my clients," she began.

"You've dated him?" Vivienne asked.

"I wish," Alicia countered. "Unfortunately our interaction has always been professional. His company's HR will usually contact me whenever they're looking to fill a position. I'm surprised they contacted me again, because you'll be the third applicant I've referred to ColeDiz International over the past four months."

Vivienne's gaze narrowed. "What happened to the other two?"

"One lasted about a week before Diego sent her packing and the other lasted a month before he was terminated. Both were supposed to be on call, but whenever he needed them they either were unavailable or didn't know how to organize his social and business schedule."

"And, what makes you think I'll be more successful than the other two?"

"You were the wife of a congressman so you're familiar with the demands of a high-powered man. Plus you have a business background and you're also bilingual. The position is for six months and pays extremely well. You won't…" Alicia's words trailed off as she averted her gaze to stare at a tiny lizard crawling up the screen.

"I won't what?" Vivienne asked, leaning forward on her lounger.

"You'll have to make yourself available 24/7. Diego's an international businessman, so if he's up at two in the morning talking to someone on the other side of the world he may need his assistant to be available, too."

"So, I'd become a live-in personal assistant?"

"Yes," Alicia said after a long pause. "I'm certain he'll hire you because you're confident and assertive. He fired the first applicant because she locked herself in the ladies' room, and refused to come out after he'd reprimanded her."

Vivienne knew her friend made a living from the fees clients paid Alicia's placement agency. But lately, Vivienne found herself tired of sleeping late and hanging around the pool bemoaning the turn her life had taken. No one other than her attorney knew at the time of her husband's death that she'd planned to divorce Sean Gregory anyway. She'd told the reporter who'd managed to get around the police barricade that she'd come to Washington to attend a fund-raiser with Sean. But, the truth was she'd come to tell her husband that her attorney had filed documents to end their four-year sham of a marriage.

She sat up. "Set up the interview, Alicia."

"Yes," Alicia whispered as she pumped her fist in the air. Her company had grown from placing nannies and au pairs with wealthy couples who were either too lazy or disinclined to care for their own children, to providing executive and support staff for several Florida-based companies, of which ColeDiz International Ltd. was one.

When she'd heard that her friend had lost her husband, she hadn't hesitated when she booked a flight to Connecticut to be with Vivienne. The public viewed Vivienne Gregory as the beautiful grieving widow of one of Washington's young rising stars. But it wasn't the loss of her husband Vivienne grieved most, but that of a marriage that'd ended before it had a chance to begin. She'd been a political widow four years before she legally became one.

Diego Cole-Thomas closed the shades to shut out the blinding rays of the summer sun before taking his seat at a round table in the anteroom of his office with his cousin and confidant. He'd asked Joseph Cole-Wilson Jr. to meet with him over breakfast because he wanted to discuss a venture that was certain to change the family-owned conglomerate forever.

Diego had celebrated his first year as CEO in April, and it'd taken twelve months to gain the complete confidence of his employees, managers and board of directors to move the company in another direction. Diego's great-grandfather, Samuel Claridge Cole, had set up the company in 1925, and more than eighty years later not much had changed. The board of directors was expanded to include nonfamily members, but every CEO was a direct descendant of Samuel Cole. Martin and David, sons of Samuel, held the position before Diego's father Timothy Cole-Thomas took over the helm. He was now the fourth generation and fifth chief executive officer of a company with holdings that included coffee plantations in Mexico, Jamaica, Puerto Rico and Brazil, vacation properties throughout the Caribbean and banana plantations in Belize.

His first action upon assuming control was to become a cotton broker. He paid cash on delivery to a Ugandan cotton grower, making ColeDiz the biggest family-owned agribusiness in the United States.

Ignoring the cup of coffee next to him, Diego stared at Joseph. He knew his cousin was still smarting because he'd requested the eight o'clock meeting the day the corporate attorney was scheduled to begin a two-week vacation with his longtime girlfriend.

"What I want to tell you will not take much of your time."

"Gracias, primo," Joseph whispered in Spanish under his breath.

A slight frown was the only indication of Diego's annoyance with his younger cousin for the unsolicited aside. He'd brought the twenty-eight-year-old into the company, but after five months Joseph still hadn't shown any initiative. If their grandmothers hadn't been sisters, Diego would've fired him his first week on the job.

Even though his last name was Wilson, Joseph's looks were undeniably Cole. He'd inherited Marguerite-Josefina Diaz-Cole, his Cuban-born great-grandmother's, olive coloring and refined features. His close-cropped curly black hair, large dark eyes and sensual mouth had many of the single female employees openly lusting after him. However, once word got out that he was dating a girl he'd met in law school, a collective groan could be heard from his admirers.

"I wanted to tell you before you leave that ColeDiz will establish its first American-based company before the end of the year."

Joseph sat forward in his chair. "What about the coffee plantation in Lares, Puerto Rico?"

Diego inclined his head. "I should've said a company on the mainland."

"*¿Dónde sobre la tierra firme,* Diego?"

Diego's expression didn't change. "*Carolina del Sur.*" The only time he spoke Spanish at the office was when he and Joseph were alone. His mother didn't speak the language, but his *abuela* Nancy spoke only Spanish whenever he and his siblings visited with her. Nancy Cole-Wilson never wanted him to forget his African and Cuban roots.

"What the hell is in South Carolina?"

Planting an arm on the table, Diego cradled his chin on the heel of his hand. "Tea."

Joseph's eyes grew wide. "Tea?" he repeated.

"*Sí, primo. Té.* ColeDiz is going to get into the business

of growing and manufacturing tea, and I'm going to put you in charge of our first North American venture."

The light that fired the jet-black orbs dimmed. "I know nothing about tea. I'm a lawyer, not a farmer, Diego."

"I'm not a farmer, yet I know the entire process of growing and harvesting coffee and bananas."

Joseph wasn't about to argue with his cousin, because he knew he would come out on the losing end. So, he decided to try another approach. "Isn't tea only grown in Asia?"

Diego lifted his eyebrows. "That's what most people believe. But, there's only one tea garden or plantation in America, and it's on Wadmalaw Island in the South Carolina low country."

"Where do you plan on setting up this plantation?"

"I had someone buy a hundred acres between Kiawah and Edisto Islands. When you return from your vacation I want you to negotiate the transfer of the property to ColeDiz. We'll put in the tea shrubs late fall and hopefully we'll be able to get our first harvest next spring and the second harvest in the summer. And if the warm weather holds throughout the winter, then we can expect another harvest."

Joseph stared at the man who looked enough like their great-grandfather Samuel to have been his twin. And, the family joke was that Diego was as driven as the man who was known as the consummate twentieth-century deal maker.

"Should I assume that you don't want anyone to know about the venture until you begin planting?"

Diego nodded. "You assume correctly."

"Have you run this by the rest of the family?"

Silence shrouded the room, swelling in intensity as the two men continued their stare-down. Diego blinked once. "Enjoy your vacation, Joseph."

The younger man pushed to his feet. His cousin had just unceremoniously dismissed him. "I will." That said, he turned on his heels and walked out of the room, slamming the door behind him. Joseph liked that he'd become part of the family-owned company, but it wasn't easy with Diego as his boss. Diego worked nonstop and expected everyone else to do the same.

He walked down carpeted hallway to the elevator in the luxury office building. Joseph wanted to tell Diego that he didn't need to set up another company. What he needed was a woman to make him aware that there was a world and life beyond ColeDiz International Ltd.

Diego stared blankly, focusing on the space where his cousin had been, his mind working overtime in anticipation of setting up a new venture. Despite being a brilliant corporate attorney, Joseph was not a risk taker. He didn't want to get into farming when in fact it was farming that afforded him his opulent lifestyle, much to the delight of his social-climbing girlfriend. Now, if Joseph worked as hard as he played there would be no doubt he would become CEO if or when Diego decided to relinquish the title and the responsibilities that went along with running the company. Their great-grandfathers, Samuel Cole and José Luis Diaz, for whom Joseph was named, were farmers. Farming had made the Coles one of the wealthiest, if not the wealthiest, black family in the States.

Reaching for his fork, he speared a chunk of fresh pineapple. He ate slowly, finishing his breakfast, which included freshly squeezed orange juice, sliced pineapple and black coffee. He'd just touched the napkin to his mouth when the intercom rang.

Recognizing the extension on the display, Diego pressed a button on the telephone console. "Yes, Caitlin."

"Good morning, Diego. I have someone in my office I want you to meet. Her name is Vivienne Neal and I believe she would be perfect for the position as your personal assistant. Are you available to meet with her now?"

He wanted to tell the head of human resources that she'd said the same thing about the other two candidates, but held his tongue because Caitlin had him on speaker. "Yes."

"I'm faxing you her résumé as we speak and I'll bring her around in about fifteen minutes."

Once he'd taken over control of ColeDiz, his respect for his father increased appreciably. He didn't know how Timothy Cole-Thomas had managed both business and social obligations without them overlapping until Timothy disclosed that his stay-at-home wife, Nichola, had become his social secretary and personal assistant. Nichola checked with his personal secretary every day to make certain dinner meetings, fund-raisers or family get-togethers did not conflict. Unlike his father, Diego didn't have a wife, so he'd decided to hire a personal assistant.

He cleared the table of his breakfast, slipped on his suit jacket and tightened his tie. Removing the pages from the tray of the fax machine, he'd glanced over Vivienne Neal's résumé, Googled her name and was standing behind his desk when Caitlin escorted her into his office. Caitlin nodded, smiling, and closed the door behind her.

Vivienne felt her heart stop, her breath catching in her chest for several seconds before she was able to breathe normally. She'd used Alicia's computer to bring up what she could on ColeDiz International Ltd., but uncovered very little about the company's CEO. The Coles, like many wealthy families, kept a low profile. Their names appeared in the press only when linked to a business deal or charitable event. They also were fortunate to have lived their lives relatively free of gossip and scandal.

The man standing with his back to floor-to-ceiling windows spanning the width of the expansive room appeared to have been carved out of stone. He was tall, broad-shouldered and it'd only taken a single glance to recognize the exquisite cut and fabric of his suit. However, it wasn't his clothes that drew her rapt attention, but his face.

He rounded the desk and she saw up close the lean, angular sable-brown face with large, deep-set dark eyes that glowed with confidence under black sweeping eyebrows. Chiseled cheekbones, a straight nose with slightly flaring nostrils and a strong, firm mouth and cleft chin completed the undeniably male image that was Diego Samuel Cole-Thomas.

Diego approached, right hand extended. "Good morning, Ms. Neal."

Vivienne felt a slight shock race up her arm when Diego's hand captured hers. She inclined her head. "Mr. Thomas."

"It's not Thomas, but Cole-Thomas."

Vivienne's eyebrows lifted slightly with his terse response. *Oh, that's what you're all about?* she mused. Mr. Cole-Thomas was the personification of an egotist. She inclined her head again, the gesture conveying her apology. "I stand corrected, Mr. Cole-Thomas."

A slight frown appeared between Diego's eyes. Vivienne Neal's body language said one thing and her facetious apology another. It was apparent the woman applying for the position as his personal assistant was not

only beautiful and tastefully dressed, but also not easily intimidated, which meant she wouldn't dissolve into tears the
way her predecessor had. Cupping her elbow, he led her
into the anteroom where he held informal meetings.
Instead of sitting at the round table, he directed her to sit
in a tan leather chair, seated her, then sat in a matching
facing chair.

Diego forced himself not to stare at the long shapely legs
under the pencil skirt that was part of a navy-blue linen suit
that Vivienne had paired with a white silk blouse and
stylish blue-and-white spectator pumps. Aside from the
pearl studs in her ears, her only other jewelry accessory was
a gold band with three rows of diamonds on the middle
finger of her right hand. While it was impossible to ascer-
tain the length of her hair, which she'd pinned up in a
French twist, it'd only taken a single glance to conclude
that Vivienne Neal was no ordinary personal assistant, pos-
sessing the style and elegance of a wealthy woman.

*"Aunque no conocí a su marido, me gustaría extender
mis condolencias sobre su muerte prematura."*

"Gracias, Señor Cole-Tomas." Vivienne replied fluidly
in the same language.

She wondered if Diego had offered his condolences on
the death of her husband in Spanish to confirm that she was
as fluent as her résumé indicated, having held a position
translating financial contracts with a leading international
investment firm.

A hint of a smile parted her lips. "Did I pass the test?"

Diego crossed one leg over the opposite knee and
pressed his forefinger alongside his face, in a gesture that
reminded her of a famous image of Malcolm X. "At least
I know you understand Spanish."

Vivienne felt a shiver of annoyance snake its way up her spine. She wanted to tell Diego Cole-Thomas that she didn't need the position as much as she needed a diversion, something to keep her mind occupied. With the proceeds from the sale of the house in Connecticut and as sole beneficiary of Sean's life insurance, it wasn't necessary for her to secure immediate employment.

Even before they were married, she'd told her fiancé that she had no intention of living year-round in the nation's capital. But that didn't stop Sean from spending a great deal of his time in Georgetown, because he'd believed that she would eventually change her mind and live with him in D.C. when the House was in session. Vivienne had proven him wrong, including the period leading up to his untimely death.

Her accountant recommended that she hold on to the Georgetown property, so she'd rented it fully furnished to a couple who wanted to use the first floor for their architectural and interior design business and the two upper floors as personal living space.

She'd dropped out of sight for six months, playing the role of a grieving widow. The police still hadn't found the car or the driver responsible for the hit-and-run that left her late husband fatally injured. But the officer assigned to the case informed her it would remain open.

Vivienne blinked once. "I understand, speak and write Spanish. I'm also fluent in French and Italian." There was just a hint of boastfulness in her tone.

She glared at the arrogant man who seemed to challenge her without saying a word. If he wanted a personal assistant who was fluent in Spanish, then she was it. But, if he thought he was going to intimidate her with veiled challenges to her competence, then she wasn't the one for the job.

However, she was forced to admit that everything about Diego exuded power and breeding, from his well-groomed hair to the soles on his imported shoes. A slight frown touched her brow. It could've been the light, but there was something very wrong with his socks. Realization dawned. He was wearing one blue and one brown sock with his dark blue pin-striped suit and black leather wing tips.

"Are you aware that you're wearing two different color socks?"

Diego lowered his leg, lifted the hem of his trousers and stared at his feet. "The laundry service must have mismatched them."

"You're color-blind." Her question was a statement.

"Yes."

"Do you see red and green?"

"Yes," Diego admitted. "It's the blues and yellows I have a problem differentiating."

The seconds ticked off as he continued to regard the woman who sat separated from him by less than five feet. There was something about Vivienne Neal he liked—and it had nothing to do with her face or body. She was professional and straightforward, and he doubted if another prospective employee would've pointed out the fact that his socks were mismatched.

"You're more than qualified for the position, given your education and work experience," Diego said quietly, in the drawling cadence of one who'd grown up in the South. "But the fact remains that I've hired two personal assistants with similar credentials and I've had to let them go."

Vivienne smiled for the first time. The expression shocked Diego as he sat up straighter. Her smile was as sensual as the rest of her. "Perhaps the third time will be the charm."

Diego nodded, praying she had more going for her than her pretty face and killer body. "Let's hope you're right, Ms. Neal. Our human resources department will contact you with my decision once they verify your references." Rising from his chair, he extended his hand and pulled Vivienne gently to her feet. What could pass for a smile softened his mouth. "Thanks for the heads-up on my socks."

She gave him an open, warm smile for the first time. "You're welcome."

He released her hand. "Someone from security will escort you to your car."

Vivienne walked to the door, feeling the heat from Diego's gaze behind her. Even if she hadn't impressed him, she knew her résumé had. And, it wasn't until she was seated in her rental car, driving back to Alicia's house that she admitted to herself that she wanted the position as Diego Cole-Thomas's personal assistant—not because she viewed the position as a challenge, but because the man with whom she would work was the *real* challenge.

Diego lost track of time as he rested his feet on the corner of his desk, staring out the wall of glass facing the West Palm Beach skyline. Twice he'd reached for the telephone receiver and both times he'd stopped himself. He didn't know what it was, but there was something so inexplicably seductive about Vivienne Neal—a sensuality he'd never encountered in any woman whom he'd met or been involved with.

She was well-spoken, appropriately dressed for an interview and conducted herself professionally. However, she had exhibited a haughtiness when he'd questioned her about her ability to read, write and speak Spanish, and he'd been forthcoming when he told Vivienne that she was overqualified. However, he didn't need her to translate contracts, because there were attorneys and paraprofessionals on staff who were well versed in languages and legal terms to do that. What he needed from Vivienne was strictly personal.

Lowering his feet, he swung around, picked up the telephone receiver and tapped an extension. It was rare that Diego made direct contact with any of his managers. He usually left that task to Lourdes Wallace, his secretary, or as she preferred—executive assistant.

"Human Resources, Caitlin Novak speaking."

The corners of Diego's mouth inched upward. Within three months of taking over as CEO, he'd instituted subtle changes that he'd believed were a long time coming. At a staff meeting the employees were informed that whenever they answered the telephone they were to identify their department and themselves, giving their full names. An incident involving a representative from an overseas bank, who was placed on hold indefinitely, had become the impetus for the mandate.

"Caitlin, this is Diego. I want you to contact Ms. Neal and let her know that she's hired."

A slight gasp came through the earpiece. "But, I haven't checked her references."

"You can check her references later. I need her for this weekend. I want you to messenger an official offer letter. Also, make arrangements to have her clothes and whatever else she'll need delivered to my house."

There came a pause before Caitlin spoke again. "Is there anything else, Diego?"

"I can't think of anything right now. Thank you, Caitlin."

"You're welcome."

It was done. He'd hired the widow of one of Washington's rising political stars to become his personal assistant. Now, he had to make one more call—this to confirm if Vivienne Neal was qualified to function as his personal hostess, also.

Diego dialed a number that went directly to voice mail. "Jacob, this is Diego. I need you to find out what you can on a Vivienne Kay Neal Gregory. She happens to be Sean Gregory's widow. Please get back to me before Friday. Later."

He hung up feeling more relaxed than he had in months. It wouldn't take weeks or even days to find out whether Vivienne Neal was suited for the position as his personal assistant. However, she would be put to the test this upcoming weekend. Face, body, intelligence and experience aside—he would let her go as quickly as the two before her.

Chapter 2

"Don't believe him, Blair!" Vivienne screamed at the television. "Todd Manning lied to you before and he'll do it again," she said, continuing her rant.

A basket filled with clothes she'd taken out of the dryer and folded sat at her feet. It'd been more than a decade since she'd watched her soap operas. *All My Children* and *One Life to Live,* as well as life in Pine Valley and Landview had seemingly stood still. The principal characters hadn't aged, while their children were now adults with children of their own.

In a way, her life had paralleled a soap opera. She'd known the moment she saw Sean Gregory that she would one day become his wife. Perhaps it was because Sean was her brother's college roommate, or maybe it was because everyone claimed they were so well suited to each other.

They became engaged a week following his law school graduation and married a year before he threw his hat into the political ring, winning the seat his father had vacated in the previous election when he retired due to failing health. The elder Gregory lived long enough to witness his son being sworn in as a member of Congress before succumbing to a rare blood disorder. Elizabeth Deavers Gregory, who'd buried her husband and then her son, was now a recluse.

Although she and Sean had talked about starting a family, their timing was always off. And whenever Congress was in recess and Sean returned to Stamford it wasn't to spend time with his wife. Congressman Gregory's social calendar was filled with golf outings, yacht and lawn parties, backyard cookouts, and lunch and dinner meetings with constituents whom he could count on to back his reelection bid.

The chiming of Vivienne's cell phone interrupted her thoughts, and she reached down between the cushions of the sofa to answer it. "Hello."

"I'd like to speak to Vivienne Neal."

"This is she."

"Ms. Neal, this is Caitlin Novak, and I'm calling to inform you that we would like to welcome you to ColeDiz International as our newest employee."

Vivienne felt her stomach muscles contract. "Are you saying I'm hired?"

"That's exactly what I'm saying, Ms. Neal."

"But…but you told me you had to check my references."

"We will, but it's just that Mr. Cole-Thomas needs an assistant this coming weekend."

Vivienne went completely still. "This weekend?" she repeated. "Are you talking about the day after tomorrow?"

"Yes, Ms. Neal. And, because we are dealing with such a short time frame, I suggest you pack whatever you'll need as quickly as possible. Mr. Cole-Thomas wants you ready to begin working Friday evening."

She wanted to tell the personnel director that Mr. Cole-Thomas was fortunate because she only had to pack her clothes and personal items, but didn't. Her winter clothes, along with her furniture, were in a Connecticut warehouse.

"You'll receive a packet from a messenger service later this afternoon. He's been instructed to wait while you sign several documents we'll need to complete your employment process. I'm also including the name and number of a moving company that will transport your possessions to Mr. Cole-Thomas's house."

Vivienne tried processing all that'd happened that morning. She'd been interviewed by a man who unsettled her more than she'd wanted to admit, hired four hours later and was expected to move in with him before the start of the weekend.

"Please let Mr. Cole-Thomas know that I'll move in tomorrow."

There came a pause before Caitlin said, "I'm sorry, Ms. Neal, but that may prove to be a problem."

There was something in the personnel director's voice that sounded ominous. "What kind of a problem?"

"Mr. Cole-Thomas expects you to move in today. If you require assistance packing, then I'll have someone come over and help you. Don't worry about moving supplies…"

"Kindly tell Mr. Cole-Thomas that it's impossible for me to move in today, even with assistance," Vivienne said, interrupting the woman.

There was no way she was going to jump just because her so-called new boss asked her. After all, as an employee she did have rights. He'd probably fired her two predecessors because they weren't willing to give in to his unreasonable demands.

There was another pause on the other end of the line. "I'll let Mr. Cole-Thomas know that you won't be available until tomorrow."

Vivienne managed a tight smile although Caitlin couldn't see her. "Thank you."

She ended the call, fuming inwardly. The nerve of him! He wasn't a boss, but a tyrant. If, and she meant *if*, they were to have an association of any duration, then he would come to know that Vivienne Neal didn't frighten easily, nor had she ever been one to play fetch.

Within minutes her cell phone rang again; she recognized the number on the display. "I guess you've heard," she said without her usual greeting.

"I can't believe he hired you so quickly," Alicia said, her voice rising in excitement.

"He wants me to move in today," she informed her friend.

"What's the problem, Viv? You only have to pack your clothes and books. I can run you over to his house when I get off."

"That won't be necessary. He's arranged to have someone move my things."

"Then what's the holdup? Don't you want this job?"

"Yes, I want it."

"Then, act like you want it, Viv. You and I both know that returning to work is what you need to deal with your depression."

Vivienne wanted to tell Alicia that she wasn't depressed, but angry. She'd allowed herself to become her mother— a trophy wife. She only visited D.C. when Sean was invited to state dinners or White House gatherings and when he needed her on his arm. In essence she'd become arm candy. She'd always been amused by the curious stares directed at her whenever Congressman Gregory introduced her as his wife. After a while she wondered if the men knew something she didn't. Did Sean have a mistress tucked away in D.C.? Had he fathered a secret love child—a child that should've been theirs?

"I am not depressed, Alicia."

"Then, what are you? You tell me you're ready to go back to work and I've managed to hook you up with the perfect position. I know you don't need the money. However, I do need the commission."

"Why didn't you tell me you needed money?" Vivienne asked her friend.

"I'm not broke, Viv. It's just that I don't want to use my personal funds to subsidize my business. The commission I'll get from ColeDiz will cover my office expenses for three months."

She knew Alicia rented desk space in a posh Palm Beach office building. She claimed her clients were more ame- nable to her fees with an exclusive address. One thing she did know about Alicia Cooney was that she was terrified of being poor again. Instead of looking to marry well the second time, she'd decided to go into business for herself. Her staffing agency was small, but her elite clients afforded her a comfortable lifestyle, and Vivienne didn't want to do anything to jeopardize her friend's commission, so she decided to compromise.

"Call Caitlin Novak and tell her that I'll be ready to begin working tonight."

Why, she mused when she ended the call, did it sound as if she'd made herself available for a rendezvous?

As promised, Diego sent two men over to pick up eight cartons containing her clothes, books and other personal items. Three hours later Vivienne came face-to-face with Diego Cole-Thomas for the second time that day. The man who stood in the foyer of his oceanfront Palm Beach condo looked nothing like the one who'd interviewed her earlier that morning. A white guayabera shirt had replaced his custom-made one. Jeans had replaced his Italian suit and a pair of sandals replaced his custom wing tips. She didn't know why, but a dressed-down Diego didn't appear as intimidating. But, that was not to say he would be any less difficult to deal with.

Stepping back, Diego extended a hand to the woman who stared up at him with narrowed eyes. He wondered what was going on behind her suspicious gaze. They were strangers, but he hoped that within a matter of days she would come to understand what he expected from her.

His new personal assistant looked nothing like the woman he'd interviewed that morning. She'd let down her hair and secured it in a ponytail that swept her shoulder blades. Diego was hard-pressed not to laugh out loud, something he rarely did. He'd hit the mother lode. Sean Gregory's widow was stunning. She was going to make an incredible hostess.

"Good evening, Vivienne. Please come in."

She shook his hand. "Good evening, Mr. Cole-Thomas."

Diego's eyebrows lifted slightly before a frown settled

between his eyes. "All of my employees call me Diego, and I'd prefer you do the same."

Vivienne wanted to ask him how many of his employees lived with him, but held her tongue. If she hoped to get along with her boss, then she had to temper her sarcasm. She forced a smile even though she didn't quite feel like it at that moment.

"Okay, Diego." His eyebrows lifted again at the same time as the corners of his mouth inched up in amusement. "What's so funny?"

Diego's smile disappeared as quickly as it'd appeared. "Nothing," he snapped quickly. "It's not often that I hear my name pronounced with a Spanish accent."

"It is Spanish for James, isn't it?"

He nodded. "It is." He released her hand. "Have you had dinner?"

It was Vivienne's turn to nod. "Yes, I have."

"If that's the case, then let me show you to your bedroom, and then we'll sit down and talk about what I need from you."

It was over quickly. The moment in which he'd almost smiled vanished, replaced with an expressionless, businesslike tone. How, Vivienne wondered, was she going to live under the same roof as her boss, yet maintain an impersonal relationship? It wasn't going to be easy—not when she had been hired to be his personal assistant and that meant getting to know him personally.

She followed him down a wide carpeted hallway with twenty-foot ceilings, recessed lights, pale walls and floors, quickening her stride to keep up with his longer legs. They passed rooms without walls and others with yawning spaces that gave the condo a sense of openness and the illusion that it was even more spacious than it actually was. A curving staircase led to a second story.

Diego lived in a secluded enclave with private roads, twenty-four-hour security and awe-inspiring views of the Atlantic Ocean. When she'd driven up to the gatehouse, she couldn't believe that she would spend the next six months waking up to the sound of pounding surf. The recently built condominium units began at seven figures, appropriate for the three- to five-thousand square feet of living spaces.

Vivienne wanted to linger a bit and examine the pieces of glass art and several large colorful paintings, but she would have time for that later. After all, she was expected to live in the duplex for the next six months. Her offer letter outlined a six-month position, renewable at the discretion of both parties. She'd also signed a nondisclosure agreement that she would be subject to litigation if she disclosed confidential information vital to ColeDiz International Ltd.

Diego stopped at the foot of the staircase. "Our bedroom suites are upstairs. My suite is on the left and yours is on the right. We share a balcony that faces the water. There's also another balcony outside the kitchen and dining area that overlooks the ocean."

Vivienne stared at his broad back. "Are there any bedrooms on the first floor?"

Shifting slightly, Diego gave her a long, penetrating stare. It was the first time he'd noted any hesitation from his new personal assistant. "There's a den that can be easily converted into a guest suite when needed. Why?"

"Wouldn't it be better if…" Her words trailed off as he leaned closer and she inhaled the subtle scent of his cologne. Suddenly she felt as if he were too close to permit her to draw a normal breath. It had been a very long time since a man had overwhelmed her by occupying the same space. And, that man she'd married.

However, that would never happen with Diego Cole-Thomas. He was her boss, and she'd made herself a promise when she'd first entered the job market that office romances were a definite no-no. Several of the women at the investment firm where she'd worked had become involved with their bosses or coworkers, and most of the liaisons ended badly for them. Either they requested transfers or were reassigned to other positions. In most cases, the men were married and had no intention of leaving their wives and children.

"Say what you need to say, Vivienne," Diego said, taunting softly. "After all, you had no problem telling me that I had on mismatched socks."

Pinpricks of heat stung her cheeks. "Don't tell me you're going to be difficult because I had the nerve to remind the CEO of his wardrobe malfunction."

"Difficult?" he repeated softly. "You really think I'm difficult?"

Vivienne lifted a shoulder under a loose-fitting yellow blouse she'd paired with black cropped pants. "If you're not, then why would you bring it up? You hired me to be your assistant—no, your personal assistant. And that means it's my job to make your life as stress-free as possible. If I have to check your socks every day, then so be it. I want you to keep in mind that I'm here to work, not play. I only asked about a bedroom on the first floor because I believe it would be more appropriate if we maintain some distance when it comes to our sleeping arrangements."

Crossing his arms over his chest, Diego angled his head and stared at Vivienne as if she'd taken leave of her senses.

"Do you actually believe I'd try to compromise or take advantage of a female employee?"

"Did I say that?" she shot back defensively.

"You didn't have to, Vivienne. You implied—"

"Don't try and put words in my mouth, Diego. I don't have a problem saying what's on my mind, so let's get that straight right here, right now."

Diego went completely still. Underneath the cool exterior of the woman with the haunting tawny-brown eyes was a quick temper and an even sharper tongue. "This will be the first and last time I'll permit you to talk to me in that tone." Though spoken quietly, his words were as sharp and cutting as a razor.

"What tone do you want me to take with you, boss man?" Her voice was dripping with sarcasm.

Diego couldn't believe Vivienne. It was apparent she either didn't need or want the position. But, he wasn't about to make it easy for her. "Are you trying to get fired?"

"No," she countered, after a pregnant pause.

He leaned closer. "Then, what's with the attitude?"

"I didn't know I had one."

"Well, you do," Diego said.

Pressing her palms together, Vivienne bowed her head as if he were royalty. "*Por favor perdone mi impertinencia,* Señor Cole-Thomas."

Diego didn't know whether to fire Vivienne Neal on the spot. His broad shoulders shook as he bit back laughter. If Vivienne was genuinely sorry for mouthing off at him, then he was the elusive Loch Ness Monster.

"Humility doesn't quite suit you, Ms. Neal."

Vivienne wrinkled her nose, winking at the man who unsettled her, unsettled her more than she wanted to be. And, that was further exacerbated because she would've preferred her bedroom on the first floor rather than the second.

"I'm glad you noticed."

Diego wanted to tell Vivienne that that wasn't the only thing he'd noticed about her. She claimed a refreshing natural beauty that hadn't come from a plastic surgeon's scalpel or a professional makeup artist. He estimated her to be around five-five or five-six, but it was her slimness that made her appear taller. If his interest in her was less of a professional nature, then he would've preferred her carrying at least ten to fifteen more pounds. Most of the women he dated usually wore a double-digit dress size, while many of the men in his family preferred tall, very slim women.

He sobered. "Now, are you ready to see what's upstairs?"

"You're not going to fire me?" Vivienne asked, answering his question with one of her own.

The seconds ticked off as they stared at each other. It was Diego who broke the silence. "No!" He turned and made his way up the staircase. "And if it'll make you feel safer at night I'll lock my bedroom door," he said over his shoulder. "Or better yet, lock yours."

She grunted as she followed him up the curving carpeted stairs. She didn't want to get fired but wanted to see how far she could push Diego, because Vivienne Kay Neal had no intention of becoming a doormat for the powerful CEO with the intimidating reputation.

"That won't be necessary," she said to his back, "because I don't do bosses."

Diego lifted his eyebrows as he glanced over his shoulder. "At least we're in agreement about two things. I don't do employees."

"What's the other thing?"

"Your qualifications. You're exactly what I've been looking for." He waited at the top of the stairs for Vivienne, who was oblivious to the significance of his statement.

They walked down a hallway wide enough for them to walk two abreast. Recessed lights reflected off the pale-veined marble floor that was only a shade lighter than the walls, which were covered with a fabric that resembled finely woven linen.

Diego stopped at the end of the hall where oceanfront windows and doors separated massive carved mahogany double doors that led to the bedroom suites. Resting his hands on the heavy brass doorknobs, he pulled them open to reveal a suite with a living room, dining area, sitting room and a bedroom with a king-size bed upholstered in cream-colored suede.

Vivienne walked into her suite as if in a trance. Diego had called it a bedroom suite, but it was more like an apartment. Her eight boxes, labeled with their contents, were lost in the enormous walk-in closet with enough shelves for Imelda Marcos's shoe collection and all of Cher and Elton John's flamboyant concert costumes.

"You like shoes," Diego said softly behind her back.

She nodded. Half the boxes were labeled "Shoes," while the others contained slacks, blouses, dresses, books and another with miscellaneous items. "Whenever I see a pair I like, I just have to have them."

Crossing his arms over his chest, Diego angled his head. He wanted to tell Vivienne that she was going to have to increase her wardrobe because his social agenda was as active as his business calendar. "Do you like shopping?"

Spinning around on the toes of her ballet-type shoes,

Vivienne gave him a look mirroring puzzlement. "Shopping for what?"

"Clothes."

"I've been known to melt the numbers on several of my credit cards with a marathon shopping spree. Why?"

A mysterious smile softened Diego's firm mouth. He'd found himself smiling more with Vivienne than he had in a very long time. The task of trying to balance his business dealings with his personal life had taken a toll on his sense of humor, something he'd been accused of lacking entirely.

"I'll tell you after I lay out my itinerary for the next few weeks," he said cryptically.

"Which itinerary, Diego?"

"I only have one itinerary."

With wide eyes, she said, "You mix business with personal?"

He inclined his head. "Most of the time they overlap."

It was Vivienne's turn to cross her arms under her breasts, bringing Diego's gaze to linger there. She lowered her arms and sat on a leather-padded bench. "Do you expect me to accompany you to your meetings?"

He lifted his shoulders in a gesture that reminded her of her favorite Italian actor Giancarlo Giannini. Diego was tall and powerfully built, yet claimed a grace that was totally incongruent with a man his size. To say he was elegant was an understatement. He had the most beautiful hands and feet of any man she'd seen. His hands were slender with long, delicate fingers. There were no ragged cuticles or uneven nails, which attested to his being well-groomed.

"I'm going to require you being present at a few, only because I'd like to get another perspective on the proceedings. I'm starting a new venture and I'm going to need your input and feedback. And remember, everything we discuss is bound by the confidentiality statement you signed."

Vivienne curbed the urge to roll her eyes at him. "I understand," she said instead. Although she wanted to stay and examine the space where she would sleep, she also wanted to know her responsibilities.

Diego extended his hand, smiling when she placed her hand on his as he eased her gently to her feet. "You can check out the house later," he said, reading her mind, "but what I want to discuss with you is a priority."

Tilting her chin, she stared up at him staring back at her. There was an emotion lurking behind the raven-black eyes that caused a shiver to race along her spine. "What do you need me to do?"

"I don't need you to do anything except to accompany me to a wedding Saturday evening."

A moment of apprehension rushed through Vivienne as she mentally replayed his statement. "You want me to be your date?" The last word was a whisper.

Nothing on Diego moved, not even his eyes. "For lack of a better word—yes, I want you to be my date."

Her gaze dropped to his chin. Apprehension gnawed at her confidence as she tried to slow down the runaway beating of her heart. Diego Cole-Thomas hadn't hired her to keep his life in order, but to become a live-in call girl sans the sex.

"If I were a man, would you've asked me to be your date?"

He flashed a sensual smile. "No. I would've asked another woman."

"If that's the case, then why don't you ask her?"

Diego increased his hold on Vivienne's hand before he tucked it into the bend of his elbow. "I'm trying to uncomplicate my life, Vivienne, not add to the craziness."

She gave him a sidelong glance. "So, you're using me to run interference with an old girlfriend?"

There came a beat. "There are no old girlfriends in my past, Vivienne."

"If they're not old girlfriends, then what were they?"

"Acquaintances."

"So, you're a love-'em-and-leave-'em kind of guy?" she whispered under her breath.

When Diego didn't respond to her taunt, Vivienne knew it wasn't because he couldn't, but because he'd chosen not to. She'd spent less than fifteen minutes with her new boss and she already knew that Diego Cole-Thomas was a very private person. If he lived alone it wasn't because he couldn't get a woman to live with him.

He was alone by choice.

Chapter 3

Vivienne sat on a chocolate-brown leather love seat in a room with a wall of pocket doors. They were open to take in the cooling breeze coming off the ocean.

She stared at Diego who sat in a matching club chair. This time, when he crossed his legs he hadn't had to concern himself with mismatched socks. Resting his elbow on the arm of the chair, he anchored his thumb under his chin and placed a forefinger along the side of his face.

She glanced around the room rather than focus on Diego staring at her as if he were a predator contemplating an attack. At that moment she was his prey, having signed an agreement to give him the next six months of her life and not to disclose any information about ColeDiz International Ltd.

Instinct told her that working closely with Diego wasn't going to be an easy task, yet she welcomed the challenge.

It would help her to maintain her fluency in Spanish, sharpen her business skills and fill a six-month employment gap on her résumé. She wouldn't have resigned her position with the investment firm if Sean was still alive. But his death had become fodder for the tabloids, and it wasn't until he was buried with all of the reverence bestowed upon an elected official that her life resumed a semblance of normalcy.

"This room will become your office," Diego said in a voice so quiet that Vivienne had to strain to hear him over the hypnotic sound of the crashing waves. "It can also double as a bedroom. The sofa converts to a queen-size bed." His eyebrows lifted slightly when she glanced at the leather sofa that completed the seating grouping. "The alcove has a small utility kitchen with a mini fridge stocked with snacks and beverages. There's also a half bath on the other side of that door." He pointed to a door at the opposite end of the room.

"The telephone has three extensions," he continued. "The first one is the house phone and the second a direct line to my executive assistant, Lourdes Wallace."

"And the third?" Vivienne asked when he hesitated.

"It's my direct line. All you have to do is press the button and the call will go to my private line at the office. If I don't pick up after four rings, then the call will be forwarded to my BlackBerry. I'll order a BlackBerry for you, so we'll be in sync."

"If the house phone rings, how do you want me to answer it?"

"Cole-Thomas residence, Ms. Neal speaking, will suffice."

Vivienne nodded, mentally filing away the information. "How are you going to explain me to your family when they call and I answer your telephone?"

Diego glared at her under lowered lids. "I don't explain myself to anyone—and that includes my family."

"Well," she said sotto voce.

"A cleaning service comes on Mondays and Thursdays." He wagged a finger at her. "And that translates into you not lifting a finger to do any cleaning. I'm going to give you a remote device for your car that will allow you to come and go without being stopped by security."

Vivienne smiled. "It's probably easier to get into Fort Knox than trying to get into this place." She'd been stopped along the private road leading to the multimillion dollar condominiums by an armed uniformed guard a quarter of a mile from the gatehouse. He'd called in her name on his walkie-talkie, and it was only after she'd been cleared that she was allowed to continue.

"The residents pay through the nose for security."

"Hiding behind armed guards and electronic gates is hardly what I call living, Diego."

"It is to those who value their privacy."

"And, are you one of those who value your privacy?"

"More than anything," he confirmed. "That's one of the reasons why I hired you, Vivienne. You were married to a politician, so you know about discretion. Secondly, you're a recent widow and if we're seen together at a social event, then it lets both of us off the hook when I explain that our liaison is strictly business-related.

"Did you ever meet Sean?"

"Not personally. I was introduced to him at an NAACP fund-raiser in D.C. a couple of years ago."

"Why were you in Washington?"

"I'm on the board of the local Florida chapter."

"Is that the only board you're on?" Vivienne asked.

Diego exhaled an audible sigh. "No. At the present time I'm an active member on five boards, either as a consultant or a fund-raiser. I've earned quite a reputation by convincing many of my wealthier friends and family members to dig deep for a good cause."

"Convince or intimidate?"

He waved a hand. "I use whatever works, Vivienne. You'll have a computer, so how you set up my schedule is your decision. Just make certain you send an update to Lourdes every day, and she'll do the same to avoid scheduling conflicts."

"Other than Saturday's wedding, what else is pending?"

"The wife of a college friend is throwing him a surprise birthday party on Sunday. What he doesn't know is that it'll be aboard a yacht that will be a birthday gift from his in-laws."

"You're kidding me?"

Smiling, Diego shook his head. "No, I'm not. His in-laws are in the oil business."

"Apparently he doesn't have to concern himself with how much it'll cost to gas up that baby."

"Do I detect a hint of cynicism?"

"Damn skippy, Diego," she countered, glowering at him. "While most people have to decide whether to fill up their gas tanks to go to work, or cut back on food for their children some guy gets a yacht for his birthday because his outlaw in-laws reap untold oil profits."

Vivienne's rant surprised Diego, especially since he knew she'd grown up in a privileged family. It'd taken Jacob Jones two hours to give him the information he'd requested on Vivienne Neal, and the information that had come through his BlackBerry was not what he'd expected. His friend had uncovered documents that Vivienne Kay Gregory, née Neal, was suing her husband Sean Bailey Gregory for divorce, citing abandonment and alienation of affection as grounds for the dissolution of their four-year marriage.

Jake had also reported that Vivienne's father had amassed a small fortune as a litigator specializing in civil rights cases. Her brother Vaughn, who'd attended Stanford Law with Gregory, lived on the West Coast with his wife and two school-age daughters. After graduating from an elite New England finishing school, Vivienne went on to Sarah Lawrence where she'd earned a degree in romance languages.

She'd taken a year off to live in Europe and upon her return she enrolled in a graduate program as an MBA student. Her grades and her father's reputation were crucial factors when she was hired by a major investment firm for their international banking division. A check on her financial and criminal background yielded nothing. She'd never been cited for a parking violation or bounced a check. Jake ended his report by concluding that Vivienne Neal was so clean, she literally squeaked.

Diego wanted to tell Vivienne that she could stop with the verbal beat down, because ColeDiz was into agriculture, but swallowed the words since he was certain it would only instigate another volley from her. Despite her sharp tongue, he respected her fierceness, her spunk. The last thing he needed was another assistant who was a crybaby. She'd asked whether he was going to fire her, but that wasn't going to happen unless she breached her contract.

What he didn't want to acknowledge was that his personal assistant was beyond his expectations. Whether in a tailored suit or casually dressed, with or without makeup, Vivienne Neal was confident, regal and claimed a strength that did nothing to compromise her femininity.

Pressing his palms together, he stared at her over his fingers. "May we please change the subject?" he asked.

Vivienne's head came up when she registered a deceptive calmness in Diego's voice that hadn't been evident before. "*Sí*, Diego, *por favor* continue."

"I'd like us to take our evening meals together, so—"

"You expect me to cook dinner?"

"No, Vivienne," he drawled as if she were a two-year-old. "Either we'll dine out, order in, or I'll cook. The refrigerator is always well stocked."

"You cook?"

"Yes, I cook," he shot back. "Now, will you please stop interrupting me?"

"*Lo siento.*"

Diego lowered his leg, planting his sandaled feet firmly on the carpeted floor. "No, Vivienne, you're not sorry."

A hint of a smile parted her lips. "But, I am sorry. I promise not to say anything until you're finished." She pantomimed zipping her lips.

Throwing back his head, Diego laughed, the warm, deep sound filling the room. "You know you're really a piece of work, Vivienne Neal." She nodded vigorously, while pointing to her compressed lips, which made him laugh even more.

"Over dinner we'll discuss the next day's agenda."

Vivienne listened intently, enthralled by the soft drawl of Diego's voice when he gave her an overview of his family-owned holdings, which included coffee plantations in Costa Rica, Mexico, Puerto Rico, Jamaica and Brazil. The family had expanded their agribusiness to include bananas in Belize, and as CEO he'd become a cotton broker with a Ugandan grower.

"The company's next venture will be based on the mainland," he said. "It goes against everything my great-grandfather wanted when he first set up ColeDiz, but it's a new century and time for a change."

"Where do you intend to start up this new venture?"

"South Carolina."

"What's in South Carolina?" Vivienne asked.

"Tea."

"Tea," she repeated. Diego nodded. "You're going to grow tea in the United States?"

"Yes." He stood up in one smooth motion, Vivienne rising with him. "We'll talk about this some other time. What I need you to do is concentrate on that stack of mail on the desk."

Vivienne glanced over at the workstation with a large flat screen monitor on an L-shaped desk littered with envelopes. "What's in them?"

Diego bit back a smile. "I don't know. It'll be up to you to discern what's important and what isn't." He sobered. "I know you probably want to get settled in, so I'll see you in the morning."

Vivienne took several steps, and then stopped. "What time do you get up?" She knew she was on call 24/7. However, she wanted to establish a schedule with Diego that would minimize confusion.

"Five."

"Why so early?"

Diego angled his head. "I'm in my office by six."

Vivienne gave him an incredulous look. "You start working at six?" He nodded. "What about breakfast?"

"I usually grab something from the food kiosk in the building lobby."

She rested her hands on her hips. "Haven't you heard that breakfast is the most important meal of the day?"

He frowned. "I don't have time to make breakfast."

"Do you have an early-morning meeting tomorrow?"

"No. Why?"

"I'll get up earlier and make breakfast for you, but only if you promise to stay and eat it."

The seconds ticked by as Diego stared at the woman who'd offered to get up at dawn to accommodate his unorthodox lifestyle, wondering if she'd done the same for her late husband. He recalled Jake Jones's e-mail about Vivienne's intent to divorce her husband because he'd neglected her—in and out of bed. What, he wondered, had happened to sour their short-lived union? He knew couples who'd been married five years and still acted like newlyweds.

"Thank you."

Vivienne gave him a dazzling smile. "You're welcome. Good night, Diego," she said as she turned and walked out of the office.

"*¡Buenas noches!* Vivienne," he said to the empty room where she'd been.

To say Vivienne Neal was an enigma was an understatement. Born into privilege, she'd attended elite schools, traveled extensively, spoke several languages, was the widow of a high-powered politician, and now lived under his roof as his personal assistant.

Diego's expression grew serious. Alicia Cooney had told his personnel director that Vivienne Neal was perfect for the position, and Caitlin's reaction had been much the same. He'd found Vivienne highly intelligent, but extremely outspoken. Women with whom he'd found himself involved were usually more reticent.

But, he had to remind himself that despite living together their relationship would remain platonic. After all, he was her boss, and he had very strong views about mixing business with pleasure.

Vivienne walked into the suite that was to become her sanctuary for the next six months. It would be where she'd sleep, read or just while away the hours when she wasn't working for Diego Cole-Thomas.

Her first reaction to the CEO was one of apprehension because of his hard-charging reputation as a man who ran his family-owned corporation like a general directing a military campaign. But she'd discovered another side to the man who'd admitted to being less than perfect when he attributed his wearing mismatched socks to color blindness.

She didn't doubt whether she'd be able to manage Diego's business and personal agenda, because it was something she'd accomplished before. In her first year of marriage, she'd hosted Sean's meet-and-greets when he decided to run for his father's congressional seat. Although she'd held down a full-time job, she mailed out invitations, kept track of the responses, met with caterers to plan menus and florists to come up with arrangements that suited carefully thought-out themes. She'd become the consummate politician's wife. But in the end she'd become a political widow, flying to the nation's capital only when it was advantageous for her overly ambitious husband to be seen with his wife.

She'd shifted her focus from Sean to her career, occasionally traveling abroad as a translator. The trips to Italy, Spain or France became working holidays where she shopped, visited museums and attended the theater, enjoying productions of popular Broadway plays.

When she'd married Sean she'd hoped to balance her career with motherhood, but even that was denied her because whenever her husband returned to Connecticut they rarely shared a bed. And a stubborn pride wouldn't let her beg her husband to make love to her, so work became the balm to soothe his estrangement and her sexual frustration. When she'd called Alicia to complain about Sean, her college roommate suggested two options: divorce, or an affair. In the end she'd decided on the former.

Her bedroom suite—a suede headboard and bedframe, marble floor, rugs, drapes and wallpaper—was decorated in neutral shades. The monochromatic color scheme continued into the bath and sitting rooms. Vivienne fell in love with the bathroom. Mirrored walls, custom moiré wall covering and cappuccino-colored onyx stone around the garden tub and countertops provided a striking contrast to the soft beige tones in an adjoining powder room. She found it odd that although Diego lived alone he'd purchased the top two floors, doubling his living space. All of the furnishings were tasteful, and there was no doubt he'd had it professionally decorated.

Vivienne glanced at her watch. It was close to ten. She knew she had to unpack a few of the boxes tonight to select something to wear to bed and for the following day. And, she'd also promised Alicia that she would call with an update. Looking around, she realized she'd left her handbag on the table in the foyer.

Retracing her steps, she made her way down the staircase and across the darkened living room to the foyer. A lamp on the table provided enough light for her to see her handbag. She'd just reached for it when a voice stopped her.

"Quitting already?"

Spinning on her toes, she saw a shadow. Then Diego stepped into the light. Why, she mused, hadn't she noticed the stubble on his lean jaw when they'd sat together in the office? He moved closer, and the lingering fragrance of his cologne mingling with his body's natural scent was a potent sensual bouquet that served to remind her how long she'd been without a man.

"No, I'm not." Her voice was low, as if she'd run a grueling race. "I came down to get my handbag." There came a beat before she asked, "What are you doing lurking around in the dark?"

Diego took another step, bringing him within inches of the woman who intrigued him and upset his equilibrium. "I didn't know I needed your approval to set the alarm. After all, I don't want to be responsible for not protecting my houseguest."

She smiled. "I thought I was your employee."

He returned her smile. "*Eso, también,* Vivienne."

She froze. It was the first time Diego had initiated speaking Spanish to her. "Houseguest and employee," she drawled. "Now, which one carries more clout?"

"I would have to say employee. My houseguests usually have to fend for themselves, while I take full responsibility for my employees."

Vivienne met the dark gaze that seemingly bored into her. She'd attempted to conceal her own feelings behind a sometimes too-bright smile and witty repartee. She'd kept up a brave front for four years, and continued the deception when she was photographed as the grieving widow.

"Lucky me." She wiggled her fingers. "*¡Buenas noches!*"

"Good night, Vivienne."

Diego waited until he was certain Vivienne had made it

up the staircase, then he followed the trailing scent of her perfume. The fragrance was like the woman herself—delicate and sexy.

But, it wasn't her face, perfume or body that nagged at him hours later when he found himself in bed tossing and turning restlessly. It was Jake's e-mail and the part about Vivienne's divorce action. If Sean Gregory hadn't been killed in a hit-and-run, then everyone would've known that he wasn't sleeping with his wife. And, the question was, if Congressman Sean Gregory wasn't sleeping with his wife, then who had he been sleeping with?

Diego peered at the clock on the bedside table at the same time as he punched the pillow under his head. It was two in the morning and he wasn't going to get much sleep this night—if any, and he knew the reason for his insomnia was a woman who slept in a suite next to his.

Tossing back the sheet, he moved off the bed. Walking on bare feet to the windows, Diego slid back the glass door and screen. The light from a nearly full moon cast an eerie silvery light on the beach. The damp ocean air swept over his naked body. His flesh pebbled, although the nighttime temperatures were in the seventies. The humidity was as thick and heavy as a wet blanket.

He went to the far end of the balcony and peered over the edge. Strategically placed lights surrounding the rear of the building and the moon provided enough illumination for him to see a couple sitting close to each other on the beach. He smiled. It was apparent he wasn't the only one unable to sleep.

Diego saw movement out the corner of his eye and turned to see Vivienne rise from a chair at the opposite end of the balcony. Time appeared to stand still; she was bathed in moonlight, the outline of her body visible through the lightweight fabric of her nightgown. Within seconds his body reacted violently, the flesh between his thighs stirring to life. Gritting his teeth, he swallowed a curse.

He couldn't remember the last time his body hadn't followed the dictates of his brain. Unable to move, and helpless to stop the blood rushing to his groin, Diego closed his eyes and waited, waited for the shadowy image of Vivienne's slender body to fade. When he opened his eyes he saw that he was alone. Vivienne had retreated to her bedroom, while he had to wait a little while longer before he could do the same.

Breathing heavily, Diego lay facedown on the bed. Shivers of self-doubt taunted him as he chided himself for not only hiring Vivienne Neal but also for mandating that a condition of her employment was that she had to be a live-in personal assistant.

He knew he hadn't made a mistake in hiring her, but in having her in the bedroom next to his. It was apparent Vivienne was more aware than he was of the proximity of their sleeping arrangement when she'd asked whether there were bedrooms on the first floor.

Cursing under his breath in English and Spanish, Diego punched a pillow with enough force to release the feathers from their casing. His plan to utilize his personal assistant's skills as his hostess had just backfired. He'd prided himself on his iron-willed self-control when it came to women. Yet he had found himself fully aroused when he'd glimpsed the outline of her body through a layer of fabric.

"I don't do bosses." He could still hear Vivienne's taunting voice.

"And I don't sleep with female employees," he whispered in the darkened room. He repeated it over and over until he fell asleep.

Chapter 4

Vivienne opened her eyes to find sunlight coming through the silken sheers at the windows. She'd slept fitfully, alternating sleeping on the cushioned lounger on the balcony and in her bed. It wasn't that the bed wasn't comfortable. It was her surroundings. She'd never been one to adjust easily to change, so she knew it would take her several days before she'd feel completely comfortable in the Palm Beach duplex. The fact that she would be alone most of the day would ease the transition from sharing Alicia's three-bedroom house for the past two months to living with a man.

And she was living with a man—albeit her boss. She knew when she called her mother to apprise her of the new change in her life she would have to endure Pamela Neal's tirade that she didn't raise her daughter to cohabitate with a man unless that man was her husband. However, she was prepared for her mother. What could Pamela say when she'd finally disclosed that she could count the number of times she and Sean slept together under the same roof and also how many times they'd made love during their short marriage.

Glancing at the clock, Vivienne noted the time. It was nearly five-thirty. She knew she had to get up, because she'd promised Diego that she would prepare breakfast. This was one morning where she'd wanted to linger in bed but knew it wasn't going to happen. Although she wasn't going into a traditional office, she still had to go to work.

Her motions were slow and mechanical as she got out of bed and headed for the bathroom. The night before she'd emptied all of the boxes and put away her clothes. Her wardrobe in the expansive closet reminded her of half-empty racks at department stores after a megasale. A shopping spree was definitely a priority if she was to accompany Diego to social events.

Twenty minutes later, she skipped down the stairs, making her way into the kitchen. The heat of the rising sun coming through the pocket doors warmed the marble floor under her bare feet. A group of seagulls had gathered along the beach, examining the remnants left on the sand with the incoming tide.

A smile parted her lips when a gull swooped down, dropping something from its beak. There was a loud commotion as the others rushed over in an attempt to claim it. Vivienne saw a large clamshell on the sand after they'd flown away. The gull had dropped the shell in order to open it, but his feathered friends had duped him out of his breakfast.

Shifting her attention from the scene beyond the glass, she examined the gourmet kitchen with granite-topped cabinetry in a pale paneled wood that gave the space a sleek but warm feeling. Most of the appliances, including the dishwasher and double refrigerators and freezer, were covered with the same light wood, while the backsplashes were covered in glass tiles.

Diego's claim that the refrigerator was well stocked was confirmed when she opened it to find everything she needed to put together breakfast, lunch and dinner. Working quickly with a minimum of effort, she set the table in the dining area, ground fresh coffee beans for the coffeemaker, cubed a mango, cantaloupe and honeydew melon, and then placed four strips of bacon on an unheated stovetop grill. She'd just begun dicing peppers and onions and cubes of smoked ham for an omelet when Diego walked into the kitchen.

She glanced up, and in the instant when their eyes met she felt the energy that made him so undeniably powerful. But she also felt the sexual magnetism that gave him a sense of self-confidence some men would spend a lifetime perfecting.

"Good morning."

He smiled. *"Buenos días."*

Diego wanted to tell Vivienne that it was more than a good morning. In fact, it was a glorious morning. He'd finally fallen asleep and when he woke it was to the resolve that nothing would ever come from his attraction to his personal assistant. This morning she looked much younger than thirty-one. Dressed in an oversize tee, jeans, bare feet and with her hair pulled back in a ponytail, she reminded him of his younger female cousins.

He placed a small square white object on the countertop. "This is a programmable remote device for your car. When you depress the right button, my name and security code will go directly to the gatehouse. You'll have to do it whether you're coming or leaving."

"What's the left button for?"

Diego gave her a long, penetrating stare. "A GPS panic button." He smiled when Vivienne's delicate jaw dropped. "If you break down anywhere along the road leading to the complex, or if you believe someone's following you, then press it and the security team will respond."

A slight frown touched her smooth forehead as she concentrated on dicing ham in precise cubes. "I don't understand something, Diego."

"What's that?"

"Why would you install a security system when you live in a complex with armed security?"

"The armed security protects us from outside intruders, the inside security from resident intruders or their unsavory guests."

"Whatever happened to background checks?"

"If you have enough money and know the right people, you, too, will be able to fly under the radar."

Placing a paring knife on the cutting board, Vivienne wiped her hands on a towel. "Come stand in the sunlight so I can check out your socks."

As Diego came toward her she noticed things about him she hadn't before. He had a quick step for a man who stood several inches above six feet and the toe of his right foot was turned in slightly. He was impeccably dressed in a stark white shirt with a spread collar and French cuffs with silver cuff links bearing his monogram. The hem of his dark gray pleated-front trousers ended at the precise break above a pair of polished slip-ons. The silk pinstripe gray tie was knotted in a perfect Windsor. Her gaze came to rest on his cleanly shaven face. Although not classically handsome, she thought Diego extremely attractive. Fastidiously well-groomed, he not only looked good but also smelled good.

Vivienne met Diego's gaze and what she saw in the dark, deep-set orbs caused the muscles in her stomach to contract. Diego Cole-Thomas's expression could not disguise the curiosity lurking behind his enigmatic gaze. Her eyelids fluttered before she was able to bring her fragile emotions into some semblance of order. She'd met enough men to recognize that particular look, and at that moment she knew what her boss was thinking even if he wouldn't openly admit it—he was more than interested in her.

"What do you want to know, Diego?"

He blinked once. "Say what?"

"What is it you want to know about me?"

His eyes narrowed. "What are you talking about, Vivienne?"

She glared at him in what would've become a staredown, but dropped her gaze. "Forget it."

Reaching out, he caught her wrist. "No, I'm not going to forget it. Something's bothering you, or you would've never asked me that question."

She struggled to free herself, but his slender fingers were like bands of steel. "I'm sorry I brought it up, Diego. Now, please let me go so I can finish making breakfast."

Diego released her wrist. "We'll continue this later tonight. If we're going to live and work closely together, then I don't want to have to deal with your moods. If I tick you off about something, then I expect you to tell me. *"¿Comprende?"*

She nodded. "Yes, Diego, I understand."

"Good." He winked at her. "You can check my socks now," he said, pulling up his suit trousers.

Vivienne leaned over, peering closely at a pair of black socks with dark gray specks. "They're good."

Diego curbed the urge to run his fingers through Vivienne's hair. There was something so endearingly domestic about her getting up to cook breakfast and check his appearance that he wondered if she'd done the same early on in her marriage to Sean Gregory.

"Do you want me to help you with anything?" he asked when she straightened.

Vivienne shook her head. "No, thank you. I have everything under control. I'm making an omelet for myself. Would you like one?"

Moving closer to Vivienne, Diego rested a hand at the small of her back when he glanced over her shoulder, the gesture as natural as if he'd executed it countless times, as she picked up the knife to finish dicing the ingredients for an omelet. "I like my eggs over easy. Hey, you're pretty good with that knife."

Tilting her chin, Vivienne smiled up at him. Even though Diego was close, very, very close, she loathed asking him to move back. There was something so natural about them standing together that it took several minutes for her to realize what she was sharing with him at that moment was what she'd wanted with her late husband. The only time Sean had entered their kitchen was to open the refrigerator to get a bottle of mineral water or a cold beer.

"That's only because I took a few cooking courses in France and Italy."

"Which do you like better—French or Italian cuisine?"

She lifted a shoulder. "I'm somewhat partial to Italian."

Diego nodded. "So am I," he said. "Do you like to

travel?" He recalled the entry on her résumé that mentioned she'd traveled extensively for her former employer.

"It all depends on where it is and the accommoda-
tions. The older I get, the less I'm willing to rough it."
Diego's hand fell from her shoulder when she moved
over to the sink to wash her hands, and she missed his
warm touch.

"I can assure you if you travel with me on ColeDiz
business, you definitely won't have to rough it."

Vivienne turned and stared at Diego as if she'd never
seen him before. "I have to travel with you?"

"Didn't Ms. Novak tell you that it was a part of your job?"

"No. What she did ask was if I had a valid passport, and
I told her yes."

"I'm sorry she wasn't more explicit. But to answer your
question, yes, you'll have to travel with me on occasion."

"How often is 'on occasion'?"

Diego stiffened as if Vivienne had struck him. He glared
at her. "Why do you always challenge me, Vivienne?"

"I'm not challenging you, Diego. I merely asked a
question."

"Well, I don't like being questioned, nor do I want to
have to edit everything I say to you because if I don't, then
you're going to mouth off at me."

Vivienne's temper flared. "Are you such a tyrant that
you're going to deny me my First Amendment right to
free speech?"

His eyebrows shot up. "Is that how you see me,
Vivienne? You think I'm a tyrant?"

Vivienne stared at the man towering above her like an
avenging angel. At that moment Diego Cole-Thomas had
become her late husband. Her frustration with and resent-

ment of a dead man had been transferred to a man who ordered her about as if she were chattel.

"Yes I do, Diego. You issue orders, and then expect me to fall in line, in lockstep like an automaton. Despite what you've been led to believe, you are not perfect, Mr. Cole-Thomas."

Diego found Vivienne's tirade amusing and somehow quite sexy. Watching her chest rise and fall under the T-shirt was definitely a turn-on. All traces of gold had disappeared from her eyes, leaving them the color of strong black coffee.

"I know I'm not perfect," he drawled, "because after all I am color-blind."

Vivienne curbed the urge to swat him with the dish towel. "I wasn't talking about that, Diego, and you know it."

"Don't try and put words in my mouth, Vivienne," he said, repeating what she'd told him the night before. "Arguing with you is not only bothersome but also tiring. Keep it up and I'll take it out on some hapless employee who needs his or her job."

Her jaw dropped, and she gave him an incredulous look. "You'd fire someone just because you're in a bad mood?"

It was Diego's turn to stare at Vivienne as if she'd lost her mind. How was she so sophisticated, yet so gullible? Had her marriage failed because she'd believed everything Sean Gregory told her until she'd had enough of his excuses? Or had she chosen to believe there was nothing wrong with their marriage because politicians were expected to spend time away from their families with the excuse that they were affecting change on behalf of their constituents?

Reaching over, he tugged on the end of her ponytail. "No, Vivienne." His voice had lowered to a sensual timbre. "I'd never take my frustrations out on someone else."

A momentary look of distress crossed her face. "What are you frustrated about?"

"Let it go, Vivienne."

"Didn't you hire me to uncomplicate your life? If you let me know what's bothering you, then perhaps I can help."

Crossing his arms over the front of his crisp white shirt, Diego angled his head. "Unless you're willing to go upstairs and take off your clothes and permit me to make love to you, then I don't think you can be much help to me."

Vivienne wasn't able to stifle her gasp of surprise. She opened her mouth, but nothing came out. It was the first time in a very, very long time that she'd found herself at a loss for words. Her shock faded, replaced by anger. Diego had lied to her. What happened to his I-don't-get-involved-with-my-female-employees pronouncement?

"Lighten up, Vivienne," he continued, smiling. "You don't have to worry about me trying to seduce you."

Picking up the towel, she flicked it, deliberately missing him by inches. "I'm going to pay you back for teasing me, and that's a promise."

His smile grew wider. "There you go issuing challenges again."

Her smile matched his. "It wasn't a challenge, Diego. It was a promise."

Diego stared at Vivienne under lowered lids, silently admiring the fullness of her bottom lip, a lip he suddenly wanted to taste to see if it was actually as soft as it looked. And it was the second time in a matter of hours that he'd found himself lusting after a woman who would sleep under his roof for the next six months.

He knew he had to put some distance between himself and his personal assistant or he would violate everything he'd been taught and had come to believe as the head of his family-owned business. With the exception of the family secret that involved his great-grandfather and his young secretary, the succeeding ColeDiz CEOs had lived scandal-free lives.

Everyone remarked about his startling physical resemblance to his maternal great-grandfather, Samuel Claridge Cole, as he was being groomed to take over the reins from his father, Timothy Cole-Thomas. It wasn't his father but his uncle Martin Cole who'd apprised him that his business style was very similar to the approach that his father had taken when he set up the company following the Great War.

His uncle refused to tell him whether he approved or disapproved of his style. He'd been prepared to accept Martin's constructive criticism, and this left him less than confident about the company's direction. Diego knew his style was very different from his father's, but a year after he'd initiated changes and had grown the company to include cotton, soybeans and eventually tea, he felt comfortable not only as the head of ColeDiz International, but also in his own skin as the corporate CEO.

He'd hired Vivienne because of his commitment to service and not-for-profit organizations, and many of his personal contacts were lifelong friends, college buddies and the sons and daughters of other business giants. For him there was no delineation between business and social life. For Diego, socializing was always business-driven, but not necessarily the reverse. He'd made it a rule not to date the daughters or sisters of the men in his social circle.

Hiring Vivienne would serve a twofold purpose. With her as his date and hostess, he wouldn't have to concern himself with female companionship, and just her presence would be enough to indicate he was unavailable.

He'd struck the mother lode with Vivienne as his assistant. She was both smart and socially astute. There was no doubt Sean Gregory was aware of her assets when he married her. But Diego would do what the flashy politician had neglected to do. He intended to capitalize on Vivienne Neal's intelligence, grace and beauty.

Diego winked at the woman standing in his kitchen, a woman who made him laugh and a woman who made him feel things he didn't want to feel. He hadn't known her twenty-four hours, yet felt as if he'd known her forever. It was apparent he'd had to shuck a few oysters before finding that rare pearl. Vivienne had become that exotic rare jewel.

He winked at her. "I can't say I haven't been warned."

Vivienne returned his wink. "As long as you don't forget, then you'll be all right."

He shook his head. "You just have to have the last word, don't you?"

She gave him an innocent look. "Yes," she said after a comfortable pause.

"I think it's time I eat breakfast, so I can go to work where I know I'll always have the last word. Be ready to go out with me this afternoon."

"What's happening this afternoon?" Vivienne asked.

"I'm taking you shopping. You're going to need a few outfits for this weekend. And while you're there, you can pick up whatever else you want or need." She lifted her eyebrows at this disclosure. There was no doubt his offer to take Vivienne shopping had surprised her.

"Where is there, Diego?"

"Miami. We'll drive down, shop, hang out long enough

to have dinner and then come back." He glanced at the watch under his cuff. "I'd love to stay and debate you, but I have to leave within the next twenty minutes."

Vivienne opened her mouth to tell Diego there was a difference between asking a question and debating, but thought better of it. It was no concern of hers if he'd decided to go to Miami to shop when they could've easily gone to Worth Avenue.

When she'd called Alicia to tell her what she thought of her new boss, Alicia had opened up about what she'd read and heard about Diego Cole-Thomas. There were rumors floating around the business world that he was a maverick. And, despite the salacious gossip, Alicia said there was a waiting list for those wanting to work for ColeDiz International Limited.

She recognized that Diego was a complex man, that he didn't like to be questioned or challenged, and she'd done both. If he wanted to take her to Paris for a pair of shoes, then who was she to complain? If she was going to understand half of what made him who he was, then she had to choose when to say something and when it was appropriate to remain silent. Working as Diego Cole-Thomas's personal assistant wasn't going to be a walk in the park, but it wasn't as if the position didn't come with perks.

All of the things she'd wanted to experience with Sean she would share with Diego—fund-raisers, private parties, business dinners and travel. Vivienne didn't need her new position as much as she wanted it. In the two months she'd lived in Florida she'd lost her drive and ambition. She was more than comfortable sitting around and watching early-morning talk shows, afternoon soaps and then afternoon talk shows. If she hadn't cleaned, cooked or done laundry, there was no doubt she would've become a permanent couch potato. It wasn't as if she could even go for an early-morning jog. The extreme Florida temperatures and humidity made it virtually impossible to engage in any outdoor activity for an extended length of time without succumbing to either exhaustion or dehydration. She'd thought about joining a health club but changed her mind when she told Alicia that she was thinking of purchasing a condo with a health club on the premises.

Alicia, not wanting to lose her friend and housemate, told her that she could stay as long as she wanted, but Vivienne had set three months as the maximum length of her stay. There was something to the adage about wearing out one's welcome.

Living in Diego's duplex for the next six months would provide her with a taste of condo living. Once her temporary employment ended she would weigh her options as to whether she'd make Florida her permanent home or return to Connecticut. Her former employer had made it known that if she wanted to come back to work for them, they would make it happen for her.

She smiled at Diego. "Breakfast should be ready in five minutes. Would you like toast?" she asked, pressing a button on the coffeemaker. Then, she flipped a switch to activate the exhaust fan above the stove before turning on the grill.

He nodded. "I'll have one slice of wheat, please."

"Dry or butter?"

"Butter, please."

"Where are you going?" Vivienne asked when Diego turned to leave.

He stopped and peered at her over his shoulder. "Do I have your permission to go upstairs to get my suit jacket?"

Heat stung her cheeks as she dropped her gaze. "Yes, you may. And, I'm sorry, Diego—"

"No, you're not, Vivienne," he countered, frowning. "And, stop apologizing for saying what you mean. I'd rather you tell me exactly what you're feeling rather than deal with half truths. Remember why I hired you."

"Aside from my qualifications and that I wasn't afraid to mention you had mismatched socks, why did you really hire me?"

Diego gave Vivienne a long, level stare. She'd asked him the very question he'd asked himself when he lay in bed tossing and turning restlessly. His reason for hiring her wasn't physical in nature, because he hadn't planned to sleep with her. Sleeping with his personal assistant would be history repeating itself when Samuel Cole slept with Teresa Maldonado, and the result of the liaison was an illegitimate child that was the reason for discord that lasted decades and became the family's deepest secret.

"I hired you, Vivienne, because I like you."

Vivienne nodded numbly like a bobble head doll as she watched Diego until he disappeared from her line of sight. *I hired you because I like you.* She didn't want to read more into his statement, but she couldn't help wondering whether he liked her because she wasn't hesitant to speak her mind, or he liked her the way a man liked a woman. She prayed it was her outspokenness. That would make it a lot easier for her.

She knew she was physically attracted to her boss and that nothing would come from it since it would compromise their working relationship. It would be a lot easier if he wasn't so attractive and she wasn't so sexually frustrated.

In the four years she'd been married, not once had she considered having an affair, although some women in a similar situation wouldn't have hesitated to seek out male companionship. Not only had she been the faithful little wife but also the sexually frustrated fool. When she finally admitted to herself that she'd had enough, it was then that she'd decided to do something about it.

It no longer mattered about Sean's political career. It was her emotional health that was paramount. As a woman aware of her strong sexual passions, she either had to end her marriage or cheat. Thankfully she hadn't had to cheat, nor had she wished Sean dead. It was not that she didn't love him, because she did. It was that she'd fallen out of love with him.

Minutes later, the smell of frying bacon, brewing coffee and eggs filled the kitchen. Vivienne carefully slid two eggs, over easy, onto a plate for Diego then added a slice of buttered toast and bacon. She'd set the plate down at his place setting when he returned to pull out her chair. She sat down, and he rounded the table to sit across from her. She waited for him to pick up his fork and spear a portion of eggs. Their gazes met while he chewed. For an instant, there was a glint of humor in his eyes.

"It looks as if I'm going to have to give you a raise."

Vivienne turned her attention to her own plate. "Why is that?"

"Your cooking skills match your other qualifications."

"You didn't hire me to cook, Diego."

"I know that and you know that. But, since you've offered to prepare breakfast, then that, also, should be factored into your job description."

"How much are you going to pay me to prepare breakfast?" Diego angled his head, a gesture Vivienne liked and had come to look for. He quoted a figure, surprising her with the amount. "I'll have to think about it."

"What's there to think about, Vivienne? I believe it's more than enough compensation."

"Shame on you, Diego," she chided softly. "As a businessman, I know you wouldn't accept the first offer presented to you."

A light fired the dark eyes staring at her. "What is it you want, Vivienne?"

She picked up on his teasing tone. "Are you prepared to negotiate, Mr. Cole-Thomas?"

He leaned over the table. "That all depends on what you want, Miss Neal."

"Double it and you have a deal." Vivienne didn't need the money, yet she wanted to know how far she could go with him.

His eyebrows flickered. "What do I get if I decide to meet your demand?"

"You will get breakfast."

Diego shook his head. "I can get breakfast at work, Vivienne. You're going to have to sweeten the deal with something else."

"Let me think about it," she said, playing along with him.

"When do you intend to get back to me?"

"I'll let you know tonight."

A grin lifted the corners of his mouth. "I'll extend the deadline until twelve midnight. After that, I'm withdrawing my offer and the deal will be off the table indefinitely."

"Twelve midnight," she repeated softly. Picking up her fork, she speared a portion of her omelet, chewing it thoughtfully. There was no doubt living with and working for Diego Cole-Thomas was going to be anything but boring. "I'll let you know before midnight."

Chapter 5

Vivienne sat in the cushioned natural rattan chair at a round glass-topped table under a sand-colored umbrella on the balcony outside the kitchen, enjoying her second cup of coffee. It was the perfect place to begin or end the day. After Diego left, she'd cleaned up the kitchen, returned to her bedroom to make her bed and retrieve her cell phone.

Staring out at the angry, pounding gray surf, she lost track of time, ruminating on the path her life had taken. She'd kept her New Year's resolution to divorce Sean when she'd directed her attorney to file the petition to end her marriage, but instead of changing her status to that of divorcée, fate had preempted legal action and made her a widow. Sean's untimely death had spared him the embarrassment of his wife suing for divorce for abandonment and alienation of affection. He would've had to come up with a plausible reason why he wasn't sleeping with his wife.

The tabloids would've had a field day with headlines offering to pay anyone for information about an alleged clandestine affair. She'd sold their dream house, settled all of her financial obligations and had relocated to West Palm Beach. For Vivienne, living in Florida for the past two months was a bit of a culture shock. She still found it odd to wake up to see palm trees instead of oaks and maples, and the smoldering humidity and weeks of ninety-plus-degree temperatures made her feel sluggish.

She hadn't missed leaving Connecticut as much as she'd missed getting up each morning and going into work. Her career gave her a sense of purpose, something that was sorely missing in her marriage. As a woman in her early thirties, she knew she would've been able to balance a career with motherhood—if she'd become pregnant.

Her fervent wish had been to become a mother and work from home. Five percent of the investment firm's employees worked from home—most were women with small or school-age children.

Now, she was working from home, but not her home. She'd become a temporary employee living and working in a luxury Palm Beach duplex. Diego had given her the remote device that would allow her to leave and reenter the private residential condominium community without being stopped at security checkpoints, but she hadn't planned to go anywhere because she wanted to begin sorting through the mail before she set up a computerized system to manage his social calendar.

Although reluctant to leave the balcony with its incredible views of the ocean, the intense heat from the sun forced her to retreat to the cooler interiors. As soon as Vivienne walked into the kitchen and closed the pocket doors she was revived by the cool air coming in through the many vents. Emptying her coffee cup, she rinsed and put it into the dishwasher with the rest of the dishes and pots from breakfast. The clock on the microwave read eight-ten.

She'd established a pattern of calling her mother and former mother-in-law Thursday mornings. She always called Pamela Neal first, because Pamela and several other women had formed a golf club and they could be found on the links several times a week during the spring, summer and fall months. Elizabeth Gregory, who reportedly hadn't left her house since the day she buried her son, was amenable to receiving telephone calls but had refused all visitors.

Wending her way through rooms without walls, Vivienne found herself in the home office. Bright sunlight pouring into the room revealed what she hadn't discerned last night. As with the rest of the duplex, the furnishings were tasteful and wholly masculine. Leather, suede and linen in neutral shades were in keeping with the tropical setting.

Exotic orchids in varying colors spilled from delicately painted ceramic pots on a tapestry runner centered down the length of a rosewood table. Framed prints of orchids from various countries graced the wall above the collection of delicate flowers. Looking closer, she noticed all the prints bore postmarks—Vietnam, République du Bénin, Cuba, Madagascar and the former Soviet Union. She never would've thought über-macho Diego Cole-Thomas would be into flowers. But then she remembered his mentioning a new venture that included growing tea in South Carolina. The CEO of ColeDiz International Ltd. was indeed a twenty-first century gentleman farmer.

Walking over to look at the ocean, she punched in the speed dial on her cell phone. Vivienne smiled when she heard her mother's familiar greeting. "Good morning, Mom."

"How are you, sweetheart?"

She smiled. Everyone, whether male or female, young or old, friend or stranger was a sweetheart to Pamela Neal. "I'm good. I found a job."

There was a slight pause on the other end. "Are you really ready to go back to work, Vivienne?"

"Yes. The truth is I never wanted to stop working."

"Am I to believe that a leave of absence wouldn't have been preferable to your resigning and relocating?"

Vivienne registered the thinly veiled criticism in Pamela's beautifully modulated voice. Her mother was an expert in getting her point across without having anyone accuse her of being overbearing. "That's not what I'm saying, Mom. I had to get away from the curious stares and inane questions about Sean's death."

"You didn't have to move a thousand miles away, because there would have come a time when the stares and questions would have stopped."

"I'm sorry, Mom, but I couldn't wait for that time to come."

"Tell me about your new job, sweetheart."

Vivienne told her mother about her position as personal assistant for the CEO of an agribusiness. "I'm on call 24/7." What she didn't want or couldn't tell Pamela was that she was living with her boss, knowing the older woman would throw a hissy fit.

"Isn't that a little extreme, Vivienne?"

She heard the concern in Pamela's voice. "It's a six-month position, not long enough for me to burn out."

"I don't want to worry about you, sweetheart."

"Weren't you the one who said it's a mother's privilege to worry about her children regardless of their age?"

"Did I say that?"

"Yes you did, Mother." Vivienne knew Pamela didn't like to be called Mother. "Have you seen Elizabeth?" she asked, inquiring about her former mother-in-law.

"I invited her to go golfing but she said she doesn't want to leave the house because she believes there's someone watching her."

"Did she tell you who?"

"No."

"I'm going to call her as soon as I hang up with you." In the past, Elizabeth's endless list of excuses ranged from her not feeling well to she hadn't slept the night before, or she wanted to stay in to finish a book. But she had never told Vivienne that she was afraid to leave her home. "Have you heard from Daddy?"

"He called last night. He'll be home Sunday afternoon."

"Give him a kiss for me."

"When are we going to see you, Vivienne?"

"I probably won't get any time off until the end of the year."

"Promise me you'll spend Christmas with us. Vaughn, Justine and the kids are coming for the Christmas break, so I'd like to have the whole family together."

"I'll make certain to ask for time off."

Vivienne doubted whether Diego would deny her a vacation to celebrate Christmas with her family. She knew how important it was to Pamela to have a family gathering for Christmas. William Neal, who was now semiretired, had embarked on a quest to play one golf course in all of the lower forty-eight states. He had begun in Maine, and so far had worked his way down the Eastern Seaboard to Maryland.

"I'm going to give you the numbers where you can reach me if my cell is off," she continued. Vivienne gave her mother numbers to Diego's house and office before ending the call.

She punched in the area code and number to her former mother-in-law, counting eight rings, then hung up. She found it odd that Elizabeth Gregory's voice mail wasn't on. Worry lines appeared between her eyes. Unlike some women who complained about their mothers-in-law, Vivienne got along very well with hers. When she'd mentioned to Elizabeth that she'd felt like a political widow, the older woman had opened up about her own marriage and told her that Sean was just like his father, that the elder Gregory spent the minimum number of days in Connecticut to make him a legal resident of the state.

Vivienne made a mental note to call Elizabeth again later that morning. Meanwhile, she knew she had to begin sorting through the stack of unopened mail on the desk. She arranged the envelopes by postmarks, opening the oldest date first. It was mid-June and some of the envelopes bore dates going back more than three months, and most of the envelopes were stamped "Personal" and addressed to Diego at the ColeDiz office. One bore a delicate handwriting in blue ink with no return address.

This one is from a woman, she mused, bringing the envelope closer to her nose. The subtle hint of perfume lingered on the heavyweight vellum. Vivienne didn't want to read the contents, but knew she wasn't given a choice. After all, she was Diego's personal assistant and that meant she was privy to anything personal in nature.

Sliding an opener under the flap, she took out a single sheet of paper. It was dated February 23.

Diego,

I know we've had our differences, but I'm willing to apologize—but only if you'll do the same. You told me early on in our relationship that you weren't anti-marriage but that you weren't ready to start a family at this time in your life. I told you that I understood your position. But after dating for more than a year I believed it was time for a commitment. After all, we were sleeping together, saw each other exclusively and my biological clock is ticking.

I'm sorry if you felt I was unappreciative when you gave me a diamond necklace for Valentine's Day instead of the ring I'd asked for. And you were uncharacteristically cruel when you told me to sell the necklace and buy myself a ring—if that's what I wanted, but just not to tell anyone it was from you.

I've tried calling you, but you won't take my calls, I'm denied access to your condo, so writing is my last resort. If, after you read this you don't contact me, then I'll take it as a sign that what we had is over.

In closing I'll say it was fun and the SEX incredible!

Fondly,

Asia

"Damn," Vivienne swore softly under her breath.

Asia was practically begging him for a reconciliation, and he hadn't bothered to open her letter. And why, she mused, had Diego taken up a year of her life without committing to a future? Dating Asia had become a win-win for Diego. He never had to go looking for a date or a lover, because Asia was always available.

She didn't blame the woman for moving on. After all, she wanted to be married and she wanted a child, and if Diego wasn't going to agree with her, then he shouldn't have taken a year of her life.

Vivienne knew she couldn't afford to dwell on the events of her boss's private life, so she put the letter aside. It took more than three hours to read all of the correspondence, sorting it into piles for community, family, fraternal and social engagements. The dates had passed for a few of the events, but many were scheduled to be held during the summer and fall months.

Turning on the computer, she waited only minutes before it booted up. Diego had bought an all-in-one system with a large, flat monitor, wireless keyboard and mouse. Staring at the icons on the screen, she realized she'd be able to watch television or movies from the state-of-the-art system. That meant she could view her soaps while working at the same time. Now that she'd gotten into them again she wanted to keep up with the fictional lives of characters that permitted her a couple of hours of escapism.

Vivienne clicked on Microsoft Works to set up an address book, calendar and scheduling database for Diego's many commitments, marveling how he was able to balance his civic and social obligations while overseeing a global enterprise. The morning passed quickly; she stopped once to get a bottle of water from the mini fridge.

Diego stood under the entrance to the home office, staring at Vivienne as her fingers skimmed the keyboard. He smiled. She was concentrating so intently that she hadn't known he was watching her.

He'd told her that he was coming home early to go to

Miami. It would save time if they shopped at the upscale shops on Worth Avenue, but he'd promised his sister Celia that he would come down to Miami to have dinner with her. It wasn't often Dr. Celia Cole-Thomas took time off from her busy schedule as an E.R. doctor to reconnect with her family. Celia had offered to cook, but Diego suggested she make reservations at her favorite restaurant because she had to learn to relax. Her comeback was, when her older brother learned to relax, then she would follow suit.

The running Cole family joke was that the offspring of Timothy and Nichola Cole-Thomas were nuptial-phobic. What they didn't understand was that he wasn't marriage-shy, but he'd created a wish list timeline—divided by decades. Marriage was included on the timeline at the beginning of the fourth decade. By forty he would've taken ColeDiz in the direction he wanted it to go, which would leave him time to concentrate on being a husband.

"Have you eaten lunch?"

Vivienne's head came up. Shifting on her chair, she stared at Diego leaning against the doorframe. He'd removed his suit jacket and his tie hung loosely from his open shirt collar.

She smiled sweetly. "I decided to work through lunch because I wanted to make a good impression. After all, I don't want the boss man to think of me as a slacker."

Diego straightened, frowning. "Stop calling me that."

"What?"

"Boss man."

Vivienne affected an expression of pure innocence. "But isn't that what you are, Diego? You're a man and my boss."

His frown deepened. "That may be true, but…"

"But what, Diego?" she asked when his voice trailed off.

She knew she'd gotten to him, had shaken the hard-nosed businessman.

"Be ready to leave in exactly one hour." Turning on his heel, he walked away, leaving her staring at the spot where he'd been.

Rolling her head on her neck, Vivienne grabbed her shoulders and dug her fingertips into the muscles. She was tight from sitting in the same position. It'd been months since her last spa treatment. It was one of the things she missed since relocating. Not only had she had standing weekly appointments for her hair, face, hands and feet but also scheduled biweekly massages. Instead of sitting and watching soaps, she planned to search out a full-service salon. Spending a couple of hours being pampered in a salon was preferable to sitting and watching television.

She saved her data, shut down the computer and walked out of the office. There was only the sound of the cool air coming through the many vents from the central air-conditioning system. Summers in Florida were very different from living in Connecticut. Floridians went from their air-cooled homes to air-cooled cars and into air-cooled malls or supermarkets. People who lived in the Northeast waited patiently for the end of winter to enjoy the longer sun-filled spring and summer days.

Diego had given her an hour to ready herself. It took forty-five minutes for her to shower and slip into a white short-sleeved blouse with a mandarin collar she'd paired with a tan linen pencil skirt. A narrow dark brown snakeskin belt matched the strappy three-inch slingbacks and wristlet. She was sitting on a chair in the foyer when she heard Diego descend the staircase.

"I'm ready," she called out.

Diego walked into the foyer to find Vivienne sitting on a chair, one bare leg crossed over the opposite knee. His gaze lingered on her legs and feet before moving up slowly to her face. Her hair was swept up in a sophisticated twist, and she'd applied a minimum of makeup, but then he'd discovered she didn't need makeup to enhance her natural beauty. Her skin was clear, her eyes bright and her lush mouth temptingly curved where he wanted to kiss her to find whether it was as soft and inviting as it appeared.

He smiled when he realized they were similarly dressed. He'd changed into a tan linen suit with a white shirt in the same fabric, open at the throat, worn outside the waistband of his slacks. His footwear was a pair of chocolate-brown woven slip-ons.

Extending his hand, he pulled her gently to her feet. "We'll eat lunch during the drive down."

Her eyebrows lifted. "You've mastered the feat of driving while eating?"

"No, Vivienne. I've hired a driver to take us to Miami."

Her jaw dropped. "Oh!"

"Yes," he countered softly. "I don't want you to report me to the Department of Labor for unfair labor practices. After all, you are entitled to meal breaks."

Vivienne gave him a sidelong glance as she preceded him out the door after he'd activated the security system, the scent of soap and his subtle masculine cologne wafting in her nose. She walked a few feet to the elevator and punched the button.

"How many units are in this building?" she asked when the elevator doors closed behind them.

Diego stared at the bright pink polish on her groomed toes. He'd sat in his office, staring out the window, trying to recall everything about his newly hired personal assistant and failed. He still couldn't believe his good fortune when his HR manager escorted Vivienne Neal into his office. He'd hoped her appearance would come close to what she'd put on her résumé, but seeing her in person had surpassed his expectations. And when he recalled what Jake disclosed about Sean Gregory neglecting his wife he realized either the man was visually impaired or he was having an affair.

But, beyond her appearance, he found her to be perfect in every way. Yes, she had a wicked tongue, yet he respected her assertiveness. Vivienne was nobody's pushover. If she confronted and challenged him, then she would stand up to anyone.

"They were configured for forty, but I purchased two units to convert them into a duplex."

"It's a lot of space for one person."

"I bought the other unit for the future. If I decide to marry and have children," he added when she gave him a puzzled look.

Vivienne thought about the letter from Asia at the same time as a frown settled into her features. Men like Diego, who treated women like temporary conveniences, annoyed her, because that's what she'd become for Sean. He married her because having a wife served to enhance his image as a politician with a stable home life.

Taking her arm, Diego led Vivienne out of the elevator and across the lobby to a side door that led directly to the parking lot and an awaiting car and driver. "What's with the attitude?" he asked close to her ear.

"I don't have an attitude."

"I've seen that look enough to know you're pissed off about something."

"From who? Asia?"

Diego stopped midstride, the action causing Vivienne to lose her balance. He caught her before she fell, spinning her around to face him. "What are you talking about?"

Vivienne glanced over his shoulder to find the driver holding open the rear door to a shiny black Lincoln Town Car. She squinted in the bright Florida sunshine, chiding herself for not bringing her sunglasses.

"A letter from her was among those on the desk. Do you want to know what she wrote?"

A muscle throbbed noticeably in Diego's jaw. "No, I don't."

"Suit yourself," she murmured, ducking her head and sliding onto the leather.

"Let it go, Vivienne," Diego warned, moving over to sit beside her.

She gave him a look that spoke volumes as she clamped her teeth. Not only was Diego a tyrant but also cold and unfeeling. She couldn't understand how he'd dated a woman exclusively then left her because she wanted what every normal woman wanted: a commitment. He asked her to let it go, and she would. It was none of her business who he saw or slept with, because her job was to uncomplicate his personal life and not add to the confusion or chaos.

Leaning forward, Diego opened a built-in refrigerator and took out a plastic container of sushi, extending it to Vivienne along with a cloth napkin. "Do you want water or pop?"

She stared at the container. "Is there anything else, because I can't eat raw fish."

He replaced the container in the fridge. "I'm sorry. I should've asked you if you ate sushi before I ordered it."

"Don't apologize—"

Diego held up a hand. "It's all right, Vivienne. We'll stop in Palm Springs to eat something before going on to Miami."

"How far is it to Miami?"

"A little under seventy miles. Why?"

"I'd like to wait until we get to Miami and order a Cuban sandwich."

Diego's eyes brightened with the mention of the sandwich. "Are you sure?"

Vivienne gave him a dazzling smile. "Very sure."

Reaching for her hand, he held it gently. "Then, that makes two of us."

Settling back, she closed her eyes, enjoying the strength in the hand of the man cradling hers and the smooth motion of the car. Her chest rose and fell in an even rhythm and her head dipped to the right.

Diego hadn't realized Vivienne had fallen asleep until he glanced over at her. Disentangling their fingers, he placed his left arm over her shoulders and held her close. It wasn't the first time a woman had fallen asleep in his arms, but it was the first time in his life that he felt as if this one belonged there.

Chapter 6

Turning his head slightly, Diego pressed his mouth to Vivienne's hair, inhaling her flower-scented shampoo. He was able to touch and smell her without the guilt of coming on to his employee. It was what he'd wanted to do the night before when he saw her on the balcony. Although he hadn't slept with any woman who worked for ColeDiz, there was something about Vivienne Neal that made him want to break his promise.

Everything about her was subtle—her natural beauty, feminine scent, perfume and the subtle sexiness that emerged when he least expected it. Most times she kept him off balance with her sharp tongue, but it wasn't enough to minimize her overt femininity. He pondered whether her acerbic retorts were the result of an unfulfilled marriage or sexual frustration. What happened between a husband and his wife in their bedroom wasn't usually a topic for public conversation; however, it was apparent that Vivienne wasn't opposed to citing it as a basis for the dissolution of her marriage to a man who'd achieved superstar status his first term in Congress.

Diego closed his eyes as he expelled a breath, his mind awash with a jumble of questions about why Vivienne Neal was different from Asia and the other women in his past. When she'd mentioned the letter from Asia Huntley it was as if a door to a chamber of horrors reopened to let the demons he'd put to rest escape. He didn't know what Asia had written, and he didn't care, because it was probably lies. Just when he'd gotten used to her head games, she resorted to lying—lies that were indistinguishable from the truth. After a while he didn't know when she was lying or telling the truth. Then, it hadn't mattered once he decided to end their year-long relationship.

It wasn't until his driver entered the city limits for Fort Lauderdale that he realized what made Vivienne so unique. She was the only woman he couldn't intimidate with a glance or command. Her attitude was show me what you've got. He'd shown her, using everything in his bully arsenal. The exception was raising his voice. But, that was something he refused to do. He'd never had to raise his voice to his employees, managers or family for fear of losing control. And his greatest strength and ultimate success had been his iron-willed control, even if Vivienne insisted on challenging him.

Diego instructed his driver to stop on Calle Ocho, Miami's Little Havana thoroughfare before gently shaking Vivienne.

"We're here," he said in a quiet voice when she woke, blinking rapidly.

Vivienne smothered a yawn with her hand as she looked out the side window. "Where are we?"

Diego smiled when she yawned again. "We're in a section of Miami known as Little Havana." The chauffeur opened the rear door and he stepped out. "Let's go, sleepyhead," he urged Vivienne as she slid slowly off the leather seat.

They walked down a street as the sound of music with a distinctive Latin beat blared from passing cars, boom boxes and speakers outside a store advertising *música latina.* A group of elderly men sitting at a card table teased one another in rapid Spanish as they slapped dominoes onto the table.

Diego wrapped an arm around Vivienne's waist as they approached a trio of young men, who stopped whatever they were discussing to stare intently at the woman who walked past them. They exchanged glances when recognizing the proprietary embrace of the tall man glaring at them.

"How did you find this place?" Vivienne asked Diego after they were shown to a booth in a small coffee shop crowded with midafternoon patrons.

"My cousin's husband told me about it."

She glanced at the plastic-covered menu printed in English and Spanish. "Do they live here in Miami?"

"No. They live in Virginia."

Her head came up. Soft light from a hanging stained-glass lamp illuminated Diego's face. It was as if she was seeing him for the first time. His large, intense, deep-set eyes were so dark she doubted if light could penetrate them. "Where in Virginia?"

"Alexandria."

"Nice neighborhood."

"It is very nice," Diego said in agreement. "In a few years there'll be as many Coles living in Virginia as in

Florida. My brother Nicholas moved to the western part of the state two years ago to take over a failing horse farm."

Vivienne's eyes lit up when Diego mentioned horses. She'd gone riding whenever she spent her summer vacations at a New Hampshire sleepaway camp. "Does he race them?"

"No. He's set up a stud farm to breed Thoroughbreds. My father was a little disappointed when he turned down a position with ColeDiz to, as he puts it, 'horse around with horses.'"

"I take it your father isn't very fond of those of the equine persuasion."

An easy smile softened Diego's mouth. "He has an intense dislike for them because as a kid he was thrown by a horse that had a reputation of not allowing anyone to ride her. My dad had accepted a challenge from another boy that not only would he ride the mare, but he'd stay on for a full minute. He stayed on about three seconds and wound up with a broken leg."

"Why did he get up on the horse if he knew she wouldn't let him ride her?"

"You'll have to ask a sixteen-year-old boy who wanted to impress a girl who wouldn't give him the time of day."

"Did he ever get her attention?"

"He did better than that. He eventually married her."

Vivienne's mouth opened but nothing came out before the skin around her eyes crinkled in a smile. "Omigosh! It sounds like a romance novel."

Resting his chin on his fist, Diego studied the animated features of the woman sitting across from him. He liked seeing her smile. The gesture made her eyes light up, softened her mouth and made her more approachable.

"I take it you read romance novels."

"I love them."

A hint of a smile played at the corners of his mouth. "What I can't wrap my head around is that they all have the same plots."

"That's not true. They're formulaic, but that doesn't make the books the same."

"My mother and sister are addicted to them, and whenever I hear them talking about their favorite books or authors they sound interchangeable."

"They're genre books, Diego. They're no different from Walter Mosley's Easy Rawlins, or James Patterson's Alex Cross. When you pick up their novels you know what to expect."

Diego lifted his eyebrows. "Do you read only romance?"

"No. I usually read other genres, but romances are my favorite."

He gave her a long, penetrating stare. "Can you answer one question for me?"

"What is it?"

"Why do women read romance novels?"

"Why are you so gender specific? Men have been known to read and write them, too."

"I didn't mean to sound sexist, but the vast majority of romances are read by women."

Vivienne closed her eyes, smiling. When she opened them she found Diego staring at her with an expectant look on his face. She didn't want to believe that the CEO of an international company was really that interested in what she had to say about romance novels.

"You're right about that, but the reasons for reading the books are probably as varied as the women who read them. Some read for escape, others to figure out what's going wrong in their lives, and I'm sure there are some who read the books because they know what's going to come walking through their doors at six o'clock is the complete opposite of the heroes in the books."

"Which category do you fall into?" Diego asked.

She wanted to say the hero that wasn't coming home after a day's work, or that her hero hadn't even bothered to come home, but decided Diego didn't need to know about her past. "I read them for pleasure."

A cynical smile touched his lips. "Pleasure," he repeated softly. "That's an interesting choice of words. Are you using pleasure to mean sensual gratification, delight or a source of joy?"

"All of the above," she answered truthfully. "It's the only genre where I can visit a different city, state or country, have affairs with different men and I am assured of a happily ever after at the end of each novel. They show women how they should be treated and respected by a man who professes to love them. They're also a guide for young women who are looking for positive male role models when it comes time for them to choose a partner."

"Is it fair for the books to set a standard most men can't measure up to?"

Vivienne detected a hint of cynicism in his question. "What is there to measure up to, Diego? The books are about men respecting women, and their commitment to be faithful to her."

"That's easy."

"Is it?" she asked. "Then, why do some men find it so difficult to be faithful?"

Diego's intense dark eyes bored into her. "I don't know."

"What about commitment?"

"What about it, Vivienne? If I'm with a woman, then I'm committed to her and our relationship."

"Committed enough to marry her?"

His eyes narrowed and he lowered his hand. "Where are you going with this?"

"You said you didn't want to talk about her—"

"By *her* you mean Asia?"

"Yes."

"You're like a dog with a bone, Vivienne. But, since you want to know about me and Asia I'll tell you. She slept with one of my friends. Now, can we talk about something else?" Talking about Asia Huntley was like pouring salt into a raw, open wound for Diego.

Vivienne nodded. "I'm sorry it ended badly."

"I'm not," he countered. "Do you believe in affairs?" He'd smoothly segued to another topic.

"Yes, if they're between consenting single adults."

"What if one or both are married to someone else?" Diego asked, hoping to shed some light on Vivienne's marriage to Sean Gregory.

"For me that's a no-no. What about you? Have you ever had an affair with a married woman?"

His expression changed, becoming impassive. "I don't sleep with married women and I don't have affairs."

"What do you have?"

"Relationships."

"Is there a difference?" she asked.

"For me there is. The basis of an affair is usually sex, and in a relationship there's a romantic attachment."

Her smile was dazzling. "You are a romance hero. Are you blushing, Diego Cole-Thomas?" she asked when he lowered his gaze. "Yeah, you are."

Diego was saved from further embarrassment when their server came to take their food. The waitress who'd seated them approached the table. *"¿Usted está listo para ordenar?"*

Diego took a quick glance at the menu. *"Tendremos la mezcla de mariscos y un sándwich cubano."*

Taking one of a trio of pencils stuck in the oversize bun perched precariously on the top of her head, the attractive young waitress batted her lashes at Diego. "Would the *señor* like something to drink?"

"I'll have a beer. You forgot to ask the *señora* what she'd like to drink," he called out when the woman turned to walk away.

Red-faced, she returned to the table. *"¿Señora?"*

Vivienne ordered iced tea, struggling not to laugh as Diego continued to glare at their server. "That wasn't very nice, boss."

"That's because it wasn't nice of her to ignore you."

"I can take care of myself, Diego."

"Remember, I told you that I take full responsibility for my employees."

Vivienne didn't need Diego to take care of her, but for the first time in her adult life she would permit him to do what Sean couldn't or wouldn't do.

"Tell me about ColeDiz."

"That's a very long story."

"And we have the next six months before my contract with ColeDiz ends."

When Diego told his human resource manager that he wanted to hire a temp for six months to straighten out his personal affairs, he'd thought it was a long time. But that was before he met Vivienne Neal. Her tenure would end mid-December—the height of the Christmas holiday season—and his social calendar was busier than usual at that time. He knew he would have to come up with a reason to extend her employment beyond the new year.

"You should've eaten your sushi," Vivienne said to Diego when their orders were placed on the table. He'd ordered a dish with shrimp, scallops, crab and grouper with a roasted red pepper sauce.

"I shouldn't have presumed you eat raw fish. Are you allergic to anything else?"

"No." She picked up a sandwich stuffed with sliced roast pork, bread-and-butter pickles and Swiss cheese on a roll and took a bite. "Oh, my goodness," she sighed after swallowing a mouthful. "This is better than the last one I had. Thank your cousin for recommending this place."

"You can tell him yourself the week of the Fourth of July."

"What's happening then?"

"The entire family's getting together for a reunion. We always come together during the week between Christmas and New Year's, but with Coles spread out over the country sometimes the weather becomes a factor."

"Is the reunion usually held in Florida?"

Diego took a deep swallow from his glass of ice-cold beer. "Yes. We get together at the family compound in West Palm. I have cousins who live in Brazil, New Mexico, Mississippi, Massachusetts, Virginia and D.C."

Vivienne's eyebrows lifted when she saw the residue of foam on his upper lip. She touched her mouth with her forefinger, smiling when Diego dabbed his mouth with a paper napkin. "You missed it." Rising slightly, she leaned over the table and attempted to wipe away the fleck of white with her thumb, but found her wrist caught in a firm grip.

"Diego," she gasped when he drew her thumb into his mouth, alternating sucking softly and gently nipping the pad.

She closed her eyes, smothering a groan under Diego's sensual assault. Did he not know what he was doing to her, how long it'd been since a man had touched her other than to shake her hand? The electric shock raced up her arm, spreading to her upper body and bringing with it a swath of heat.

Grinning, Diego let go of her thumb but not her wrist. Using the napkin, he wiped her finger. Vivienne jerked her hand away, frowning, while her heart thumped erratically against her ribs as she attempted to regain a modicum of poise.

"Are you okay, Vivienne?"

She rolled her eyes at him. "Eat your food and leave me alone."

"I'm sorry."

"No, you're not, Diego."

He sobered quickly. "I said I was sorry if I embarrassed you. What I won't do is grovel."

"And I don't want you to," Vivienne countered.

Diego held out his hand. *"¿Tregua?"*

She stared at the long delicate fingers as if they were a venomous reptile. While he'd asked for a truce, she detected an underlying hint of arrogance. Reluctantly, she took the proffered hand. "Okay."

He didn't know what had gotten into him and Diego chided himself for teasing Vivienne, aware that it wasn't going to be easy to remain unaffected by her. Not only was she the most intriguing woman he'd ever met, but she also lived with him.

They hadn't spent twenty-four hours together, yet he was reacting to her the way he'd done as an adolescent when he didn't know whether to tease or kiss a girl he liked. Most times he teased them because it was preferable to rejection. However, it was very different with Vivienne Neal. She wasn't a girl, and he wanted to kiss her and at thirty-six he was emotionally stable enough to deal with her rejection. In fact, he'd welcome it if only to maintain their platonic relationship, and as she so emphatically stated, "I don't do bosses."

Diego knew he had to be careful not to blur the lines so that it became impossible to distinguish business from personal and pleasure, although that is exactly what he wanted to do. Reaching into the breast pocket of his jacket, he took out a monogrammed money clip and peeled off two large bills.

"Aren't you going to finish your food?" Vivienne noticed he'd barely touched his meal.

He glared at Vivienne under lowered lids. "I just lost my appetite."

She blinked once. "I hope you're not blaming me for that."

"Did I say you were the reason?"

She met his hostile stare with one of her own. "If you were a woman I'd think you were PMSing."

"Well, since I'm not, I can assure you that I am not PMSing."

Vivienne tossed her napkin on the table and picked up her tiny purse. "That's disgusting."

Diego slid out of the booth. "You started it, Vivienne, so don't look so put out."

"Are you always so crotchety?" she asked, sliding off the vinyl seat.

His eyebrows shot up. "I'm not old enough to be crotchety."

"Okay. Is ill-tempered a more appropriate word?"

He stared down at her staring up at him. Even with her heels, Diego still was a good head taller than Vivienne. "Try irascible."

"I prefer grumpy."

"There you go, Vivienne. You just have to have the last word, don't you?"

"No."

"Zip it," he warned softly.

"Yes, boss."

Cradling her elbow, he led her to where their driver awaited them. "We have to get to South Beach before it gets too late," he said as if what had happened between them was an everyday occurrence.

Stunned by his abrupt shift in mood, Vivienne wondered how she was going to make it through the next six months with a man who was a chameleon. She wanted to know who the real Diego Cole-Thomas was. Was he the man who barked commands at her like a general in private, or the sexy, uninhibited man whose public display of affection left her wanting more?

Diego nodded to his driver, who held open the rear door. He assisted Vivienne into the car and slid in beside her. "Thank you, Henri."

Beads of perspiration dotted the driver's dark brown shaved head as he nodded his head in acknowledgment. He hadn't removed his jacket, despite the intense heat. It was only when he raised his arm to close the door that Vivienne saw the butt of a holstered handgun under his left arm. She settled back against the leather seat, the importance of the man for whom she worked unsettling her poise.

How had she forgotten that Diego headed a successful

international business, that he was a member of one of the wealthiest African-American families, and he traveled with an armed driver and lived in a maximum security gated community. Her Connecticut home was built in a private community where visitors had to stop at a gatehouse before they were permitted access to the grounds, but it wasn't a fortress. Diego said he'd moved to the newly constructed condos because it afforded him the utmost privacy, but she suspected it had more to do with security than privacy. As CEO for a billion-dollar conglomerate, did he fear being kidnapped and held for ransom, or was he afraid of retaliation from an enemy or business rival?

She stared out the side window as different scenarios crowded her mind of news footage and movie plots of the kidnapping of wealthy people and their children. The most vivid one was *Man on Fire* where Denzel Washington portrayed an ex-CIA agent hired to guard the daughter of a wealthy Mexican businessman.

On a business trip to Caracas, Venezuela a while ago, Vivienne became aware of the extreme social and economic disparities between the haves and have-nots when she was met at the airport by a private paramilitary quartet hired by an affluent gem dealer who lived behind high, electrified gates with armed guards patrolling the perimeter. He'd hired tutors for his children because he feared for their safety outside the property.

"Why are we shopping in Miami when we could've gone to Worth Avenue?" Vivienne asked Diego when he closed the partition separating them from the driver.

Diego turned to stare at her averted face. "I promised my sister that I would have dinner with her."

"What role am I to play tonight?"

"What are you talking about?"

Vivienne turned to meet his questioning gaze. "When we have dinner with your sister will I be your personal assistant or your date?"

A beat passed before he smiled. "I hadn't thought about it, but since you're bringing it up, then I'll have to say my date."

A mischievous grin tilted the corners of her mouth. "Let me warn you in advance that I never kiss on the first date."

"What about the second date?" Diego asked, playing along with her. She shook her head. He lifted his expressive eyebrows. "The third date?"

"Yes," she said smugly.

"You're hard, Vivienne Neal."

"I have to be to put up with you. I don't plan to lock myself in the restroom to have a good cry."

"You know about that?"

"Yes, I do. You didn't hire me because you like me, Diego. You hired me because you know I'm not easily intimidated."

Diego knew Vivienne was right, but he wasn't going to let her know that. As it was she knew exactly what buttons to push to keep him slightly off balance and had him questioning why he wanted her as his social companion. Her intelligence and social grace would prove invaluable, but it was the woman herself that'd enthralled him. He was mentally prepared for the gossip about his association with the widow of a politician who hadn't been dead a year yet.

What he had to prepare for was the day when Vivienne Neal's six-month contract would expire.

Chapter 7

Vivienne stared at her reflection in a mirror in a boutique on 8th Street between Washington Avenue and Ocean Drive as a saleswoman stood off to the side with her hands clasped together as if she were praying. The boutique was her last resort after visiting upscale shops featuring Versace, Marc Jacobs and Kenneth Cole.

"It's perfect," the woman with coiffed champagne-pink curls whispered reverently. "You have excellent taste, Ms. Neal."

Vivienne smiled. "Thank you, Mrs. Chapman."

She'd spent close to two hours in the shop trying on slacks, tops, skirts, dresses, gowns and swimsuits, while Diego opted to spend the time watching ESPN in a space that doubled as the employees' break room. After she'd selected a dress and an outfit for the upcoming wedding and yacht party, Stella Chapman brought her garments that complemented her taste and style. What was ironic was that every article of clothing was blue and/or white—her favorite color combination.

"Do you think you're going to need accessories, because we have some lovely pieces that just came in yesterday? We have an orange wood necklace by Nathalie Costes that would look great with the navy sheath dress. And then there's a bracelet made of rosewood with a touch of gold that would be just darling with your white wrap dress."

"No, thank you. I have accessories," Vivienne replied.

She had enough shoes and handbags. Rings, necklaces and bracelets she'd inherited from her grandmothers, along with pieces Sean had given Vivienne for her birthday and their anniversaries, were in a D.C. safe-deposit box—jewelry she only wore whenever she'd accompanied her late husband to a political gala. She made a mental note to empty the box and close out a joint savings account.

Stepping out of the slacks, she handed them to the saleswoman. "I'm going to have a meltdown if I try on another piece."

Stella Chapman was hard-pressed not to give her customer a Cheshire cat grin. When the attractive woman walked into her shop with the most delicious-looking man she'd seen in a very long time, she thought they were tourists who were just browsing. Ms. Neal not only knew what she wanted, but her taste was impeccable. She favored clean lines that flattered her slender body and would make her a knockout at social events.

"I'll have my assistant bring your blouse and skirt." The assistant appeared on cue, as if Stella had willed it. She'd hung the garments on a padded hanger.

Vivienne gave the gracious woman a warm smile. She'd

offered to steam out the wrinkles in her skirt and blouse. "Thank you."

Her motions were slower than they'd been when she first walked into the specialty shop whose inventory surpassed those she'd seen in the designer boutiques. What she hadn't wanted was to attend an event and see another woman wearing the same garment. And, she'd been truthful when she said she couldn't try on another garment without screaming at the top of her lungs, because she'd literally shopped until she was ready to drop.

When she'd sorted through Diego's correspondence there were invitations from the Florida Education Foundation, The Parkways Foundation's annual "Garden Party," an America Cancer Society fund-raiser, birthday parties for an aerospace corporate president and prime-time television anchor and several retirement celebrations. He was also invited to attend weddings in Savannah, Georgia and upstate New York.

Vivienne slipped the narrow belt around her waist and buckled it. By the time she'd slipped into her shoes, gathered her tiny purse and walked out of the dressing room, Diego had settled the bill as shopping bags filled with her selections sat on the floor beside him.

"Did you get everything you needed?" he asked as she approached him.

She gave him a tired smile. "I think so."

"Do you want to go to another shop? We still have some time before we meet my sister for dinner."

Vivienne shook her head. "Please do not mention shopping for at least another month."

He leaned closer and pressed a kiss to her forehead. "What's the matter, baby? Can't hang?"

Too exhausted to acknowledge Diego's endearment, she leaned into his warmth and strength. "Guilty as charged."

Diego curbed the urge to take Vivienne into his arms and communicate that she didn't have to continue her tough-girl act with him, that he couldn't make up for what her husband should've done, but made a silent promise to make the next six months fun—not only for himself but also for her.

"I called Henri to bring the car around. As soon as he arrives we'll head over to the restaurant where we'll meet my sister."

Tilting her chin, Vivienne stared up into Diego's raven gaze, experiencing emotions she didn't want to feel. Not only did they live together, but he was also her employer and that made him forbidden fruit. And she was mature enough to recognize that Diego was as intrigued by her as she was by him. That was the sole reason why she'd come back at him with everything she had in her verbal arsenal.

Under another set of circumstances she never would've spoken to her boss as she had with Diego. He was terse and curt, but that wasn't a reason for her to challenge or question him. She also had to remember that at the end of her six-month position she would have to ask him for a reference.

Vivienne doubted whether she would return to Connecticut to live, which meant a favorable reference from the CEO of ColeDiz was certain to grant her access to some of the top Florida corporations.

"Weren't you the same woman who boasted that she'd melted the plastic on a few of her credit cards?"

She gave him a tired smile. "It could be that I'm out of practice. Or maybe it's the heat. It doesn't get this hot in Connecticut until July or August."

"How long have you lived here?"

"Two months."

"That's certainly not long enough for you to become acclimated to our weather. But I think it's more than the heat that has you dragging."

"What are you talking about?" Her voice was soft, nonconfrontational.

"Sleep, Vivienne. I saw you last night on the balcony when you got up to go back into your bedroom. A few hours later you were up making breakfast."

"I promised you that I would make breakfast."

"And, I'm not going to hold you to that promise," he countered.

"I don't know about you, but I always eat breakfast, Diego."

"That shouldn't change. What I'll do is change my hours so that we can eat together."

"But, I thought you wanted to be in your office by six." A slow smile spread over his face, bringing her gaze to settle on his sexy mouth and chin. "What's so funny?"

"Tú," he whispered in Spanish. "When are you going to get it into that beautiful head," he continued, "that I run ColeDiz, and that means I can set my own hours. If I choose to go into the office at four in the morning, or four in the afternoon no one's going to question me. Now that you're living with me I'll try and act like a normal human being instead of the monster you make me out to be. If you agree to make breakfast, then I'll stay around and eat whenever you eat."

A rush of heat burned beneath Vivienne's cheeks. "I didn't say you were a monster."

"Not in so many words."

"You are not a monster, Diego."

"*Gracias, m'ija.*"

"*De nada, m'ijo.*"

"*Cuidado,* Vivienne, or you'll have me believing that you like me."

The warmth of Diego's smile quickened her pulse. "Why shouldn't I like you? Didn't you tell me that you liked me?"

His reply was preempted when Henri walked into the boutique and gathered up the many bags, leaving Diego to escort Vivienne to the car.

Barton G.'s maître d' led Diego and Vivienne through the dining room and out into the courtyard. The restaurant was located in a residential neighborhood away from the frenzy of Ocean Drive.

Diego had explained during the short drive that the restaurant, which was originally called Gatti's, was a dining hangout for the famous and infamous. Legendary gangsters Meyer Lansky, as well as FBI head J. Edgar Hoover were frequent guests at the 1925 Deco-styled building.

Vivienne only caught a glimpse of the dining room's color palate that combined cool color blends of brown, copper and bronze with shocking bursts of vibrant green, deep red roses and shimmering light orchids. Seeing the orchids reminded her of the plants in Diego's home office. She'd wanted to linger at the stunning onyx bar, but the maître d' told Diego that his party was in the courtyard's Orchid Garden waiting for his arrival.

She smothered a gasp when they were led into an area that resembled a rain forest with an overgrowth of trees, vines and stalks of bamboo. A tall woman with a dimpled smile and a curly natural hairdo framing her round face rose to her feet with their approach. The man sitting beside her pushed back his chair and also stood up.

Diego pulled his sister close, kissing her cheeks. "*¿Cómo estás,* Cee Cee?"

Celia Cole-Thomas's smile vanished when she rolled her eyes at her older brother. "Please don't call me that awful name," she admonished softly. Reaching for his hand, she smiled again. "I'm good. In fact, I'm deliriously happy."

Diego's impassive expression didn't change. It'd been several months since he last saw his sister, and she was thinner than he'd ever seen her, and that included when she'd been in medical school and studied around the clock, eating only enough to keep going. If her face had been any more gaunt he would've suspected that she was anorexic. The simple black sheath dress she'd chosen to wear made her appear even slimmer.

Peering over her shoulder, he studied the man watching him with Celia. It was the first time since she'd moved to Miami more than three years ago that he'd seen her with a man. If she wasn't working double shifts at Miami's municipal hospital, then she was always trying to catch up on her sleep. Her date appeared to be in his forties, ten years his sister's senior. "Aren't you going to introduce me to your friend?" he asked sotto voce.

Celia's smile grew wider. "Yale's not my friend. He's my roommate and fiancé." She turned and held out her hand. "Yale, this is my brother Diego. Diego, Yale Trevor-Jones."

Diego's eyes narrowed as he studied the man with sandy-brown graying hair and cool gray eyes. He was only an inch or two taller than Celia and very slender. Reaching for his sister's left hand he stared at the diamond solitaire on her finger.

Smiling, he extended his free hand to Celia's fiancé. "Congratulations. You're a very lucky man." Releasing his future brother-in-law's hand, he turned to Vivienne. "This is Vivienne Neal. Vivienne, I'd like to introduce you to my sister Celia and my future brother-in-law, Yale Trevor-Jones."

Vivienne exchanged handshakes while mouthing appropriate phrases before Diego pulled out a chair to seat her. She found it odd that Celia and Yale both had hyphenated surnames. The first two years of her marriage she'd signed her name Vivienne K. Neal-Gregory until she finally dropped Neal. However, within months of becoming a widow she'd legally reverted to her maiden name.

She stared at Celia under lowered lashes, biting back a smile. The sparkle of the ring on her left hand matched the twinkle in her dark eyes. There was nothing about her features that indicated she and Diego were related except for their eyes. Both had deep-set, intense, very dark brown eyes. There was something about Celia's face that reminded Vivienne of a doll's. It was small and oval, her dimpled smile infectious.

Dropping an arm over the back of Vivienne's chair, Diego met Celia's questioning gaze. He knew she wanted to know who Vivienne was, but decided to make her wait. After all, she hadn't told him that she was dating, or that she was contemplating marriage. If family members teased him about being married to ColeDiz, then it was medicine for Celia.

"If it's all right with everyone, I'd like to order a bottle of champagne to celebrate my sister's engagement." There were nods from those at the table.

Vivienne smiled at Celia. A light sheen of moisture dotted her flawless olive-brown bare face. "May I please see your ring?"

"Of course." Celia extended her left hand.

"It's exquisite," Vivienne said. And it was. The center stone was a trillion-cut diamond flanked by matching baguettes. The diamonds were large, but not ostentatious.

Celia blushed. "Thank you."

"When did you two get engaged?" Diego asked.

"Last Saturday," Yale answered. "I wanted to wait until the July Fourth weekend to go up to Palm Beach and ask your father's permission, but with Celia and my schedule at the hospital I wasn't certain if we could get off at the same time."

"You're also a doctor?" Diego asked.

Yale nodded. "Celia and I work together in the E.R."

Diego's eyebrows lifted with this disclosure. "How long have you known each other?"

"A year," Celia answered quickly. "But, we just started dating seriously a couple of months ago."

Diego wanted to tell his sister that dating a man for a couple of months wasn't nearly enough time for her to consider marrying him—even if they were living together. But he held his tongue, because he didn't want Celia to think he wasn't happy for her.

"Did you tell Mom or Dad that you're getting married?"

"Not yet. We want it to be a surprise, but I wanted you to know first." Celia looped an arm through Yale's. "I've always confided in Diego, because I think of him as my knight in shining armor."

Diego's left eyebrow lifted a fraction. "Now that you're getting married Yale can take care of you."

A bright flush suffused Yale's lightly tanned face in the waning sunlight. "I intend to give Celia everything she wants or needs."

Diego's fingers tightened on the back of Vivienne's chair in a punishing grip. He wanted to tell the man sitting across from him that Celia could afford to buy any and everything she needed because she was a trust fund baby. Unlike many students, she hadn't had to get loans to finance her education. The money came out of her trust until at twenty-five she took control of the fund set aside for her at birth. All Dr. Yale Trevor-Jones could do for his sister was make her happy.

"That's very noble of you."

The other three people at the table stared numbly at Diego. Celia recovered first. "Diego." There was no mistaking the cool disapproval in her tone.

Ignoring her backhanded reprimand, he asked, "Have you set a date for the wedding?"

"No," she answered. "It probably won't be for another year."

"Why the wait?" Diego questioned.

Yale gave Diego a direct stare. "We're not certain whether we want to remain on staff at the hospital."

Celia placed a hand on Yale's back. "With my specialization in internal medicine and Yale's in pediatrics we've thought about setting up a private practice in a low-income neighborhood."

Yale smiled at his fiancée. "I've inherited quite a bit of money from my father and grandfather both of whom were doctors. I know Celia is concerned about the initial start-up cost of setting up a practice, but my inheritance will cover purchasing a building and most of the equipment. If we run out of money, then we'll take out a loan."

Diego looked at his sister, who gave him a surreptitious wink. It was apparent Celia hadn't revealed her net worth to the man she planned to marry. "Can either of you get off from the hospital one day next weekend?"

"What's happening?" Celia asked.

"Nothing much but a little R & R at my place on Jupiter Island."

Celia pressed her palms together. "I'll get off even if I have to call in sick." She turned to Yale. "Darling, my brother bought a spectacular house overlooking the ocean. The last time I saw it the contractor had just put down the floors. When I stood on the second floor cantilevered balcony watching the sun set over the ocean I felt as if I'd been transported to another world. Have you seen the house, Vivienne?" she asked without taking a breath.

"Not yet."

"Then you and Yale are in for a big surprise. You are bringing Vivienne, aren't you, Diego?"

"Damn, Cee Cee," Diego murmured. "There've been occasions when you've accused me of being rude, but do you really think I'd be so tactless to mention going to Jupiter Island in front of Vivienne and not invite her to come along?"

Vivienne gave Diego a sidelong glance when she wanted to kick him under the table. It was apparent that he was not only brusque with her, but also with his sister and future brother-in-law.

Celia sat up straighter. "I don't know what to think when you decide to do something, Diego."

Diego glared at his sister. "This is not the time or the place for a family spat, Celia," he warned softly. "We're here to celebrate a happy event, so can we put aside petty differences and enjoy ourselves?"

Celia smiled. She'd never been able to remain angry

with Diego for more than a few seconds. He'd always been the one to run interference between their parents whenever she wanted to do something they hadn't approved of. And Diego had been there for her when her first boyfriend broke her heart, and he was the one who championed her dream to become a doctor.

"You're right—as usual, Diego."

Diego opened his mouth to come back at his sister, but remembered they weren't alone. He raised his hand to signal a passing waiter. "Can we please have a wine list?" The waiter reached around his back, handing him a small leather book which Diego offered to Celia. "Please order what you like."

"Yale and I like Moët."

He stared at his sister under lowered lids. "Are you planning on having a large wedding?" If Celia and her future husband liked Moët, then he would order a case as an engagement gift.

"Even if I invited only Coles it'll still be a large wedding. And, then there's Yale's family. He's one of six."

Yale dropped an arm over Celia's shoulders. "Don't forget the clan in Wales."

She smiled at her fiancé. "Yale has family in Connecticut, England and Wales."

"Where did you live in Connecticut?" Vivienne asked Yale. She knew he wasn't from the South the instant he'd opened his mouth.

"Cos Cob. And you?"

Her eyebrows lifted. Yale had grown up in an affluent Fairfield County suburb. "Stamford."

Yale winked at Vivienne. "It's not often that I meet a Connecticut Yankee in the Sunshine State."

Celia studied the woman sitting next to her brother. She found Vivienne Neal very different from most of the women he'd dated. Not only was she slimmer, but she appeared very reserved. The others were chatty and tried too hard to impress Diego and his friends. There were two women who'd managed to hang around longer than the others, but once they began talking about marriage, Diego ended the relationships. He'd confided to her that he wanted to be the one doing the asking, not the reverse.

"How long have you lived in Florida?" she asked Vivienne.

"I've only been here two months."

"Do you plan to live here permanently?"

Vivienne blew out a breath. "I'll consider it if I can make it through the summer heat. If not, then I'm going back North."

A frown creased Diego's smooth forehead. "Didn't you promise me that you'd stay until mid-December?"

A pregnant silence descended on the four at the table as Yale, Celia and Diego stared at Vivienne, who forced a smile she didn't feel. Diego wanted her to pretend she was his date when it was he who wasn't following the script. He knew she'd signed a contract to act as his personal assistant, so she couldn't understand why he'd put her on the spot with his query.

Resting a hand on the nape of his neck, she leaned over and pressed her lips to his jaw. "Thank you for reminding me, *m'ijo.* I told you I'm not used to this heat."

Celia's eyes sparkled like polished jet. "You speak Spanish?"

Vivienne explained that she'd majored in Romance Languages, lived in Europe for a year and had recently resigned her position with an investment company. She didn't tell the newly engaged couple that she was Sean Gregory's widow. She'd asked Yale where he'd lived because she didn't know if he was from her late husband's congressional district. She was spared revealing more about herself when a waiter approached their table with menus and rattled off a litany of recommended favorites.

"I'd like to suggest that we order different appetizers and entrées, then share," Celia suggested when the waiter walked away.

Diego studied the extensive menu. "What do you recommend?"

"The coconut crusted voodoo shrimp is a must," Yale said.

Diego turned to Vivienne. "What if we let Celia and Yale order for us?"

She smiled. "Okay."

Within minutes another waiter appeared with a bottle of chilled champagne in an ice bucket and four flutes. Quickly and expertly, he uncorked the bottle, filling the glasses with the pale, bubbly liquid.

Diego raised his flute, his gaze fixed on his sister's smiling face. "I raise my glass in a toast to Yale and Celia. Remember, my man, in the words of the illustrious Oscar Wilde, 'Women are made to be loved, not to be understood.'"

Yale, grinning from ear to ear, touched his glass to Diego's. "I'll drink to that."

Instead of kicking Diego under the table, Vivienne dug her nails into his thigh, encountering solid muscle in her effort to silently chastise him. A soft gasp escaped her parted lips when his hand rested on her knee, then moved higher, fingers caressing the warm, bare, silky flesh on her thigh.

Leaning to his left, Diego pressed his mouth to Vivienne's ear. "Don't start something you don't intend to finish, *m'ija*," he whispered.

Vivienne recovered when Diego removed his hand to offer her toast to the newly engaged couple. "I'd like to offer a toast in the words of the great Roman poet Virgil, 'Love conquers all things. Let us give in to love.'" She touched her flute to Yale's and Celia's, deliberately ignoring Diego.

Nothing in her voice or expression revealed the riot of emotions racing through her body. He had ignited a sensual fire that only he could extinguish. She knew they were playing a dangerous game that would become more perilous as time passed. She was pretending to be his date, and she would step into the role again on Saturday and Sunday, while behind closed doors she would become Ms. Neal, personal assistant.

Celia sat, stunned by the scene unfolding before her. She'd never seen her brother exhibit a modicum of overt affection with any of the women he'd dated. Most times he appeared bored, while they seemed totally oblivious to his indifference. Several of the single female doctors had asked to meet Diego, but Celia was forthcoming when she told them that her brother wasn't interested in a serious relationship. But there was something very different about Vivienne Neal. She hadn't draped herself over Diego as the others had done.

"How long have you two been together?"

"Not very long," Diego said quickly.

"How long is 'not very long'?" Celia continued with her questioning.

Vivienne stared at her date's stoic expression. "This is our first date."

Yale drained his flute and reached for the champagne bottle. "Where did you meet?"

A silence ensued and Vivienne knew it would only be a matter of time before Diego's family became aware of their relationship. "I'm working for Diego."

Celia went completely still. There was an unwritten rule that went back eighty years that the head of ColeDiz would never become involved with any of the employees. "You work at his company?"

"No. I'm your brother's social secretary." Vivienne felt social secretary sounded more professional than personal assistant.

"*¡Eso es estupendo!* You don't know how long my father has been after him to hire someone to organize his social calendar. Diego will always arrive at a family get-together late, or miss it entirely because of a scheduling conflict."

Vivienne was spared having to answer more questions from Celia when their server approached the table to take their orders. Yale ordered appetizers and entrées of fish, meat and poultry with accompanying side dishes. He also ordered a round of Cody's mojitos, a potent concoction of lime, sugar and fresh mint leaves and seven-year-old rum. Vivienne took one sip and knew immediately it would last her throughout the meal. Glasses were raised again, as the pediatrician toasted the best mojitos north of Havana.

Dinner became a three-hour affair and when Diego offered the services of his driver to take Yale and Celia back to their apartment, both refused, opting to walk the four blocks.

Diego hugged and kissed his sister before offering her fiancé a handshake and rough embrace. "I hope you guys can make it up next weekend."

Celia gave him a warm smile; he returned it with one

of his own. She'd seen Diego smile more in the past few hours than she'd remembered since he'd taken over the reins as CEO of ColeDiz. Perhaps having a social secretary had eased some of the anxiety of attempting to balance his business and personal life.

"We're going to try. Even if Yale can't get off, I'm coming."

The two couples parted, Vivienne heading to the parking lot, Diego following, where Henri waited for them. She slipped onto the rear seat, kicked off her heels, tucked her legs under her body and closed her eyes.

"Are you all right?"

She smiled, but didn't open her eyes. Diego's deep voice floated over her like a sensual fog. "I'll let you know tomorrow. I ate and drank too much."

"Was that your first mojito?"

"Yes."

Diego tried making out her expression in the vehicle's dim interior. Vivienne admitted that she'd eaten and drunk too much, when in reality she'd eaten only small portions of the dishes. As for drinking she hadn't finished her flute of champagne or the excellent mojito.

"I'll make you one tomorrow that's not too strong."

Vivienne remembered they were to attend a wedding and birthday celebration, both of which were certain to serve alcoholic beverages. She opened her eyes. "What's happening tomorrow?"

"We're going to Jupiter Island."

Vivienne sat up straight. "I thought you were going next weekend?"

"We are. The wedding and the birthday celebration are both on Jupiter Island. ColeDiz's offices close on

Fridays during June, July and August. We'll drive up early tomorrow afternoon to unwind before the weekend's festivities."

"I'd planned to go to a salon tomorrow for my hair and a mani-pedi."

It took Diego a full minute before he realized a mani-pedi was a manicure and pedicure. "Do you have an appointment?"

"No. Where I go has walk-in services."

"We'll leave whenever you're finished."

Vivienne closed her eyes again. She felt relaxed, more relaxed than she had in months. The ongoing tension she'd felt that kept her off guard and off balance for years vanished the day she'd met with her attorney to go over the conditions of her divorce decree. She hadn't requested alimony, but was willing to compromise to split the proceeds from the sale of their Connecticut home.

"I'll get there when they open."

"Don't rush, Vivienne. I usually sleep in late Fridays."

"I guess you don't want breakfast before I leave."

He chuckled softly. "Have you agreed to make breakfast for me?"

"Yes, I have."

"Thank you."

Silence descended for several miles until Vivienne said, "Thank you for my new wardrobe."

Several beats passed. "There's no need to thank me, Vivienne. A beautiful woman should wear beautiful clothes."

Instead of being buoyed by Diego's compliment, she felt as if she'd been punched in the gut. "So, it's all about image."

The seconds ticked off. "That's all it's ever about,"

Diego said. "Success and image are not only synonymous but also interchangeable."

Something inside Vivienne sank like a stone. Diego had admitted to hiring her because of her qualifications, but the truth was he'd hired her for the same reason Sean had married her: she enhanced his image.

However, the difference was she wasn't married to Diego Cole-Thomas and her association with him would end mid-December. Within seconds her dark mood lifted when she decided to use whatever Diego was offering to her advantage. She would hobnob with the Palm Beach and Jupiter Island elite, and then, come the new year, she planned to move on with her life.

Chapter 8

Vivienne stopped at Alicia's house after leaving the salon to pick up her mail and to give her friend a recap of her first full day of work. Her anxiety about her mother-in-law eased when she received a letter with E.D. Gregory and a Stamford, Connecticut post office box address instead of her home address on the flap. She thought about what her mother had said about Elizabeth, who believed she was being watched. Perhaps she would find out what was going on with the older woman after she read her letter.

Sitting on the lanai with Alicia, she took a sip of sweet tea. "My life has become a rerun. I was an accessory for Sean and now again for Diego Cole-Thomas."

Alicia narrowed her eyes. "Why are you protesting so much, Viv? Do you want Diego to see you as a woman or an employee?"

"Both."

"You can't have both, girlfriend. Either you're an employee or a woman willing to get involved with her boss."

"I don't do bosses and he doesn't do employees."

"Says who?" Alicia asked.

"Diego told me that he doesn't get involved with his female employees."

"Mr. Cole-Thomas is a liar, because he is involved with you, Viv. The man hired you to straighten out his social calendar, but yet you're doing double duty as his date. It just doesn't add up. I know he hired you because your qualifications are impeccable. But so is your face and body. Any man, and that includes the sexy bastard, would want you on his—"

"What did you call him?" Vivienne said, interrupting her friend.

"A sexy bastard. There was a write-up about Diego in a local magazine and the journalist referred to him as a 'sexy bastard' and the moniker stuck. Come on now, you have to admit that he is sexy as hell."

"I'm not going to deny that."

Alicia waved a hand. "Then, stop complaining and enjoy the ride, Viv. If I had your background not only would I jump at the chance to work for Diego, but I'd also jump his bones. He'd probably fire me rather than charge me with rape, but at least I'd get to sample what Asia Huntley prattled on about after their breakup."

Alicia's mentioning Asia's name garnered Vivienne's complete attention. "Who was she?" she asked, pretending ignorance.

"She used to be a local TV weather girl. It appears she and Diego were going at it hot and heavy for almost a year. Then, like that—" Alicia snapped her fingers "—it was over.

The word was that Asia was reassigned to another station on the West Coast, but I heard through the grapevine that Diego dropped her like last week's kitty litter. He refused to talk about the breakup, while Asia dropped hints about their sex life like Hansel and Gretel dropping bread crumbs."

The sex was incredible! The last line of Asia's letter was branded into Vivienne's brain. Either Diego was that good, or Asia had been undergoing a sex drought. She took another swallow of tea, then set the glass on a low table and pushed to her feet.

"What was his reaction to her spilling her guts?"

"His reply was always 'No comment.'"

Good for him, Vivienne mused. At least he wasn't one to kiss and tell. "I'd better head out now," she told Alicia, who also stood up. Vivienne hugged her former college roommate. "Call me next week so we can get together over dinner."

The delicate lines around Alicia's green eyes deepened when she smiled. "Do you think your boss will let you off?" she teased.

Sucking her teeth, Vivienne gave her a baleful look. "Very funny, Ms. Cooney. Of course I can take time off. Call me," she repeated as she walked around to where she'd parked her car.

Diego had urged her not to rush, so she'd had her hair styled, a manicure, pedicure, facial and a thirty-minute massage. Slipping behind the wheel of her car, she started up the engine. But, before backing out of the driveway she pulled down the visor and stared into the mirror, not recognizing the image. Vivienne realized she'd changed the instant she instructed her lawyer to draw up the divorce papers, and again when she boarded the plane to D.C. to tell Sean that she was divorcing him. She'd changed again when informed that her husband had been killed in a hit-and-run. Now, she'd changed once more, because she was totally bewildered by her response to Diego Cole-Thomas.

Vivienne was more comfortable relating to him in her role as social secretary. But, whenever she had to pretend she was Diego's date she experienced mixed feelings. She had to pretend that she liked him. The problem was his response to her made it very easy to like him. What she had to keep in mind was that it was only a pretense, that he wasn't a substitute for Sean. Flipping up the visor, she backed out of the driveway and headed to Palm Beach.

Less than a mile from Diego's condo Vivienne maneuvered off the road and parked when she remembered Elizabeth Gregory's letter. Slipping her finger under the flap, she took out the single sheet of paper. She smiled. Elizabeth's slanted, precise handwriting harkened back to another century. The cursive letters resembled calligraphy.

My dearest daughter,

I've moved. I decided to close up the house and stay with my niece for a while. Her teenage children are driving me a bit crazy, but I've come to relish noise over the silence that had me believing that I was living in a tomb.

I told your mother that I suspected someone was watching me, because each and every time I looked out the window I saw a strange car parked across the street from the house. Perhaps I've become a bit paranoid, but I'm not taking any chances. I opened a post office box in the branch where my niece's husband works, and had my mail forwarded. So, if you choose to write, then use the return address. That nice police officer assigned to Sean's case called me last week. Unfortunately, he hadn't come up with anything. But, I'm praying that the horrible person who hit my son and left him dying in the street will be caught.

Write back soon.

Love,

E. D. Gregory

Eyes filling with tears and her hands shaking, Vivienne folded the letter and returned it to the envelope. Mentally she willed the tears not to fall, but was unsuccessful. She wasn't crying for herself—she'd done enough of that to last a lifetime—but for her grieving mother-in-law. Elizabeth had taken her marriage vows to heart and stood by her husband through sickness and death. She'd become the dutiful caretaker as she shared her husband's last days, confiding that in the two-plus decades of marriage she had to wait until her husband was terminally ill to have him to herself.

It was this disclosure that prompted Vivienne to end her sham of a marriage. Not that she wanted anything to happen to Sean, but she didn't intend to play the grieving widow. But fate had thrown her a curve when she did become the grieving widow as bits and pieces of Sean's life and political career became fodder for the press. One tenacious journalist had reported the absence of Mrs. Sean Gregory in many of the photographs where the wives of other congressional members were present. Many of her articles contained veiled innuendos as to Sean's infidelity and/or sexual predilection, while suggesting that the congressman's marriage was in jeopardy before his premature death. An outpouring of resentment and cries of insensitivity from Sean's supporters prompted her to print a retraction.

Reaching into her bag for a tissue, Vivienne blotted her cheeks. She didn't have Elizabeth's niece's address or phone number, which meant she would have to write her. Aware that her mother-in-law was partial to greeting cards—the funnier and sillier the better—she planned to pick up a few in an attempt to lift Elizabeth's spirits.

Diego sat up straight when he heard the distinctive chime of the front door opening. He hadn't realized he'd been waiting for Vivienne, waiting to see her again. She'd come into his life two days ago, but he felt as if he'd known her much longer. She had a sharp tongue and quick comebacks—something he admired yet wouldn't openly admit to her. He'd learned quickly that she was opinionated and not easily intimidated. If they were doing business together he would've considered her more than a worthy opponent.

And, as an actress in a role, she was flawless. Each time she touched him, called him *m'ijo,* he'd wanted it to be real. There was something about Vivienne that was so different from the other women he'd known or been involved with. Looks and intelligence aside, he'd found her poised and utterly enchanting. There wasn't a need for her to talk about herself or her attributes as Asia had done constantly. As a television personality she didn't know when to turn off her professional persona when away from the cameras, and after a while he'd learned to turn off and tune her out.

Diego realized he'd grown bored with Asia Huntley long before she slept with one of his friends, but hadn't wanted a repeat of what he'd had with Lisa Turner. Lisa was the only woman who'd managed to slip under the barrier he'd erected to keep women from getting too close to him. She was the only one he'd proposed marriage to, but she'd turned him down because she was trying to grow her cosmetic company and hadn't wanted any distractions. It was the first time a woman had referred to him as a distraction. It was only after they mutually agreed to stop seeing each other that she admitted that she couldn't see herself in the role of wife and mother. He thanked her for her honesty and moved on mentally and emotionally.

Now, Vivienne Neal was another matter. Not only did she work for and with him, but she also lived with him. It wasn't as easy not to be affected by her when they slept under the same roof. His rationale for not watching her try on clothes at the Miami boutique was because he'd wanted to be surprised when they went out together. The anticipation of seeing her in soft, flowing fabrics that flattered her slender body was akin to a child waiting to open the gaily wrapped presents nestled under the Christmas tree.

What Vivienne hadn't realized was that she was his present. He could take her out and show her off without the pretense that there was more to their association. They were both adults who were fully cognizant of what had become a business arrangement. And, in another six months the charade would come to an end.

He walked into the entry at the same time Vivienne turned to close the door behind her. The night before he'd given her an extra magnetic card key that permitted her to come and go at her leisure. A slow smile tipped the corners of his mouth when she turned around. Her hair was a mass of tiny curls that moved as if they had taken on a life of their own.

Vivienne sucked in her breath when she saw Diego standing only a few feet away. He was dressed down in a pair of faded jeans, running shoes and a cornflower-blue linen shirt she'd come to recognize as a guayabera. Many of the men in Little Havana favored the long and short-sleeved versions in different fabric and colors. The one Diego wore was similar to a camp shirt with four patch pockets without the pleats.

"Have you been waiting long?" Her voice was breathless, as if she'd run a long, grueling race.

She didn't know why, but she preferred seeing Diego dressed down and unshaven. His tailored suits, custom shirts and silk ties made him appear less approachable.

Moving closer, Diego stared down at her upturned face. "No."

A slight shudder shook her when she met the raven gaze smoldering with a lazy seductiveness that reminded her of how long it'd been since she'd slept with a man. And as much as she wanted to lie with Diego at that moment she knew it would never happen. He'd been emphatic when he said he didn't sleep with his employees, and she'd been equally emphatic when she declared that she'd never sleep with her boss. She'd always thought women foolish to engage in office romances, but the masculine specimen standing only feet away made her aware of how easy it was to succumb to temptation.

She forced a brittle smile. "I packed this morning, so I just have to get my bags."

"What did you do to your face?"

Vivienne touched her cheek. "What are you talking about?"

"It looks different."

A slight frown appeared between her eyes. Other than a facial and having her eyebrows waxed, she hadn't done anything else. The aesthetician had applied an oil-free moisturizer to her skin and applied a coat of lightly tinted lip gloss.

"I had a facial," she admitted. Diego continued to stare at her, making Vivienne more uncomfortable with each passing second.

"You look beautiful."

His compliment caught her completely off balance. Pulse points throbbed with the rush of blood pounding her body. Lowering her gaze in a gesture that was completely demure, she nodded. "Thank you."

Diego took her hand and examined her fingers. The color on her nails reminded him of ripe raspberries. "Very nice," he crooned.

Vivienne curbed the urge to snatch her fingers from his loose grip. "If you don't stop you'll give me a swelled head."

A shadow of annoyance tightened his jaw. "I doubt that, Vivienne. You have to know that you're an incredibly beautiful woman. I told you last night it's all about success and image. Having you around enhances my image appreciably. You are one of those women who are a rare find—beauty, poise and intelligence. What you have to learn to do is use it to your advantage."

"I did," she shot back angrily, "when I married Sean Gregory."

"True," Diego conceded. He wanted to tell Vivienne that she'd married a man with the star power of a Hollywood A-list actor, a D.C. pol who some predicted would one day occupy the Oval Office, a selfish, overly ambitious man who'd neglected her in his pursuit of personal power. "I'm ready to leave whenever you are," he said instead.

Vivienne was still fuming when she climbed the stair-case to the second floor. Just when she thought she was be-ginning to understand her boss he verbally body-slammed her with his constant reminder of why she was working and living with him. Her delicate jaw tightened. It was the last time she intended to accept his comments. After all, she was an employee and there were laws against harassment in the workplace. It didn't matter whether the workplace was an office or someone's home, the law still applied.

She knew she was on edge because of Sean's mother's note. What if, she mused, Elizabeth wasn't paranoid or de-lusional? What if someone was watching her? What if Sean's hit-and-run wasn't an accident? What if someone had deliberately run him down?

The what-ifs bombarded her like missiles as she picked up a large tapestry bag and matching garment bag with her dresses for the wedding and yacht party. She'd clenched her teeth so tightly that when she descended the staircase her jaw ached.

Diego took one look at Vivienne's face and knew she was upset. Reaching for her overnight bag, he punched a button on the security pad, opened the door and closed the door behind them. He took the garment bag from her loose grip as they waited for the elevator. When the elevator arrived, she stepped in and stood at the opposite end of the car with her back to him.

Using his elbow, he hit the button for the lower level. "Sulk on your own time."

Vivienne rounded on him. "How can I do that when my time is your time?"

"What the hell is bugging you, Vivienne?"

Her eyes gave off angry sparks. "You, Diego. I don't need

you to keep reminding me that I'm nothing more than a paid companion."

"You're not my companion," he countered.

"You're delusional, Diego Cole-Thomas, if you think not. You buy me pretty clothes so I can make a good impression for your friends and business associates. And you pay me the big bucks because you know I won't embarrass you."

"That's not the only reason."

"Yeah, I know," she drawled sarcastically.

His sweeping eyebrows lifted. "No, you don't know, Vivienne. I told you that I like you, but it goes a little deeper than that."

"And, pray tell, what do you mean by deeper?" The flame she saw in his coal-black eyes startled her. She had her answer. He liked her the way a man liked a woman.

"Even though I find myself quite attracted to you, I know nothing will ever come of it."

Her expression didn't change. She hadn't been mistaken. Diego being attracted to her was going to complicate everything. Vivienne knew she wouldn't be able to keep their relationship in perspective now that she knew her boss was attracted to her. What she hadn't wanted to or couldn't openly admit was that she, too, was quite attracted to him.

The elevator slowed, coming to a stop at the building's underground garage. The doors opened, but they didn't move. Vivienne blinked, shattering the spell. "Thank you for being forthcoming."

Diego gave her a half smile. "You're welcome."

They exited the elevator, nodding to the security guard in a small booth. Vivienne still felt uncomfortable with the number of security personnel safeguarding the property and privacy of the residents of two twenty-story buildings.

"Where's Henri?" she asked, staring at the empty space where the driver usually parked the Town Car.

"He's off on Fridays during the summer. I'm driving to Jupiter Island."

She rolled her eyes at Diego. None of the ColeDiz employees worked Fridays during June, July and August— none but her. But then, attending a wedding and yacht party could hardly be interpreted as work. Her mood brightened. She planned to have fun and party like a rock star.

"My car is over here."

Vivienne followed him over to a shiny yellow classic Jaguar roadster with a black leather interior. "Is this really your car?"

Diego unlocked the trunk, placing her bags inside, then closed it. Rounding the two-seater, he unlocked the passenger-side door. He winked at Vivienne. "Yes, it's really my car."

Waiting until he was seated beside her, Vivienne turned and smiled at Diego. "Where did you get a 1973 Jaguar, four-speed XKE Series III in mint condition?"

He stared at her as if she'd grown a third eye. "Where did you learn about cars?"

"I learned from my dad. Last year he bought a 1964 Mustang from a collector for an obscene amount of money."

Diego started the car, the engine roaring to life before purring like a contented cat. "It's not obscene if he really had to have it."

"Like you had to have this Jaguar?"

Grinning broadly, he maneuvered out of the parking space toward the garage exit. "Yes. My cousin's husband is into vintage cars, so when I told him I was looking for one he told me not to buy anything until I saw one he'd just restored. I took one look at this baby and wrote him a check on the spot."

"You're as bad as Daddy. My mother said he gave the man a check without road testing the car."

"It doesn't matter, *m'ija,* because he could've always had a competent mechanic put in a new engine or transmission."

"Isn't it just like a man to buy something without trying it out?"

Diego wiggled his eyebrows. "That's because we are hombres!"

"Hombres absurdos," she said under her breath.

"It's not silly, Vivienne."

"He's like a big kid," Vivienne told Diego about William Neal's golf quest. "He and his law partner, who just happens to be named Theodore, have embarked on a midlife Bill and Ted's excellent golf adventure."

Diego accelerated after leaving a security checkpoint. "Is your mother a golf widow?" He winced when he realized he'd mentioned widow. How could he have forgotten that Vivienne had recently lost her husband? He gave her a sidelong glance. "I'm sorry for my insensitivity."

"Why are you apologizing?"

"I shouldn't have said *widow.*"

Vivienne took a deep breath as she stared through the windshield. She wasn't in front of cameras or microphones, so she knew she didn't have to pretend she was the grieving widow.

"It's all right, Diego."

"Is it really all right, Vivienne?"

Her head came around and she stared at his distinctive profile. His expression made him appear as if he'd been carved from stone. "Yes, it is, Diego. Sean's gone and I have to get on with my life. If the situation were reversed I'm certain Sean would do the same."

"How was it being married to a politician?"

A heavy silence descended inside the car. "Lonely."

Diego's fingers tightened on the gearshift. Vivienne had just confirmed one of the facts in Jacob's e-mail. "Weren't you aware of what you were going to encounter when you married him?"

"When I married Sean he wasn't a politician," she said defensively. "He was working out of the D.A.'s office when his father got sick and was forced to give up his congressional seat. Sean ran and won the seat that had been his father's for almost two decades. He loved his constituents and they loved him back. He lived and breathed politics, and in the end I became the casualty of his fight for truth, justice and the American way. He'd become Superman in every sense of the word.

"When Sean and I married we'd promised to support each other's dreams, but along the way his dream for power controlled his life. If I wanted to have breakfast with my husband I had to go through his chief of staff and make an appointment. The one time I flew to Washington unannounced and walked into the restaurant at the Hay-Adams Hotel where Sean ate breakfast I thought he was going to stroke out. But he recovered quickly, introducing me to a senator and a cabinet member, then ordered French-style tournéed potatoes, cornflake-crusted brioche French toast with fresh berries and freshly squeezed grapefruit juice for me as if it was something I ate on a regular basis. When breakfast ended he took me aside and chastised me about not telling him that I was coming to D.C., and that I wasn't to do it again unless he invited me. When I reminded him that it was our fourth wedding anniversary he couldn't stop apologizing. But his pathetic excuse that he'd been so busy he hadn't remembered had come too late. It was the final straw. I'd had enough. The next time I went to D.C. it was to tell Sean I was divorcing him. My flight touched down around the same time someone had run him down. The medical examiner said he was struck with such force that even if he'd survived he would've been left in a vegetative state. The cause of death was massive head trauma."

Diego concentrated on the road ahead of him. The pain in Vivienne's voice sliced through him like the blade of a sharp razor. He didn't know what she'd expected from her marriage, but she didn't deserve to be relegated to her home state and summoned whenever her husband deemed it advantageous to his grand scheme as a D.C. power broker. He couldn't imagine a man not wanting to see his wife when she'd traveled miles to celebrate their wedding anniversary. Had Sean Gregory married Vivienne because he'd loved her, or had he seen her as an accoutrement for a man of his stature? Had she become an accessory like a piece of jewelry or article of clothing, to be taken out and put on display for special occasions? For Congressman Sean Gregory it'd been about image and only image.

The instant the word flashed through his mind, Diego knew he was no different than Vivienne's late husband. Yes, he'd hired her to set up and monitor his social calendar, but he'd also hired her for the same reason Sean Gregory married her: she complemented him. The difference was he'd been forthcoming with Vivienne. She couldn't go back in time to right the wrongs, but he would try and make certain that she would enjoy their time together.

Chapter 9

Vivienne saw for herself what Celia felt when standing on the second-story balcony overlooking the turquoise waters surrounding Jupiter Island. Approximately twenty-five miles north of Palm Beach, the small, private, seventeen-mile island community had become a sanctuary for the rich and famous. She hadn't known of Jupiter Island's existence until Tiger Woods purchased property on the island with large private estate homes and condos, wide intracoastal, eighteen-hole golf course, fourteen tennis courts, a saltwater pool and docking facilities for large boats.

Diego's oceanfront house, erected on a two-acre parcel behind a private gate and lush vegetation, was designed in classic Spanish-Mediterranean architecture that blended with the natural tropic surroundings.

Massive palm trees flanked the limestone path leading to an arched doorway and solid, carved mahogany doors.

Arched mahogany windows and doorways and an imposing tower made Vivienne feel as if she'd traveled back centuries. When she'd asked Diego about the design of the house, he said he wanted a home with an old-world feel. The builder had compromised when he used stone, wrought iron and Honduran mahogany. The result was the prevalence of wood in the windows and doors, true, half-round doors, and the ceiling of the outdoor living room was covered with tongue-and-groove decking. He'd admitted that an aunt had decorated his Palm Beach condo for relaxation and the Jupiter Island house for elegant living and entertainment.

Vivienne left the balcony, closing the French doors, and entered the bedroom with a king-size, carved, four-poster mahogany bed, matching triple dresser and armoire. A ceiling fan with blades shaped like leaves circulated the salt-filled air around the room.

She still had to unpack, shower and change before joining Diego, who'd offered to prepare dinner. Reaching for her overnight bag, she took out a change of underwear, tank top and a pair of cropped pants. Gathering a quilted toiletry bag, she headed for the bathroom, but stopped when she heard her cell phone's ringtone. Retracing her steps, she picked up the tiny instrument. Her gaze narrowed when the area code for Washington, D.C., came up on the display.

"Hello."

"Mrs. Gregory?"

"Who's calling?"

"Detective Larson, D.C. Homicide."

"This is she," she confirmed.

"Mrs. Gregory, I've taken over your husband's case from Detective Cotter, who's been reassigned."

Vivienne closed her eyes, sucking in a lungful of air. Every phone call from the police was akin to opening a wound that refused to heal. She'd buried him, but not the memories—the good ones and the not so good ones.

"Has Detective Cotter come up with anything?" She heard the sound of pages turning.

"Not since his last notation that he'd called you. But, if I come up with anything I'll be certain to let you know."

Vivienne recalled what Elizabeth had written her. "Detective Larson, has anyone from your department been in touch with Mrs. Elizabeth Gregory?" There came the sound of more turning pages through the earpiece.

"Not since February twenty-third. Why?"

"I was just asking."

"You have to have a reason for asking, Mrs. Gregory," he spat out.

She wanted to tell the detective that she didn't care much for his tone, but hadn't wanted to alienate the man. After all, she did want the person or persons responsible for Sean's death brought to justice.

"I lost my husband and Mrs. Gregory her son, so I thought someone from your department would keep her abreast of the ongoing investigation without my having to act as a go-between."

"Look, Mrs. Gregory, I'm merely making this call as a favor to Detective Cotter."

"Did you not tell me that you're taking over the case?" Vivienne said waspishly, not bothering to disguise her annoyance.

"As I said before, my call is just a formality. After all, the DCPD is a second-stringer in Representative Gregory's hit-and-run investigation."

A slight frown appeared between her eyes. "What are you talking about?"

"The feds are handling this case."

"Since when?"

"Since day one, Mrs. Gregory. Bill Larson knew your husband personally, so he asked our chief to let him cover the case. It's not that we don't want to catch the person or persons who killed your husband, but we must let the proper authorities do what they do best."

Vivienne nodded, even though the police officer couldn't see her. She wanted the police to find the driver, because then she'd be able to move forward. Guilt weighed heavily on her when she'd been apprised of Sean's death, because she'd wanted to divorce him, not bury him.

She'd fallen in love with Sean Bailey Gregory because of his lust for life, but she'd also fallen out of love for him because his lust for power was greater than any love he could have for another human being. The adage she'd told her husband many times, that "power corrupts and absolute power corrupts absolutely," had fallen on deaf ears. Sean claimed he was David fighting the Washington Goliath for the "little people," and they worshipped him. In his election bid he won by a wider margin than any other representative in the district's history.

"Thank you, Detective Larson. Please call me if you uncover some new information."

"You can count on that, Mrs. Gregory. We're going to catch the bastard who killed your husband."

Vivienne thanked him again, and then ended the call. At first she'd thought her mother-in-law's revelation was the result of grief and paranoia, but now she wasn't so certain. Were the men in the cars parked across the street from Elizabeth's home federal agents? Had they suspected Sean's accident wasn't an accident?

The questions flooded her mind as she walked into the bathroom. Even though Sean Gregory was gone, he wasn't gone completely. It wasn't what the detective had said but what he hadn't said that had her believing that her husband's accident wasn't an accident. And if someone had deliberately murdered Sean then the question was why.

Diego glanced up when he saw movement out of the corner of his eye. Vivienne had walked into the kitchen. His gaze took in everything about her in one sweeping glance. She'd pulled her hair off her face with a narrow yellow headband that matched a body-hugging tank top. He felt like a pervert when he stared at the soft swell of breasts above the revealing neckline. He'd been wrong. Vivienne Neal wasn't skinny, but lushly slender.

He returned his attention to chopping the ingredients for an Asian slaw rather than stare at her rounded hips. "How's your bedroom?"

Vivienne took a seat at the cooking island. "It's perfect. Where's yours?"

Diego winked at her. "It's downstairs." When they'd arrived he'd shown Vivienne to one of the second-story bedrooms, leaving her to settle in while he put together dinner.

She flashed a sensual moue. "I guess that means I won't have to lock my door."

His eyebrows shot up. "Have you been locking it?"

"No."

Staring at her under hooded lids, Diego said, "Then, don't start now."

Resting her elbows on the marble countertop, Vivienne

stared at the large clear bowl filled with thinly sliced cabbage, red onion and bell pepper, bok choy, julienne carrots, snap peas, green onions and bean sprouts.

"Would you like some help?"

"No thanks."

Vivienne glanced around the large kitchen that was constructed to handle a lot of cooking for a lot of people. Top-of-the-line appliances and stainless-steel hanging fixtures above a marble-top center island flowed into a walnut butcher block with seating for three. Recessed lights above the double sink and a wide arched window trimmed in mahogany let in an abundance of sunlight. The sweeping fronds of palms trees bowed in the warm breeze outside the window.

"How often do you come here?" she asked Diego.

"I try and come every weekend." He gave her a sheepish grin. "The reason I instituted no-work Fridays was to take off and hang out here."

"Hey, that's selfish."

Diego halted mincing ginger. "Should I pass your remark on to the other ColeDiz employees?"

Straightening, she shook her head. "On that note, I think I'll take a look around."

Turning on the faucet in the sink at the cooking island, Diego washed his hands. "Before you take off I want you to taste something."

Vivienne watched her boss as he walked to the refrigerator-freezer. He appeared as comfortable and secure in the kitchen as in the boardroom. She liked his hands, walk and intense gaze. Whenever he stared at her she felt as if he could see inside the woman who he accused of challenging him at every turn to sense that she wasn't as tough as she appeared, that she'd challenged him because she didn't want to like him in the way a woman liked a man.

It'd only taken three days—seventy-two hours—to find herself ensnared in a web of longing that was like an itch she couldn't scratch. And she was mature enough to know it was because she hadn't slept with a man in a very long time. She couldn't remember when she and Sean had last made love, and there were times when she felt like a cat in heat. Now was one of those times.

"What did you make?" she asked when Diego took a pitcher filled with a pale yellow liquid and a red-and-green apple from the refrigerator."

"Diego's double apple mojito."

Vivienne put up a hand. "No, Diego. I had enough last night."

"I promised to make you one that's not too strong. Just take a sip and let me know if you like it." He placed mint leaves from a small plastic container in the glasses, crushing them with a muddler. Within minutes Diego had garnished the concoction with two slices of red-and-green apple. Slivers of apples floated in the concoction and he topped it off with ice cubes and a sprig of mint leaves.

Smiling, he handed her a glass. "Here's to working well together," he said, raising his glass.

Vivienne touched her glass to his. "To a rewarding working relationship." She took one sip and then another as a slow grin spread over her face. "It's delicious. Kudos to the mixologist."

Diego inclined his head. *"Gracias, m'ija."*

"De nada, m'ijo." The cooling liquid slid down the back of her throat, chest, warming her body. "What's in the Kool-Aid?"

He moved closer, his warmth seeping into her. "Apple juice, vodka and simple syrup."

Vivienne stared up at him through her lashes. "Yummy."

Diego set aside his glass, pulling her into the circle of his arms. "You're right about that, *m'ija*. You are yummy."

"How would you know? You've never tasted me." Vivienne couldn't believe the words that had come out of her mouth. Had she been celibate so long that she was ready to seduce her boss?

Diego smiled as one hand cradled her narrow waist, the other easing the glass from her grip. "But I will," he predicted. Dipping his head he attempted to slant his mouth over hers, but Vivienne pulled back.

"Didn't we agree that we wouldn't kiss until the third date?"

"You agreed *m'ija*. Third date, third day, it's all the same to me."

"But, Diego—"

"But nothing, Vivienne," he whispered, cutting her off. "I am going to kiss you and if you want you can slap me for doing it."

He stared into the round, tawny eyes that reminded him of the eyes of one of his sister's dolls—eyes he'd poked out after viewing the horror movie, *Chucky*. When Celia discovered her disfigured doll she screamed, waking the entire household. He was grounded for a month with a stern lecture never to touch his sister's dolls again.

But Vivienne wasn't one of his sister's dolls and he could touch her. Her fragility didn't come from being made of porcelain. It came from the emotional abuse of a self-centered man who was too vain to appreciate a faithful wife. Any other woman would've had an affair, or series of affairs. And, as much as he treasured fidelity, Diego wouldn't have blamed Vivienne if she had cheated on Sean Gregory.

Vivienne attempted to blink back the tears filling her eyes. "Why, Diego? Because I can't remember the last time a man held or kissed me, because you see me as the lonely widow? Well, I'm going to let you in on a little secret. I was married for four years, and I doubt if my husband made love to me more than twenty-five times. He was always too busy, either campaigning—no I take that back. He was always campaigning even when it wasn't an election year. Everything and everyone was more important to Representative Sean Bailey Gregory than his wife. I was nothing more to him than an adornment, something to take out and put on display but only when it was advantageous for him."

Cradling her face between his hands, Diego wiped away her tears with his thumbs and touched his mouth to hers. "I see you just as you are. You're a smart, beautiful, sexy woman who has turned my life upside down."

Vivienne's eyelids fluttered wildly. "You hired me to make your life manageable."

His expressive eyebrows lifted. "True, but there's something about you that makes me go against everything I profess to believe in."

She stared at the attractive cleft in his chin. "I think it's because I'm not afraid of you."

It wasn't Diego Cole-Thomas the CEO she feared as much as Diego Cole-Thomas the man. She knew when he'd entered a room without seeing him and she'd come to look forward to having him come home, like a wife waiting for her husband. In her head, she'd substituted Diego for

Sean. Her boss had become everything her late husband hadn't been or couldn't be.

His thumbs made sweeping motions over her cheek-bones. "I don't want you to be afraid of me, Vivienne. We're only going to be together for six months, so let's make the best of it and have some fun."

She closed her eyes. "Remember, I don't do bosses, Diego."

He smiled. "And, I don't do employees."

"But—"

Whatever she was going to say was preempted when Diego's mouth covered hers in a soft, tender joining that buckled her knees. If he hadn't been holding her, Vivienne knew she would've sunk to the floor.

His lips, tongue, caressed hers, coaxing a response to his slow lovemaking. The involuntary quiver of arousal began in her breasts, moving slowly down her body like hot wax and settling between her legs.

Diego tightened his hold on Vivienne's body, molding her curves to his length, fitting her against his length from chest to knees. She tasted good, felt good and smelled delicious.

The tip of his tongue explored the recesses of her mouth, flicking over the roof, caressing the inside of her cheek and along the ridge of her teeth. He'd promised not take her to bed but hadn't promised not to kiss her.

Vivienne pushed against Diego's shoulder as she strug-gled to catch her breath. "Diego, please."

"What is it, baby?" he whispered against her parted lips.

"I can't breathe."

He smiled. "Neither can I." His chest rose and fell heavily. Taking a step backward, he released Vivienne when it was the last thing he'd wanted to do.

"Thank you."

"For what?"

"For reminding me how nice it feels to be kissed." Picking up her drink, Vivienne turned on her heels and walked out of the kitchen.

"How do you like your steak?" Diego called out to her retreating back.

"Medium well," she said without turning around.

She walked in and out of rooms, familiarizing herself with the layout of the house. An exquisite crystal chandelier was suspended above a long walnut table with dining for ten in the formal dining room. A series of arches in the living room, including a bar with a niche repeated the arched shapes of the exterior facade. Open half-round doors led to an outdoor living room that was more like a loggia. The walls of the family room, breakfast room and kitchen—the less formal spaces—were painted in brighter, more cheerful colors, reflecting their functionality. Diego's five-bedroom, six-bath house set on two acres with an inground pool was nothing short of spectacular.

Returning to the outdoor living room, she collapsed into a cushioned oak love seat, wishing she could disappear. Had she been that desperate, curious or sexually deprived that she let a man—her employer no less—kiss her? And, he'd done it without the slightest hesitation.

Vivienne took a deep swallow of her mojito, then covered her face with her free hand. Diego admitted that kissing her had gone against everything he'd believed, and it was the same for her. She'd been forthcoming when she told him that she didn't believe in office liaisons, so why hadn't she put up the slightest protest. What was next? Begging him to take her to bed?

However, Vivienne knew sleeping with Diego would spell certain disaster. She'd never been one to engage in frivolous affairs. It hadn't happened before she married Sean, and it certainly hadn't happened after she married him.

She was a thirty-one-year-old woman who'd stopped denying her own needs. For more than four years she'd ignored the truth because it'd always been Sean's needs; but that was the past and now it was up to her to control her own destiny.

But not with my boss, she groaned inwardly.

Vivienne opened her eyes, kicked off her mules and pulled her legs under her body. The outdoor living room was the perfect place to relax. The ceiling was covered with tongue-and-groove decking, the floor with terra-cotta tiles, and the lanterns attached to the walls flanking the doors and ceiling fans complemented large jade planters filled with ferns. A quartet of cushioned love seats, matching oaken table and built-in bar added to the relaxed ambience.

"Do you mind if I join you?"

Glancing over her shoulder, Vivienne saw Diego leaning against the open door. "Please."

He sat across from her, stretching out long legs. "How's the mojito?"

She stared at the half-filled glass. "It's delicious."

Diego's eyes narrowed as he studied Vivienne's averted gaze. "Are you okay?"

"Yes," she said much too quickly. "Why do you ask?"

"You won't look at me."

"That's because I'm embarrassed, Diego." She met his gaze before it shifted to the massive columns holding up the upper floor. "I've never done anything like that before."

"There's always the first time."

"And it will be the last."

"I doubt that."

This time she did look directly at Diego. "Why would you say that?"

"I enjoyed kissing you, and when I enjoy something I usually do it again and again."

"How can you be certain I'll oblige?"

"I'm not certain, *m'ija*. Call it wishful thinking."

"We hug, we kiss and then what's next, Diego? We both know that the next step is sleeping together."

The seconds ticked by while Diego stared at the woman who'd managed to twist him into knots. He'd known he was going to hire her within minutes of her walking into his office, and when he saw her that first night on the balcony wearing nothing more than a revealing nightgown, he'd wanted to make love to her.

His eyes narrowed. "Is that what you want to do, Vivienne? Do you want us to sleep together?"

"No, Diego, that's not what I'm saying. I'm trying to be realistic. We're two normal people who're not only attracted to each other but also living together. And, in my book that's a scenario for a sexual liaison."

Resting an elbow on the arm of the chair, Diego placed a finger alongside his face. "Would that be such a horrendous thing?"

"No," Vivienne said quickly. "It's my working for you that complicates things."

"What if I rectify that?"

"What are you talking about, Diego?"

Lowering his hand, he leaned forward. "What if I fire you with a generous severance package and then ask you to stay on as my girlfriend?"

Vivienne closed her eyes as she attempted to process the significance of his offer. She opened her eyes to find Diego staring at her with an expression of expectation on his handsome face.

"You're going to terminate me, then in the same breath ask me to work for you?"

"Work with me, *m'ija*. Remember, I'll no longer be your boss and you my employee."

"What's makes you think I won't take the money and run?"

Diego shook his head. "You won't run, Vivienne. You're too principled for that."

She flashed a half smile. "You're right about that. This is not about money."

He smiled. "You're right. We're both consenting adults, so there's no reason why we should concern ourselves with unrealistic expectations or a promise of commitment. And as long as we're together I'll protect you."

A frown replaced Vivienne's smile. "Protect me from what?"

"Every woman, no matter how financially independent or liberated, needs a man's protection." Something your late husband didn't provide, he added silently.

A comfortable quiet descended on them as they stared intently at each other. Everything appeared magnified: the sound of their measured breathing, the twitter of birds perched high in trees, the scurrying of insects and tiny lizards.

Vivienne blinked, shattering the enthrallment. "I'll let you know."

"*¿Cuándo?*"

"I'll let you know before we go back to Palm Beach."

Diego inclined his head in acknowledgment. Vivienne

hadn't said yes, but she also hadn't turned down his proposal. Always the optimist, to him the glass wasn't half-empty but half-full. If she did accept his offer, then they would continue to occupy separate bedrooms until Vivienne decided otherwise.

Standing up, Diego took two steps and sat down next to Vivienne. Dropping an arm over her shoulders, he pulled her close. "You asked me to tell you about ColeDiz, and I told you that it's a long story. Would you like to hear about it now or wait until after we eat?"

Vivienne raised her chin and smiled up at the man who'd promised to protect her. "Tell me now, please."

Diego pressed a kiss to her forehead. There was something about Vivienne that was so incredibly childlike under the facade of toughness she'd affected to shield herself from the emotional pain she'd had to endure while being married to Sean Gregory. When he'd promised to protect her, he meant protecting her from physical and emotional harm.

"Samuel Claridge Cole was my great-grandfather who started ColeDiz eighty-five years ago with the money he'd saved selling black market goods during the Great War."

Vivienne sat up straighter. "He was a black marketer?"

"Yes, and apparently a very good one."

"Go on, *m'ijo*. I promise not to interrupt again."

"That's okay, baby. You can interrupt anytime you want."

She settled back against his body, closed her eyes as she listened to his soft, mellifluent voice.

An Important Message from the Publisher

Dear Reader,

Because you've chosen to read one of our fine novels, I'd like to say "thank you"! And, as a special way to say thank you, I'm offering to send you two more Kimani™ Romance novels and two surprise gifts – absolutely FREE! These books will keep it real with true-to-life African American characters that turn up the heat and sizzle with passion.

Please enjoy the free books and gifts with our compliments...

Linda Gill

Publisher, Kimani Press

Peel off Seal and Place Inside...

THE EDITOR'S "THANK YOU" FREE GIFTS INCLUDE:

- ▶ Two Kimani™ Romance Novels
- ▶ Two exciting surprise gifts

YES! I have placed my Editor's "thank you" Free Gifts seal in the space provided at right. Please send me 2 FREE books, and my 2 FREE Mystery Gifts. I understand that I am under no obligation to purchase anything further, as explained on the back of this card.

PLACE
FREE GIFTS
SEAL
HERE

▼ DETACH AND MAIL CARD TODAY! ▶

168 XDL EVGW   368 XDL EVJ9

FIRST NAME	LAST NAME

ADDRESS

APT.#	CITY

STATE/PROV.	ZIP/POSTAL CODE

Thank You!

(K-ROM-09)

The Reader Service — Here's How It Works:

Chapter 10

"Samuel was twenty-six in 1924 when he booked passage on a freighter to Havana, Cuba to negotiate the purchase of a sugar plantation. What he hadn't known or anticipated was the anti-American sentiment among Cubans following the Spanish-American War. It wasn't his color as much as it was his nationality that preempted his purchasing the property. He'd framed a quotation from the man who refused to sell him the plantation: Never go to a country to negotiate a business deal without prior knowledge of that country or its people. That quotation has hung on the wall of ColeDiz International Ltd. for eighty-five years."

"Why didn't he buy a plantation here in the States?"

"He knew running a plantation in the States would be risky, because he believed it would be viewed unfavorably by blacks and whites. He'd fought with the 369th Infantry, the first black U.S. combat overseas unit that the Germans called "Hell Fighters." He was one of 171 who'd earned a Croix de Guerre, or a Legion of Merit, France's highest military medal, but no U.S. medals of honor were awarded to any black troops. He'd been a black soldier returning from World War I, and he refused to march in the back of the victory parade because a segregated parade seemed completely at odds with the principles they'd supposedly fought for.

"He didn't get his Cuban sugar plantation, but got something he hadn't expected—a wife. He met Marguerite-Josefina Isabel Diaz, the daughter of a Cuban aristocrat at a formal dinner and as they say the rest is history."

"Her father approved of her marrying an American?"

"José Luís Diaz was going to marry her off to a man more than twice her age because of her unbecoming behavior, given her station. Apparently she'd posed in a skimpy garment for an artist, and the photographs were circulated all over Havana, which proved an embarrassment for my great-great-grandfather. He saw Samuel as a wealthy American willing to marry his willful daughter, and take her to America where she wouldn't be able to bring shame on the family."

"Was her behavior really that shocking?"

"It was for upper-class Cubans in the 1920s. M.J., as she referred to herself, was too modern for what was deemed modern Cuba."

"Samuel never got his sugar plantation?"

"No. What he did was go to Costa Rica and purchase a banana plantation, and several years later he became involved in growing coffee in Costa Rica, Jamaica and Puerto Rico."

"Did he speak Spanish?"

"No. He hired someone who did speak the language. Samuel met Everett Kirkland in Costa Rica and hired him to act as his interpreter and accountant. He and Everett worked well together until a woman and the Great Depression came between them."

"Was that woman Samuel's wife?"

Diego expelled a lungful of breath. "No. It was Samuel's mistress. My great-grandfather slept with his secretary and got her pregnant. Meanwhile M.J. was pregnant with her third child. Somehow Samuel and Everett conspired to pass the child off as the accountant's and he convinced Teresa Maldonado to marry him."

Vivienne's delicate jaw dropped. "That's so wrong!"

"I agree. But, you have to remember it was the 1920s and a woman having a child out of wedlock was frowned upon. Samuel wasn't going to leave M.J., and Teresa as the only daughter of a poor immigrant family would've brought unmitigated shame on her family. She had a son whom she named Joshua, but she and Everett would never have a child of their own because of a difficult delivery."

"So, your father never acknowledged him as his son."

"Not publicly. M.J. had another girl and it was twelve years later before she gave Samuel his second legitimate son."

"Whatever happened to Teresa and Everett?"

"Everett left when Joshua was a teenager. My uncle doesn't talk much about his childhood, but I suspect he and Everett didn't get along too well. One time I walked in on him talking to my uncle Martin about shooting Everett in the head if he hit his mother again. Unfortunately, Teresa died from T.B. the year she turned thirty-seven.

"I'm ashamed to say that my grandmother and her sister weren't very nice to Joshua because he was a reminder of how their father's affair nearly destroyed the Coles."

"It doesn't make sense, Diego. They were children themselves when it happened."

"That's true, but all hell broke loose years later when Martin discovered he had another brother and sought him out. He then forced Samuel to acknowledge that he'd fathered a fifth child—a child who was a Cole, but refused to have anything to do with the family. For many years it was just Martin and Joshua until the others came around."

"What about now?"

Diego smiled. "Uncle Josh *es mi familia.* You'll get to meet him, his children and grandchildren at the family reunion. I'd like to get back to ColeDiz. Samuel had Everett to thank when he told him not to put all of his money in the bank, because a recession always follows a financial boom. When the market crashed and the banks failed in 1929 Samuel lost a mere five thousand compared to the hundreds of thousands he would've lost had he not withdrawn his money.

"He rode out the Depression and with the New Deal, ColeDiz was up and running better than before. He diversified, setting up vacation properties throughout the Caribbean. When Samuel retired, his son Martin took over. After that it was Martin's brother David who served as CEO for nine years. David sold the Costa Rica holdings and set up several banana plantations in Belize.

"My father, Timothy, stepped in when David resigned to set up his own recording company, running ColeDiz for thirty years. I took over as CEO last year and brokered a deal with a Ugandan cotton grower to pay cash on delivery of cotton to the States, making ColeDiz the biggest family-owned agribusiness in the States. After the Ugandan deal I asked for complete autonomy from the board and surprisingly they granted it by a vote of nine-to-one. I plan to do something Samuel Cole swore not to do—set up a company on the U.S. mainland."

Vivienne met Diego's resolute gaze. "Are you referring to the tea plantation in South Carolina?"

"Yes, and I'm also in negotiations with the owner of several vacant buildings in West Palm that have been rezoned from business to residential."

"Do you plan to turn them into condos?"

"Three-quarters of the units will be condos and the remaining fourth rentals. I'm not as focused on becoming a landlord as I am with the properties."

Realization dawned when Vivienne realized why ColeDiz would want to get into the business of real estate. "Don't tell me you're buying them for the air space."

A glint of surprise lit Diego's dark eyes as he stared at the woman pressed to his side. "To use your words, 'you're damn skippy.' That's exactly why I decided to buy two square blocks of abandoned warehouses."

Lowering her lashes, she offered him a sensual moue. "Pretty smart, huh?"

Diego dropped a kiss on her hair. "Very pretty and very, very smart."

Vivienne unfolded her legs, resting them over Diego's thighs. "I could hang out here forever." Sunlight streamed through the fronds of towering palm trees.

"That can easily be arranged," Diego replied, massaging her ankles and feet. "If you want, I'll close up the condo and we can stay here."

"You'd do that," she said, totally surprised by his suggestion.

"Of course. In fact, I prefer staying here, because it allows for complete privacy."

"But, you'd have a longer commute."

"I don't mind the drive."

"You don't have to do this for me, Diego."

He gave her feet a gentle squeeze. "Please don't say anything else."

"What about my work? I'm going to need a computer."

Diego gave her a pointed stare. "I'll get a computer, printer and separate phone line."

"*Gracias, m'ijo,*" she drawled.

"You're very welcome."

They sat together, talking quietly as the sun slipped lower in the sky, taking with it the intense daytime heat and throwing shadows over the sand-colored stucco walls and columns as the lights in the outdoor sconces came on automatically.

"Do you want to eat indoors or out here?" Diego asked Vivienne when a slip of a moon appeared with the encroaching dusk.

"I prefer eating outdoors."

Releasing her feet, he stood up as she pushed her feet into her shoes. "Can I help with anything?"

Diego winked at Vivienne. "You can set the table."

"Do you have a vase?"

"I don't know. Why?"

Vivienne slipped her hand in his as they made their way inside the house. "I'd like to pick a few flowers from the garden for a centerpiece."

"I'll see what I can find for you."

Diego knew he was in too deep with Vivienne Neal the instant he'd agreed to their living together on Jupiter Island. Although the property on the island was larger than his Palm Beach condo, it was the isolation that would prove the deciding factor leading to a more intense involvement.

Offering her the alternative of not being an employee would free them from the guilt of engaging in an office romance. But he had to ask himself, if they did take their relationship to another level, would he be able to remain objective when it came time for Vivienne to leave?

He'd lost count of the number of business deals and board meetings in which he'd been involved, but none compared to his arrangement with the woman sleeping under his roof that had nothing to do with business.

Vivienne Neal had done what no other business rival had been able to do. Some family members questioned his business tactics, referring to him as a rogue, but his sole objective was always sealing the deal. The deal he'd made with Vivienne had survived a mere three days. She'd derailed his agenda with her sensual beauty, extraordinary intelligence and spunk. He'd dated women, slept with some of them, had fallen in love with one, but none had affected him like Vivienne.

But there was one nagging question Diego wanted answered. Had Vivienne married Sean Gregory with stars in her eyes, believing their lives would play out in a happily-ever-after fairytale, or had she intimidated him with her poise and intelligence and, as a result, been relegated to the back-ground? He'd felt her pain and vulnerability when she revealed her late husband's abandonment, and he had promised to protect her. But he hadn't promised to love her, even though he knew it would be so easy to fall in love with Vivienne.

The fact was they would live together until the end of the year, then go their separate ways to live their separate lives.

Diego rose slowly to his feet when Vivienne appeared to glide into the room, afraid that if he moved too quickly he would lose his balance. He'd tried imagining what she would look like, what she would wear to the wedding, but the woman standing before him had surpassed his expectations. She'd brushed her hair until there were no curls, fastening it into an elegant knot on the nape of her neck, while leaving wisps to fall sensuously along her ears.

His gaze shifted from her smoky lids and vermilion lip color to the cobalt-blue gown with spaghetti straps that clung to every curve of her slender body. A soft swell of breasts was visible each time she took a breath and a front slit showed a generous expanse of legs whenever she moved. At six-four, he towered over her, but a pair of blue peau de soie stilettos made the top of her head level with his nose.

Wrapping an arm around her waist, Diego pulled her close. The subtle scent of her perfume wafted in his nostrils, making him slightly light-headed. He went completely still when his fingertips made contact with bare skin instead of fabric. Peering around her shoulder he saw that the straps crisscrossed her shoulders above the small of her back. He compressed his lips to cut off the expletive poised on the tip of his tongue.

"Where's the back of your dress?"

She glanced over her shoulder. "Diego, the dress is backless."

A frown settled into his features. "I know it's backless,

but I can almost see all the way to your..." His words trailed off.

"My what, *m'ijo?*"

"Forget it." He didn't want to say anything that would spark an argument. "You look beautiful."

Smiling, Vivienne reached up with her free hand to straighten Diego's midnight-blue silk tie under the spread collar of his white shirt. He looked resplendent in his tuxedo. "And you look incredibly handsome."

He forced a smile that didn't reach his eyes. "Thank you." Diego was still smarting about the precarious amount of flesh on display for every man at the wedding to enjoy. If it was Vivienne's intent to seduce him, then she'd succeeded. What he preferred was for her subtle seduction to be acted out in private.

Vivienne tightened her grip on her evening purse. "I'm ready."

Diego reached for her hand, leading her out of the house to where he'd parked his car, praying he was ready for the attention Vivienne would garner as his date. The formal wedding, scheduled to begin at seven with a reception following immediately after the ceremony, was supposed to last well into the morning hours. His hungry gaze lingered on Vivienne's bare legs as she settled herself into the low-slung sports car. Rounding the vehicle, he took off his jacket, hanging it behind his seat before he got behind the wheel.

Vivienne reached over and covered Diego's hand, stopping him from inserting the key into the ignition. "Please wait, Diego."

He stared at her staring back at him. "Did you forget something?"

A hint of a smile softened Vivienne's mouth. "No, but I want you to fire me."

It took several seconds before Diego realized what she was asking. She wanted him to change her status from that of an employee to someone with whom he could have a personal relationship.

Leaning closer, he pressed his mouth to her ear. "Miss Neal, you are fired!"

Vivienne and Diego shared a smile before he started up the classic car and maneuvered out of the driveway. His uneasiness about her revealing attire was replaced by the knowledge that he could pursue Vivienne without her doing double duty as his assistant and date. He pressed a button on the remote device on the visor and the electronic gates opened smoothly, silently, then closed automatically when the car sped past.

Vivienne stared out the windshield. She knew asking Diego to fire her as an employee would change her and her relationship with him. She hadn't made the request because she wanted him to sleep with her, but because it would give her the opportunity to engage in a liaison with a man whom she could trust, a man who wasn't one to kiss and tell and someone who sought to protect his reputation.

"Where's the wedding?"

"It's at the estate of the groom's parents on the western side of the island near the Indian River."

"You live alone, yet you have a house here and a condo in Palm Beach."

"I use the condo strictly for business. It's where I sometimes hold business meetings and get-togethers. The Jupiter Island property is for family and personal use."

"Can you write off the expenses for the condo if it has bedrooms?"

Diego's eyebrows flickered slightly with her query. It was apparent earning an MBA had served her well. "My accountant writes off a portion of the expenses for the first floor. The upper floor is for residential use only."

"May I make a suggestion?"

He gave her a quick glance. "Of course."

"Replace the convertible sofa. If you're ever audited by the IRS they will disallow your in-home office deductions because the sofa doubles as a bed."

"Now why didn't my accountant tell me that?"

"It could be that he or she didn't know it converted into a bed."

"It's a he, and he still should've mentioned it when I told him that I was going to use one unit for business. I'll contact my aunt and tell her to order the identical sofa without the bed." Taking his eyes off the road, he gave her a wink. "Thank you."

"You're welcome."

"Do you want to make any other suggestions?" Diego asked.

"I can't think of anything right now."

Taking his hand off the gearshift, he placed it over her exposed knee. He drove for several miles with his hand caressing the silken skin on her inner thigh until he was forced to downshift, slowing the Jaguar when he turned off onto a road leading to the property where the wedding would take place. Guests, in formal evening wear, made their way along a wide path leading to one of the most opulent estates on the island. A valet approached the car, and Diego got out and came around to assist Vivienne.

It was a perfect day for an outdoor wedding and reception. The cloudless sky was a brilliant blue, and a cooling breeze coming off the ocean and the setting sun made for a warm, comfortable summer evening. After slipping on the tuxedo jacket, Diego cradled Vivienne's hand in the bend of his elbow. He nodded to a couple who'd recently expanded their house on a nearby lot, but didn't stop to talk.

Vivienne pressed closer to Diego's length. "Are you a guest of the bride or the groom?"

"Both. I'm pleased to say that I had the honor of introducing Peyton to Raquel. She's the daughter of a business associate."

"Why didn't you hit on her for yourself?"

"I have a rule never to date a woman related to those with whom I do business."

Vivienne was forced to admire Diego's ethics. "Are you the best man?"

"No. They decided not to have any groomsmen or attendants."

The sound of bagpipes grew louder as they approached an area where a gigantic tent hovered over cloth-covered tables and chairs swathed in white organza and tied with a red, white and green tartan plaid. Centerpieces of white and red roses, ferns and baby's breath in vases were tied together with matching tartan plaid ribbon. Baskets of flowers lined the perimeter of the pool and an area set aside where the bride and groom were to exchange vows.

The waitstaff circulated, balancing trays of crudités and hot and cold appetizers, while handing out napkins to the guests crowding into an area outside an Olympic-size swimming pool. A portable bar was doing a brisk business with bartenders filling flutes with champagne and wine-glasses with premium wines.

"Can I get you anything to drink?" Diego asked Vivienne.

"Club soda."

"Are you certain you don't want anything stronger?"

She rolled her eyes at him. "I'm quite certain." After two nights of drinking champagne and mojitos she woke with a headache.

Pressing his mouth to her hair, he whispered, "Don't run away."

Vivienne watched Diego as he walked over to the bar; her gaze lingered on the breadth of his shoulders, finding him an incredible male specimen. To say he was tall, dark and handsome was without a doubt an understatement.

Whenever she recalled the feel of his mouth on hers her stomach did flip-flops. At first she'd thought she was losing her mind when she agreed to become Diego Cole-Thomas's, for lack of a better word, girlfriend; her physical attraction to him was so strong that it was palpable. She hadn't known Diego a week, yet she wanted to share his bed. At first she felt it was because she was trapped in an invisible web of unfulfilled desire that was of her own choosing for far too long, but knew that wasn't true.

There were occasions when she could've slept with other men, yet hadn't. It hadn't taken her long to realize that some men preferred having an affair with a married woman because they considered her "safe."

Vivienne turned when someone tapped her shoulder, staring at a young blond woman with a pair of enormous diamond studs in her ears. "Yes?"

"Can you tell me who styled your hair?"

The woman, who appeared either in her late teens or

early twenties, had pulled her hair off her face in a French twist that was too severe for her age and narrow face. "I styled it myself."

Her lashes fluttered wildly as if she was going to faint. "Are you a stylist?"

Vivienne bit back a smile. "No, I'm not. It's quite easy to create a bohemian knot. All you have to do is split your hair in two sections, making certain to avoid a center part in front, and create two low ponytails just below your ears. Holding a tail in each hand, twist them down and in toward each other. If you try twirling the tails around your index fingers it will make it much easier. Make the twists as tight as you can comfortably stand it, because they're going to naturally loosen when you pull them together."

"How can I get my hair not to slip out? It's so stick-straight."

"You'll have to pull the ponytails toward each other at the nape of your neck, gathering them into one ponytail. Get an elastic band that matches your hair color and secure it just below the original twists, then pull the ponytail through the elastic, but not all the way. This way you leave the ends loose. If you want, you can lift the loop up and in toward the scalp in order to hide the elastic between the two original twists that are now at the center of the head."

"It sounds so easy."

Vivienne smiled. "It is. It works better if your hair isn't squeaky clean."

The woman stuck out her hand. "Hi. I'm Alison Sanderson."

She took her hand. "Vivienne Neal."

"Do you live on Jupiter?"

"I'm staying here with a friend."

"Who's your friend?"

"Ali Sanderson, it's been a while," Diego crooned.

Vivienne wanted to kiss Diego. He'd returned just in time. She took the glass with a clear, bubbly liquid and a sliver of lime. "Thank you."

Alison stared at the ground rather than look at Diego. "Hi." That said she ran away as if she were frightened.

Diego smiled at Vivienne. "I see you made a friend."

"She was asking me about my hair and if I live here."

"You have to be very careful about what you say to Ali. She appears innocent enough, but she's like a mynah bird. She repeats everything she hears."

"When she asked if I lived here, I told her that I was staying with a friend." Vivienne took a sip of her drink. "Do you normally party with the people who live on the island?"

Diego put an arm around her waist. "No. I decided to buy property here because the parents of two college buddies lived on the island. The first time they invited me to a gathering I made a decision that one day I'd own a home on Jupiter Island."

Tilting her chin, Vivienne stared up at the man who'd gotten his wish. It wasn't enough that he had the money, but the determination to make his dream a reality. "I'm glad your dream came true."

"What about you, Vivienne? What do you want for your future?"

The seconds ticked while she pondered his query. "There was a time when I wanted what most women want—career, marriage and children."

"What about now?"

She expelled a breath. "Now, I really don't know. I'm not worried about my career, because I could always go back to my old position."

"Is that what you want to do?"

"I didn't say it's what I want to do, Diego. It's what I could do."

"What about marriage and children?"

"That's not even an option—at least not now. I don't want to remarry, and I'm definitely not going to have a child or children when I'm not certain what I'll be doing, or where I'll be next year."

"Would you be in this dilemma if you'd divorced your husband?"

"No. I'd hoped to divorce Sean quietly and then continue with my life. But, his murder—"

Diego's fingers bit into her flesh. "You believe he was murdered?"

"Someone hit him and left him for dead in the middle of the street. How else is that not murder?"

"You're right. Please go on."

"His being killed changed everything because the press made my life a living hell. They wanted answers and I couldn't give them the answers, but that didn't stop them from calling me either at home or at work, showing up unannounced at my home, sending me e-mails. It reached the point when I decided to quit my job, close up the house and move to Florida to stay with Alicia."

"Don't worry, *m'ija,*" Diego whispered, his breath hot against her ear. "I promised to protect you, and I always keep my promises."

"Don't forget why we're together, Diego."

"Just because I take business seriously that doesn't

mean I can't be passionate about other things. I care about you and that has nothing to do with business."

Vivienne wanted to tell Diego that Sean had said almost the exact same words, except he'd substituted politics for business. What Diego didn't know was that she wasn't the same woman she'd been before her husband's death. She wasn't so naive that she didn't know what he wanted from her. He wanted to sleep with her and she wanted to sleep with him. She planned to take advantage of everything he offered and then when it came time to walk away she would without an iota of regret.

The noise level escalated as more people arrived. Vivienne found herself the object of curious stares, but she either ignored them or flashed a smile at those who nodded and smiled at her. She wasn't certain whether any of them recognized her as Sean's widow, and if they did then her being seen with Diego Cole-Thomas was definitely something for them to talk about.

Ushers wove their way through the crowd, telling everyone to be seated because the ceremony was beginning. Vivienne sat with Diego as a hush fell over the assembly when the groom, dressed in Highland regalia, took his place under a pergola trimmed in snow-white roses. Peyton Cleary's darkly tanned face, coal-black hair and brilliant blue eyes had several women whispering under their breaths as to whether he had on anything under his kilt. The pipers played the distinctive chords for the wedding march and everyone rose to their feet as a petite figure in white, clinging to the arm of her father, made her way over a white carpet covered with red and white rose petals.

The rays of the setting sun caught the brilliance of the diamond engagement ring on her hand as she reached over to take her groom's hand. The dark-haired beauty was ravishing in a lace off-the-shoulder ball gown. White roses and baby's breath were tucked into the elaborate twist on the nape of her neck.

Vivienne felt the heat of Diego's gaze on her face when the couple repeated their vows. She knew he was wondering whether she was remembering when she had done the same. The couple exchanged rings and shared a kiss as husband and wife for the first time. The piper played a lively ditty as Peyton swept his wife up in his arms and executed a vigorous Scottish jig. His antics set the stage for an evening of unrestrained frivolity.

Diego eased Vivienne from her chair. "Come with me. I want to introduce you to Peyton and Raquel." They stood in the receiving line as the newlyweds chatted with their guests. When Peyton spied Diego, he caught him up in a bear hug, nearly lifting him off his feet.

"C.T.!"

Diego pounded his friend's back. "You better watch that your kilt doesn't blow up and put your jewels on display," he teased, surreptitiously handing him an envelope.

"I only put on this damn thing to please my folks. But, I must say it's rather liberating. I kinda enjoy the ocean breeze on my junk."

Taking a step backward, Diego reached for Vivienne. "Peyton, Raquel, I'd like to introduce you to Vivienne Neal."

She shook hands with the bride and groom. "Congratulations."

"Thank you," Raquel and Peyton chimed in unison.

"Please go sit and get something to eat. Peyton and I will come around to see everyone later," Raquel said in slightly accented English.

Diego led Vivienne to the tent where they were escorted to their table. Over the next three hours the seventy-five invited guests were served a seven-course dinner accompanied with wines, followed by wedding cake and champagne.

A D.J. replaced the pipers and it was close to midnight when Peyton and Raquel got up to dance together as husband and wife for the first time. They danced with their respective parents, then invited everyone to join them.

Vivienne rested a hand on Diego's sleeve. "Do you mind if we dance back at the house?"

His eyes glittering like burning coal, Diego smiled. "Let's go."

Chapter 11

Pulling her close to his chest, Diego smiled down at Vivienne as she tilted her delicate chin. They'd left the wedding reception and come back to the house in under ten minutes. He'd plugged in an MP3 player with hundreds of his favorites tunes, some dating back to the eighties, and pressed a button on a state-of-the-art system that had been programmed to play music in every room in the house. Each room was equipped with hidden speakers that could be turned on or off with a flip of a dedicated wall switch.

"How did you know I wanted to leave?"

Vivienne lifted her eyebrows and flashed a sexy moue. Diego had removed his jacket and tie and had unbuttoned several buttons on his shirt. The heat from his bare chest seeped into her. "Whenever you're bored you massage your forehead with your first two fingers."

"You think you know me that well after being together less than a week?"

"I know enough," she said confidently. "Whenever you're thinking about something you rest a finger alongside your jaw, but it's your eyes that give you away. They say things you'd never say aloud."

He spun her around and around, as she followed his intricate steps. "What do my eyes say, Ms. Neal?"

"They say you like me."

"What else do they say?" he asked, not confirming or denying her statement.

"They also say that you want me, but you're not sure how to proceed."

"That's because whenever I go after something I want, I usually get it. And once I get it most times I don't let it go."

"Are you talking about me or a piece of property?"

A slow smile parted his lips. "Both."

"Why me, Diego, and not some other woman?"

"You're different, Vivienne. If I'd met you under other circumstances I wouldn't have hesitated letting you know that I was interested in you. But what changed everything was that you were an employee. It could be because of my great-grandfather's indiscretion, but we have an unwritten rule never to get involved with a woman working for the company."

"I thought I was fired."

"You are fired."

"You know you really weren't that slick, C.T."

"Hey, only my college buddies can call me C.T."

"I thought I was your girlfriend and in my book girlfriends rank higher than buddies."

"That's true, but my girlfriend is a little miserly handing out hugs and kisses."

"Slow down, slick. They're coming."

"When?"

"Before I go to bed."

"Tease."

"Am not," she drawled.

"Are, too," he shot back.

"Back to you trying to be slick, Mr. Cole-Thomas. I figured out what you were up to when you told me that I had to stand in as your date and hostess."

"Am I that transparent?"

Vivienne lifted a shoulder. "Maybe not to others."

His arm tightened around her waist, pulling her even closer. "Why you and not the others?"

Rising on tiptoe, she pressed her lips to his. "I don't know, *m'ijo.*"

"You use that word rather loosely, *m'ija.*"

Vivienne deepened the kiss. "So do you," she whispered.

Diego went completely still. He'd never been one to play mind games, but he enjoyed the sexual sparring with Vivienne. There wasn't anything about her he did not enjoy. His earlier annoyance about her dress was forgotten when he realized a majority of the men at the wedding were over forty and married. Even if they'd wanted to stare at his date, they weren't willing to risk it with their eagle-eyed wives watching their every move. Women who married very wealthy men were notorious for staying very close to them at social affairs for fear of losing them to a more attractive younger woman. The exceptions were the women in his family. Cole women or the women who'd married Coles were strong, intelligent and extraordinarily secure about who they were and what they wanted. His father had chased his mother for a year before she agreed to stand still long enough for him to catch her.

He wanted to tell Vivienne that he was falling in love with her—her intelligence, beauty and the morsels of passion she doled out like a miser. Diego kissed her slowly, his lips moving and tasting every inch of her mouth. When her breathing deepened, he pulled back slightly, then fastened his mouth to the column of her scented neck. He returned to her mouth, his tongue easing inside while caressing, tasting and coaxing until she moaned with passion summoned from deep within her throat.

When he felt the hard need of desire pressing against her thighs, Diego knew if he didn't stop now then he wouldn't be able to. A rush of fire settled in his groin and he was helpless to stop the groan slipping between his lips. The blood in his erection grew hotter, sweeping upward until the flames threatened to incinerate him—whole. His hands went to her shoulders, pushing the delicate straps down her arms and exposing her breasts to his hot gaze.

His head dipped and he suckled her like a starving infant as the nipple swelled between his teeth, eliciting a keening from Vivienne that made the hair stand up on the back of his neck. One hand slipped between the split in the front of her dress, moving up her thighs until he found the source of her feminine heat. The scrap of fabric that made up her panty was damp from her arousal. He pressed his thumb against her mound and her hips moved against his hand in an untutored rhythm as old as time.

Vivienne felt herself floating beyond herself as a desire she'd never known left her shaking and struggling for her next breath. Her legs were trembling as she tried stemming the voracious craving for the man doing wonderfully crazy things to her breasts. She wanted Diego, wanted to lie with him and have him remind her that she was a woman with normal urges, but she didn't want him to get her pregnant. Once she realized Sean had no intent of making love to her, she'd stopped taking the Pill.

"Diego, don't!"

He released her breasts, his eyes filled with confusion, and pulled the bodice of her dress up to cover her breasts. "What's the matter?"

"We can't… I can't sleep with you without contraception."

Cradling her face between his palms, Diego kissed her forehead. "Baby, do you think I would sleep with you without using a condom? Didn't you say that you didn't want a child?"

"It's not that I don't want children, just not now."

Diego knew the moment of madness had passed when he felt his erection go down. "You're going to have to learn to trust me, Vivienne."

She nodded. "It's going to take time for me to be able to trust a man again."

He kissed her again. "Take all of the time you need."

"Thank you."

"You're welcome. Why don't you go upstairs and turn in. The birthday celebration is scheduled for an onboard brunch at eleven before we sail to the Keys for dinner."

"Okay." Leaning forward, Vivienne pressed a light kiss to his cheek. "Good night."

Diego curbed the urge to pull her into his arms again and carry her to his bedroom, where he had a supply of condoms in the drawer of one of his bedside tables. He wanted Vivienne like the earth needed rain, craved her like an addict hungered for drugs, and he needed her to help him forget all the women in his past.

Vivienne claimed she knew him, but she was wrong. No one knew him that well, because even he didn't know up until the time he'd taken her into his arms to dance with her that he wanted Vivienne Neal to be the last woman in his life.

At thirty-six he had everything he'd wanted with the exception of a wife and child. Vivienne said she didn't want to remarry or become a mother. His goal was to convince her to trust him enough to try and make her happy. And he was willing to wait until she came around.

What she hadn't known was that he was patient, a risk taker and venture capitalist. He'd taken a risk to become a cotton broker and it helped him double ColeDiz's profits. When he'd inquired about the vacant warehouses he was told that it would take the zoning board more than a year to vote to rezone the area from commercial to residential, and now he was willing to risk all of his personal net worth in order to hold on to Vivienne Kay Neal.

Ribbons of sunlight slipped through the partially closed blinds, inching their way over the California king-size bed where Diego had spent a restless night. It was after three before he was able to finally fall asleep. Whenever he recalled the taste of Vivienne's mouth, the firm roundness of her breasts and the soft moans of desire that'd slipped past her parted lips, his body betrayed him. His penis had gotten so hard it hurt when he rolled over on the mattress. And it took a very long time for his erection to go down.

The increasing heat settled over his face and he opened his eyes and stared up at the ceiling fan, the blades designed to resemble large banana leaves. Turning his head, he glanced over at the clock on the bedside table. It was only seven-ten. Reaching for the BlackBerry, Diego switched it on, noting he had a voice mail message. Punching several keys, he accessed the message. His South Carolina real estate broker had left him a message asking him to return the call irrespective of the hour. Scrolling through the directory, he tapped a button.

"What's up, Harry?" he asked when hearing the familiar voice.

"Diego, I'm glad you called back. I'm scheduled to go to contract on a tract of land over in Bluffton this coming Thursday, but I'm having a cash flow problem. Unfortunately, with the current real estate crisis they're asking fifty percent down."

"Joseph won't return from vacation for another week, so I'll come up to see the property and give you a check from my personal account. Joseph can settle the matter later."

"Thanks. I really appreciate it, Diego."

"I'm the one who should be thanking you. Will you have time to give me a tour if I come up Monday afternoon?"

"Sure. Plan to spend the night, because it's best to see the property during the daylight hours. You coming up will give Anissa an excuse to do a little entertaining, so be prepared to meet one or two of her single girlfriends."

Diego grimaced. "I'm afraid that's not going to be possible. Right now I'm involved with someone."

"Then, please bring the lady with you. You two can stay in the guest cottage."

"That sounds good."

"How are you coming up?"

"I'm flying."

"Call me when you touch down. I'll come over and get you."

"Don't bother. I'll have a driver pick us up."

"Suit yourself. We'll be looking for you sometime on Monday."

Diego ended the call. He knew Lourdes had scheduled a meeting for him with the board members of a West Palm Beach community center, but he would have to postpone it. Going to Charleston had become a priority. He tapped in a memo on the cell to call his banker in the morning to cut a bank check, payable to Harry Ellis.

Swinging his legs over the side of the mattress, he left the bed and walked into the adjoining bathroom. He'd instructed Harry to purchase the one-hundred-acre tract although he hadn't seen it. For all he knew it could've been swampland, except that he trusted the real estate agent to act in his best interest. Harry had already had an independent geologist test soil samples for levels of acidity.

He smiled when he recalled Harry's comment that his wife wanted to set him up with her single friends. But that wasn't going to happen, because the only woman he wanted to be hooked up with occupied an upstairs bedroom.

Vivienne lay on a deck chair with thirty other passengers on the sleek yacht, her hair and eyes protected by a baseball cap and oversize sunglasses. A scrumptious breakfast, prepared by an onboard chef and his staff had left her disinclined to move until the elaborate brunch she'd eaten had settled.

The menu, music and those who'd come to celebrate Brant Ryker's thirty-seventh birthday were different from the guests at Peyton and Raquel Cleary's wedding. The music was R & B and hip-hop, and the twenty- and thirty-something couples had come to party, while the boat's captain and crew were on hand to see to the needs of the passengers aboard the sleek sixty-foot sailing vessel. Tall, lanky, shaggy-haired Brant and his wife, Bay, were the consummate hosts, circulating among their guests, making certain everyone was enjoying themselves.

Diego had waited until they'd boarded the yacht to inform her that he wanted her to accompany him to Charleston, South Carolina. She was to pack enough for several days, including jeans, boots and long-sleeved shirts. When she told him that she didn't own a pair of boots, his reply was "We'll pick up a pair before flying up to Charleston."

"All you all right, *m'ija?*"

Vivienne smiled but didn't open her eyes. "I've never been better."

Diego sat on the deck chair next to Vivienne's and pulled gently on her big toe. Like everyone on board, she'd removed her shoes in order not to mar the deck that was as smooth as glass. Her shoes, a pair of blue-and-white-striped espadrilles, matched her cotton boatneck top. A pair of white stretch cuffed pants ending at the knee completed her nautical outfit. Today she'd swept her hair up into a ponytail, covering her head with a navy-blue baseball cap to protect her face from the sun.

If his friends were surprised to see him with Vivienne, they didn't say anything. Most of them were familiar with Asia Huntley; a few of them predicted he would eventually marry her. There had been occasions when he'd tried imagining Asia as his wife, but something wouldn't let him think that far ahead into the future. When he and Asia stopped seeing each other, Brant and his other college friends had called to ask him whether he was okay. He wanted to tell them he was more than okay, because what he'd expected for some time was finally confirmed.

Diego and Rosario Collier had practically grown up together and their mothers were best friends who'd attended the same schools. Ro, as he was affectionately called, had earned a reputation as a playa. He was able to get a woman, even if she professed not to like him, into bed. His prowess with the opposite sex began in high school, continued throughout college and into his career as a professional pilot.

Once Diego became CEO of ColeDiz, he hired his friend to fly the company's new G550 company jet. ColeDiz's older Gulfstream jet had logged so many miles that the cost of repairing or replacing parts had become prohibitive. The initial thirty-six-million-dollar price tag for the private jet was quickly recouped after he'd become a cotton broker. The growing trend for clothes made from natural fibers had spurred a resurgence in the sale of garments made from cotton.

The salary Rosario received from ColeDiz far exceeded any he would've earned flying commercial jets. And what pained Diego most was that Rosario hadn't seemed even slightly remorseful after he discovered his friend and Asia in bed together. It was Asia who'd become hysterical, but Diego reassured her that he was okay and walked out of her condo without a backward glance. The next day Rosario handed in his resignation and it was months later when he'd heard from Rosario's mother that her son had moved to Hawaii, where he was engaged to marry a local girl.

Unfortunately, Asia refused to accept the fact that they were no longer a couple. Her ringing his phone at all hours of the day and night, and leaving tearful and sometimes hysterical messages on his voice mail bordered on harassment. Fortunately for him, she couldn't get past security at his condo, or he would've been forced to take out a restraining order. He continued to ignore her, and eventually she went away.

What he'd tried to understand was her rationale for sleeping with his friend. She'd admitted that it was nothing and that she wanted to find out if the hype about Rosario Collier was true, and when she compared him to Rosario the latter came up sorely lacking in the fore- and afterplay.

Diego told Asia that she was a woman, not a curious child, and that he had no intention of continuing a relationship with a woman he couldn't trust. Unlike some men, he'd never been able to sleep with more than one woman at the same time. If he found one that didn't satisfy him sexually, he ended their association quickly and smoothly. He hadn't wanted to use them any more than he wanted to be used.

Staring at the woman reclining on a chair less than a foot away, he was fantasizing about making love to Vivienne as he had every night since she'd come into his life. When he first saw her on the balcony in the moonlight wearing a diaphanous nightgown, he knew then that he wanted to lie between her legs.

He'd wanted her their first night together. He'd wanted her last night when they'd danced together under the stars. And he wanted her now! What he feared was that once he made love to Vivienne it wouldn't be enough, that he'd want more. And more wouldn't be the next six months or six years, but forever.

She'd said that she'd never felt better and it was the same with him. Whenever they were together it was as if nothing else mattered except making her happy, righting the wrongs of Sean Gregory.

"How long do you think we'll be in the Keys?"

Vivienne's query broke into Diego's thoughts. "I don't know. Why?"

"I'd like to do a little sightseeing."

"Don't worry, Vivienne, we can always come back, if that's what you want."

Reaching up, she removed her sunglasses and stared at him. "Why is it always what I want, Diego? What if it's not what you want?"

Diego sat up and stared at her. "Don't confuse me with your ex-husband."

"Late husband," she shot back, correcting him.

"What—eva," he drawled sarcastically. "Weren't you the one who said that your late husband used you? That you'd become nothing more to him than an accessory, someone he'd take out when it was convenient and parade you in front of his friends like a prized show dog. You have to know what you look like, Vivienne, because fortunately mirrors don't lie. You have a beautiful face, hot-ass body, and the fact that you're intelligent and articulate adds to the package.

"The difference between me and your late husband is that I like you for more than your face and body. I'm not going to lie and say that I don't feel good with you on my arm. Hell, I'm a man, and as one I've seen other men with beautiful women and found myself fantasizing about how it would be to be with her. It's no different when I take you out and see other men staring at you. That's why I got a little bent out of shape about the dress you wore last night." He paused, staring at the diamond stack ring on the middle finger of her right hand, a ring Sean Gregory had probably given her. The man she'd planned to divorce was dead, yet she still hadn't let him go. "I don't want other men lusting after what I consider mine," Diego said in a voice that was just above a whisper. "And, there's something else you should know about me."

Vivienne stared at Diego, while at the same time holding her breath. She didn't know whether she wanted to know any more than what she now knew about him. He'd admitted to liking her, but what she didn't want was the word *love* to become a part of his or her vocabulary, because she feared that she was falling in love with him. It wasn't an emotion based on a physical need as much as an emotional necessity. All she needed from Diego was what he'd promised—protection.

Earlier that morning, she woke up drenched in perspiration with her heart beating uncontrollably, believing she was having a panic attack. Then she realized she was waking up from a nightmare. In her dream she'd gone to the house in Georgetown to see Sean, who'd called to tell her that he hadn't been feeling well. But when she arrived she found it empty except for a skeleton in a closet in their bedroom.

She'd tried to interpret the dream, thinking that skeletons in a closet meant hiding something, or keeping secrets. But what she couldn't make sense of was why the town house had been abandoned.

Her late husband had always been a very private person, and she respected that because Vivienne knew Sean would never disclose any of the details of their marriage. The reason she'd directed her attorney to file the papers necessary for granting a divorce before she had the opportunity to talk to Sean was because she knew he would try to talk her out of it. His argument wouldn't have been to try and negotiate to save their marriage because he loved her, but she was ready for his line of reasoning. He wouldn't be the first, nor would he be the last divorced politician.

The one and only time she'd asked Sean if he was having an affair, he laughed in her face, saying that if he didn't have time to sleep with her then he didn't have time to sleep with another woman. It was weeks later when she recalled his comeback that she wondered, if he wasn't sleeping with a woman, then perhaps he had been sleeping with a man. Somehow she didn't want to think of her husband as a gay or bisexual, but anything was possible.

"What is it I should know about you?" she asked Diego after a pregnant silence.

"I'm going to hire an independent investigator to look into Sean's accident."

"Why?"

"You're still wearing your wedding ring, which means you still don't have closure."

Vivienne stared at her right hand as if she'd never seen it before. She'd switched her ring from her left to right hand the day she'd come to Washington to inform Sean that she was divorcing him. She wasn't certain why she hadn't taken off the ring, but it had nothing to do with not having closure. Sean was gone and she'd accepted that.

"You're wrong, Diego."

He extended his hand. "If I'm so wrong, then give me the ring."

Vivienne thought Diego was joking, but when she looked at him she realized he was deadly serious. She blinked once. Underneath the soft, controlled voice, tailored wardrobe and impeccable manners beat the heart of a man born into great wealth and used to getting whatever he wanted.

"No." The single word was emphatic.

He withdrew his hand, smiling. "Thanks for proving me right."

Her temper flared as she twisted the ring off her finger and threw it at him. It bounced off his chest and landed in his lap. "Take the damn thing if it bothers you that much!"

Diego picked up the ring, feeling the weight of the heavy metal. There was no doubt it was made of platinum and the number of diamonds in the three-row eternity band was probably displayed with a price-upon-request tag. "I'll put it in the safe at the condo."

He knew she was angry about his mentioning the ring, but he didn't want a third person in their relationship—if they were going to have a relationship. He stared at the lighter band of color around her middle finger before shifting slightly in the chair and pushing the ring into the pocket of his slacks.

Vivienne folded her arms under her breasts. "I don't care what you do with it," she mumbled under her breath.

And she didn't care. In fact she didn't know why she'd continued to wear her wedding ring when her marriage had ended soon after it'd officially begun. She'd fooled everyone when they believed she and Sean had the perfect marriage, and as a couple they complemented each other. A political journalist had reported in her column after she'd attended a party with Sean, hosted by the National Black Caucus, that they were a part of the next wave of D.C. power couples.

Even when she met with her attorney to tell him that she'd decided to divorce her husband, she'd still wanted to believe she could save her marriage. She had him file the petition, because Vivienne knew if she'd met with Sean without legal leverage he would've used his persuasive powers to talk her out of ending their marriage.

"You're right, Diego, about me not having closure, and it won't be until the police catch the person responsible for running down Sean."

Diego's expression didn't change as he reclined on the deck chair, a baseball cap pulled low over his forehead. "This really isn't about me being right and you wrong, but about reconciling your past life. It was the same with me and Asia."

He told Vivienne about the television weather girl whose lust for life was what initially attracted him to her. For her, life was one big continuous party with a perfect forecast for every day of the year. She was the antidote to his eating, breathing and sleeping ColeDiz. He also told her about Asia sleeping with Rosario, which resulted in the loss of a childhood friend and employee.

"Asia's cheating paled in comparison to the loss of someone I regarded as a brother, Vivienne. If it had been anyone else, I would've kicked the shit out of him. But I didn't because our mothers are close friends."

Vivienne shifted on her side to stare at Diego. He was so still he could've been carved from marble. "I'm sorry, Diego. I didn't know. Her letter made it sound as if you'd dumped her because she wanted marriage and children and you didn't."

A sardonic smile twisted his mouth. "You can't believe everything you read."

"I know that now."

She told Diego about her conversations with Detectives Larson and Cotter and Elizabeth Gregory's suspicions that someone was watching her. "Detective Cotter told me that the feds are involved in the investigation, and he's confident they'll come up with something."

"He's right, *m'ija*. With today's technology they'll come up with some evidence the police probably overlooked and it'll be enough to crack the case." He would call Jake Jones and ask him to check with his contact at the Bureau to see what they'd come up with on Gregory's hit-and-run accident.

Vivienne hoped the detectives were right. Not only did she need closure but so did Elizabeth. If Diego wanted to hire a private investigator, then she wasn't going to interfere. She wanted to move on with her life, but realized that wasn't possible until she reconciled her past, and dating Diego Cole-Thomas was the first step in that direction.

The music blaring from the ship's speaker changed to a slower pace as everyone settled down on chairs to relax and enjoy the ocean breezes that offset the intense heat from the Florida sun as the yacht sailed south toward the Keys.

Although Diego's friends were diverse, they all had one thing in common: wealth. They were the sons and daughters of corporate executives, prominent surgeons, owners of sports teams and even a movie producer. Most of the women claimed names that sounded like the earth, flora and fauna: Amber, Viola, Holly, Brook and Laurel. Their male counterparts had names that were taken from the Bible: Daniel, Ephraim, Andrew, Matthias and Seth. All had attended prep or finishing schools before enrolling in Ivy League colleges, and most had gone on to work in the same field as their parents.

Diego revealed that he'd met Brant and Peyton as a freshman at Brown, and they'd hung out together because they were all Floridians. They'd studied and partied together, and at times dated the same girls, but only with the other's consent.

Brant and Bay had arrived at Peyton's wedding reception minutes before midnight, because their flight from the West Coast had been delayed. But by midnight she and Diego were back at his house dancing and kissing under the nighttime sky.

The past three days had become one continuous party for Vivienne: sharing dinner with Celia and Yale, Peyton's wedding and now Brant's birthday yacht party. Once on board, Bay had informed everyone that the ship would dock at the Keys for several hours to give everyone a chance to regain their land legs and browse the many shops. The captain had scheduled a six o'clock boarding and a sit-down dinner would be served promptly at seven-thirty. Their estimated time of arrival at Jupiter Island was ten that evening. The tall, thin woman with a mane of dirty blond hair had flashed a knowing smile when she said the party would've gone on much later except that the next day was Monday and some people had to work for a living. Her quip was followed by smirks and an exchange of amused glances. None of them had to work for a living, since they were trust fund babies.

Vivienne hadn't grown up poor, but her parents weren't wealthy, either. They were upper middle class rather than lower upper class. She and her brother had attended private schools, had traveled abroad several times before graduating from high school and had applied to and gotten into elite private colleges. It wasn't until after she'd married Sean that he told her that he'd married up. Marrying the daughter of one of the country's best civil rights litigators had enhanced his social standing. It was the first indicator that he'd married her for his personal gain, and he continued to use her until she'd decided that she'd had enough. It took a lot of courage to initiate divorce proceedings, and she knew she'd finally taken control of her life and her future with the action.

Diego wanted a temporary girlfriend and she'd be just that—temporary. He'd also offered to hire someone to uncover the person responsible for killing Sean—and she'd let him do that. She would give him what he wanted, and he in turn would give her what she wanted—closure.

In the end both of them would get what they wanted.

Chapter 12

Vivienne felt as if she'd come to one of the Caribbean islands when she strolled along the narrow streets and alleys of Key West. Diego explained that the Florida Keys attracted a lot of tourists and over the years had become quite commercialized.

They stopped in front of the Ernest Hemingway House and Museum on Whitehead Street to watch a bride and her attendants as they flitted into the beautifully landscaped gardens like delicate butterflies.

"What a lovely place for a wedding."

Diego smiled and nodded. "I remember my great-grandmother telling me about visiting Hemingway's house in Cuba. She said it was restored to look exactly the way it had when Ernesto lived there, writing and hanging out with the locals."

"Have you ever been to Cuba?"

"No."

"Do you still have relatives there?"

He nodded again, reaching for Vivienne's hand. "I have a few distant cousins in Pinar del Río. I've never met them, but my grandmother and her sister Josephine keep in touch with them."

"What's happening in Charleston tomorrow?"

"We're going to look at the land that will eventually become a tea garden."

Vivienne gave Diego a sidelong glance as they continued walking. "You've never been there?"

"No."

"How can you buy land sight unseen?"

"I have a very competent representative."

"Competent or not, it's like someone buying a piglet in a sack and when they get home discovering it's a rabbit instead."

Throwing back his head, Diego laughed loudly. "That's not a very good analogy because a piglet weighs a great deal more than a rabbit—even if it's a big rabbit, and pigs squeal and rabbits don't."

She punched him softly in the shoulder with her free hand, encountering solid muscle. "You know what I mean."

He chuckled. "No, I don't." She drew back her arm to hit him again when he caught her fist. "I'm sorry for teasing you."

Vivienne rolled her eyes at him. "You should be. What do you know about growing tea?"

"At first I knew very little about the crop, but after an intense course I know as much about growing and cultivating it as I do coffee. Just as with coffee, tea has thousands of varieties of one single plant, the camellia sinensis. Tea is no different than coffee or grapes for fine wines, because the variety of tea is the result of where it's grown. India's legendary Darjeeling or black tea is grown in the Himalayan foothills where the leaves are picked by hand, unlike the tea garden on Wadmalaw Island where they're harvested by a special machine."

"Do you plan to use a machine, too?"

"No. Harvesting by machine no matter how carefully can sometimes bruise the leaves. Hiring tea pickers will add to the island's economic base. The actual processing of the leaves will be done by machines."

"What varieties do you intend to produce?"

"We plan to start with black, green and white. Maybe we'll stay in South Carolina long enough to take a tour of the Charleston Tea Plantation."

Vivienne felt a shiver of excitement to be in on the planning stages of a ColeDiz project. The privately held family-owned company had been shrouded in mystery since its inception, and would probably remain that way for decades to come.

For the past three days she'd been involved in nonstop socializing, but that would come to an abrupt end when she accompanied Diego to South Carolina's Lowcountry. She'd survived the rigors involved with becoming his social companion, and now she would have to switch gears when he morphed into his role as CEO of the largest family-owned agribusiness in the States.

Vivienne woke Monday to discover that Diego hadn't waited for her to prepare breakfast. He'd left a note on the kitchen countertop informing her that he would return at eleven to take her shopping for boots before they were scheduled to take a two-thirty flight out of the West Palm Beach Airport.

They hadn't returned to Palm Beach until eleven the evening before, and instead of packing she'd taken a shower and gone straight to bed, sleeping peacefully throughout the night. She ate a hasty breakfast of sliced fruit, toast and coffee, then returned to her bedroom to pack. Diego had mentioned staying in Charleston for several days, and she decided to pack enough for four.

She still had two hours before Diego was scheduled to return, so she wrote a short note to Elizabeth Gregory, then continued inputting the information for his social calendar. There were weekends when he had back-to-back meetings or fund-raisers. Vivienne must have lost track of time, because when she registered movement behind her she turned to find Diego standing in the doorway, his arms crossed over his chest.

Resting a hand over her heart, she took a deep breath. He wore a suit, but had loosened his tie. "I didn't hear you come in." Shifting her neck from side to side, she tried to alleviate the stiffness.

"That's because you're working much too hard," Diego said, walking into the room and stopping behind her. His fingers circled her neck. "Don't move." Vivienne moaned softly as he massaged the muscles in her upper back.

"That feels so good."

"You're tight as a drum."

She closed her eyes. "It's from tension."

He leaned closer. "What do you have to be tense about, *m'ija*? Have I been that hard a taskmaster?"

"No," she moaned when his fingers kneaded a knot in her shoulder blade.

Diego pressed his mouth to her ear. "What has you so tense?"

"I don't know."

"While we're away I want you to relax."

Vivienne smiled. "Is that a direct order, boss?"

His fingers stilled. "I'm no longer your boss." Reaching into the breast pocket of his suit jacket, he pulled out an envelope and placed it on the keyboard. "This makes it official."

Vivienne picked up the envelope and took out two checks in the same amount. "What's all this?"

"Six months salary plus a bonus for preparing breakfast, and the other check is a matching severance package. I had the bookkeeper withhold taxes from the salary and bonus, then with whatever was left she was able to determine the severance payout."

"That's illegal, Diego."

His fingers tightened on her nape. "Mind your business, Vivienne. I have enough tax accountants on staff to deal with the IRS."

"I was just—" Her words were cut off when he moved quickly, easing her gently off the chair.

"That's enough," he ordered softly.

Vivienne narrowed her eyes at him. "I suppose that's your way of telling me to shut up."

His eyebrows shot up. "I'd never tell you to shut up."

Rolling her eyes, she sucked her teeth loudly. "You could've fooled me."

Diego knew of one way to make her stop talking, and he employed it when he slanted his mouth over hers, stealing the breath from her lungs. Her hands went to his chest as he deepened the kiss, his tongue slipping between her lips.

Even when he and Vivienne were apart, he was able to recall everything about her. He was able to remember the natural scent of her skin beneath her seductive perfume, call to mind the velvety feel of her cheek next to his when they'd danced, and the sweet taste of her mouth when he'd brushed his lips over hers. Utilizing the utmost restraint, he kissed her when he really wanted to devour her mouth.

Cupping her hips, he eased her between his legs. "There are times when you talk entirely too much," he whispered, "and the only time you stop is when I'm kissing you."

Vivienne didn't want to talk now, not with his mouth doing things to her she'd forgotten existed. Burying her face against the strong column of Diego's neck, she inhaled the lingering scent of sandalwood and bergamot. She was overwhelmed by the masculinity he exuded just standing there.

He stood up and a soft gasp escaped her when she felt the stirring hardness in his groin pressed to her middle. The size of his erection under the fabric of his trousers elicited a rush of wetness between her legs that left her shaking uncontrollably. "Diego," she whispered hoarsely.

"What is it, baby?" Diego heard desperation in her voice. He knew what she wanted, because he wanted the same. He wanted to sweep the desk of everything and put her on her back and push into her celibate body like an animal in heat.

And he was in heat, he was on fire! Desire singed his brain, leaving him shaking with a need to make love to Vivienne that came close to hysteria. The magnitude with which she responded to him was astonishing, and as he aroused her his own passion grew hotter, more intense.

His hands moved up to her head and he held her still. Dipping his head, he took her mouth again—this time his tongue plunging in and out of her mouth until both were gasping. He heard a sound and froze.

The ringing penetrated the fog of lust in Vivienne's brain, then she realized it was her cell phone. The only people, other than Alicia, who had her cell number were her family, and they usually didn't call her unless it was an emergency. Since she had relocated to Florida she'd always called them.

"Let me go, Diego. I have to answer my phone."

Smothering a vicious expletive under his breath, Diego dropped his hands. "I'll be back after I change." Turning on his heels, he turned and stalked out of the office, struggling to control the throbbing desire in his groin.

Waiting until she was alone, Vivienne pressed a button to take the call. The display had come up with a private number. Whenever her mother called she never cleared her number.

"Yes."

"Mrs. Vivienne Gregory?"

She frowned. It wasn't her mother, and the masculine voice wasn't her father's or brother's. "Who's calling, and how did you get this number?"

"My name is James Kane, and I am a close friend of your husband, Sean. He gave this number in case I couldn't reach him at the others he'd given me."

"I'm sorry, Mr. Kane, but you couldn't have been a friend of Sean because he died six months ago."

There came a pregnant pause before the slightly accented British voice came through the tiny earpiece again. "I've been out of the country, so I wasn't aware of your husband's passing. Please accept my condolences."

"Thank you, Mr. Kane."

"I called your—Sean, because I'd given him a book last year and I need it back."

"What's the title of the book?"

"It's not that type of book, Mrs. Gregory. It's more like a notebook or date book containing handwritten names, addresses and telephone numbers of people who had supported his reelection. I need that information for another candidate."

"I know nothing about the book. I suggest you get in touch with his former chief of staff and ask whether he has any knowledge of what you're looking for." The governor of Connecticut had appointed someone from her party to serve the remaining year of Sean's two-year term.

"I spoke to Mr. Jaffe and he said he hasn't seen it."

"Again, I'm sorry, Mr. Kane, but I can't help you."

"Have you checked through all of his personal effects?"

"Sean never brought his work home, so whatever personal effects that had to do with politics he left at his D.C. office."

"I'll check with Mr. Jaffe again. I'm sorry to have bothered you, Mrs. Gregory."

"No bother, Mr. Kane. I hope you find what you're looking for."

"Thank you. Goodbye, Mrs. Gregory."

"Goodbye, Mr. Kane."

"Please call me James. Mr. Kane makes me feel like my father, whom everyone addresses as Mr. Kane."

Vivienne smiled. "Okay, James. Again, I wish you luck."

"Thank you."

She depressed a button, terminating the call before the man could engage her in further conversation. The warming passion Diego had evoked had completely faded. If a number she'd recognized had come up on her cell, she wouldn't have answered it and no doubt she and Diego would've wound up in bed together.

Clenching her teeth tightly, she saved the data she'd put into the computer and walked out of the office to retrieve the bag she planned to take with her to South Carolina.

Henri held the door open as Vivienne climbed into the rear of the limo, Diego following closely behind her. An overcast sky and rumble of thunder signaled they were in for a thunderstorm, which she hoped would hold off until they were airborne. Taking off and landing during thunderstorms always made her uneasy.

Diego had changed out of his suit and into a short-sleeved white shirt, jeans and running shoes. At thirty-six he was in peak physical condition, and despite sitting behind a desk for hours there wasn't an ounce of excess flesh on his tall frame. She stole a surreptitious glance at his profile when he stared out a side window. They hadn't exchanged more than twenty words since leaving the condo, and Vivienne suspected he was still smarting because the telephone had abruptly ended his intent to make love to her.

He'd carried both their bags when they took the elevator to the lower level where Henri waited to drive them to Worth Avenue for her boots, then to the West Palm Beach Airport. It hadn't taken more than a quarter of an hour to select a pair of boots from the Coach store. She'd decided on a water-resistant-coated, signature, black-and-white rain boot with the recognizable horse-and-carriage logo.

Moving to her right, she reached for his hand, lacing her fingers through his. She smiled when he squeezed her hand. "I didn't bring my phone with me."

A slow grin spread over Diego's face, softening his features. "Speaking of phones I have a BlackBerry for you. I'll give it to you when we come back." He let go of her hand, dropping an arm over her shoulder to pull her closer. "I had Lourdes cancel all of my meetings until Thursday."

"I thought we were only going to spend two days in Charleston."

"This is my first trip to the Lowcountry in years, so if I'm going to set up business there I believe it would be in my best interest to familiarize myself with the region."

"Do you have a distributor for your tea?"

He nodded. "I plan to use the same distributor we use for our coffee and bananas."

The rain was coming down in rivulets when Henri maneuvered into a private airstrip where a number of private jets were arriving and taking off. Umbrella in hand, he held it over Diego as he alighted from the car. Diego took it and shielded Vivienne as she climbed out of the limo. A rumble of thunder shook the earth, followed by flashes of lightning crisscrossing the darkened sky.

A flight attendant in a navy-blue pantsuit and white blouse stood in the doorway of the sleek jet with the ColeDiz logo emblazoned on the side and aircraft identifying numbers and letters on the tail. A name tag was attached to the breast pocket of her jacket.

Vivienne thought they were going to stand in line at a commercial terminal and go through a security checkpoint, but then she remembered Diego assuring her that if she traveled with him on ColeDiz business, then she definitely wouldn't have to rough it.

"Welcome aboard, Ms. Neal. I'm Carrie-Ann, and I'm here to make certain you have a pleasant flight. As soon as we're airborne you'll be served a light lunch."

She returned the petite brunette's friendly smile. "Thank you, Carrie-Ann."

The flight attendant nodded to Diego. "Welcome aboard, Diego. We've been cleared for takeoff."

Diego ducked his head as he stepped into the large, modern cabin. The seats in the Gulfstream Aerospace Corporation G550 were configured to recline into queen-size beds, the bathrooms were equipped with showers and flat screen televisions were mounted throughout the cabin. He directed Vivienne to a seat and sat beside her.

Carrie-Ann pulled up the stairs, then closed and locked the cabin door. She picked up a microphone and spoke softly into it. "We're ready, Captain." Taking a seat in the rear of the aircraft, she secured her seat belt as the jet pushed back in preparation for takeoff.

Vivienne shared a smile with Diego when he reached for her hand. "We won't be in the air long enough to view a movie."

"Most times when I take a flight to the West Coast or out of the country, I usually sleep instead of watching a movie. It's the only way I'm able to stave off jet lag. After touching down I always eat a light meal, then go directly to bed. Even if I wake up during the night because my body's still on East Coast time, I force myself to remain in bed."

"Does it work when you go to Uganda?"

"No. Just say if it's six at night here, then it's already two o'clock Tuesday morning. Once I pass the International Date Line my circadian rhythms go haywire. It will usually take me two days to feel in control of what I need to do or say."

"You're always in control, Diego."

He gave her a long stare. "I wasn't earlier this afternoon when I kissed you."

"Nothing would've happened," Vivienne said glibly.

"Wrong," Diego countered. "If your phone hadn't rung I would've made love to you on the desk, sofa or floor."

"Not if you hadn't had a condom on you. Right now I'm fertile myrtle, and if you get me pregnant I'm going to hurt you real bad."

"Wrong," he repeated. "If I got you pregnant I'd marry you."

"What if I didn't want to get married?"

"It wouldn't matter, Vivienne. I didn't get this old to become a baby daddy. I was raised to be responsible and to take care of my responsibilities. The fact remains that if you found yourself pregnant, then be prepared to either marry me, or find yourself involved in a very nasty custody battle."

"You'd try to take my child?"

"It wouldn't be just your child, *m'ija*. It would be our child. What I don't want is for history to repeat itself. My great-grandfather denied his son, and the result was almost forty years of a deep-rooted enmity that splintered my family. It was only when Samuel suffered a debilitating stroke and he believed he was dying that he made peace with his illegitimate son. As a child, I heard the ugly stories, how my grandmother and her sister refused to speak to Joshua, or whenever he walked into a room they walked out. When I met with my uncle, I told him I was ashamed to be a Cole because of the way he'd been treated. He said he understood, then gave me a stern lecture about family loyalty."

"Maybe your grandmother and aunt tried to protect their mother."

"I'm sure that's true, but what happened years before was between Samuel, M.J. and Joshua's mother and had nothing to do with their other children. Nancy and Josephine should've never insinuated themselves into their parents' business. Nancy was two and Josephine was only two months when Joshua was born."

"When did they find out that Joshua was their brother?" Vivienne asked.

"Both were college students and much too old to start a family feud that lasted almost twenty years."

Vivienne was saved from further conversation about illegitimate children and cheating husbands when the jet picked up speed, then lifted off, climbing rapidly until reaching cruising speed. She didn't intend to rely solely on Diego to protect her against an unplanned pregnancy. When they returned from South Carolina she planned to go on the Pill.

The Fasten Seat Belt light went off, and they were served a lunch of flaky crab cakes, carrot salad and a dark chocolate mousse topped with ground pistachios. She and Diego opted for sparkling water instead of wine. Vivienne felt that if she were to bleed then she would bleed champagne rather than blood. She'd drunk champagne to toast Celia and Yale's engagement, at Peyton and Raquel's wedding, and then again when Bay gave Brant a key to the yacht on which he and his friends had celebrated his birthday.

The nonstop eating and drinking reminded her of the few times she'd accompanied Sean to various D.C. social functions. After the first hour she found herself bored to tears. Most of the conversations were what I can do for you if you do this for me, and she'd learned quickly that being the wife of a politician wasn't as exciting as she'd thought it would be.

It appeared as if they'd just taken off when the jet began its descent. She stared out the large windows as the

Charleston landscape came into view. Palmetto trees lined the wide boulevards along Charleston Harbor as the pilot turned westward toward the airport, bringing the aircraft down smoothly on a private airstrip.

The cabin door was opened, the stairs lowered, and when Vivienne and Diego disembarked they were cloaked in a heavy mist that settled on their hair and clothing like diamond dust. The driver, a tall dark-skinned man with the body of a professional ballplayer, alighted from a car parked a few feet from the jet and approached them.

"Mr. Cole-Thomas?"

Diego smiled. "Yes."

The driver reached for their bags. "I'll take those." He scooped up the three bags as if they were packed with tissue paper. He headed for the black Town Car, Diego and Vivienne following.

She shivered noticeably when she got into the car. The driver had turned the air-conditioning to its highest setting. Within seconds of Diego getting in beside her, she scooted over and slipped her hands under his shirt, her fingers tunneling in the crisp hair on his broad chest.

"Are you cold?" he asked in Spanish.

Vivienne smiled. "Not now."

Resting his arm over her shoulders, Diego pulled her closer, sharing his body's heat. He'd been truthful with Vivienne when he admitted to almost losing control. And he hadn't lied when he told her that if perchance she found herself pregnant with his child, he'd marry her. The truth was he'd marry her even if she wasn't pregnant, something he would've preferred. However, there were no guarantees they would remain married for the rest of their lives, because even so-called perfect marriages ended. What he didn't want was for his child to live with his mother in another state and see him during school holidays or summer vacation. He'd grown up with both parents and he wanted no less for his children.

He closed his eyes as the driver maneuvered away from the airstrip toward Sullivan's Island. It'd been years since his last visit to the Lowcountry. The first time had been when he'd come to Parris Island to witness the graduation of Jacob Jones from the Marine Corps. He met Jacob the summer he'd driven to Miami to blow off steam before leaving for college. Unfortunately, he found himself in the wrong place at the wrong time when shots rang out from a drug deal gone wrong. Diego lay on the ground as bullets whizzed around him, and it wasn't until a strong hand pulled him off the pavement and shoved him into a car that he realized he wasn't going to die. The man who rescued him was off-duty Miami-Dade police officer Stephen Jones. The officer had just returned from a Florida Marlins baseball game with his teenage son when he saw Diego facedown on the street corner. Although three years Jake's senior, the two of them had become good friends.

Jake graduated college, and then joined the Marine Corps. Diego never asked Jake about his life in the military because he'd occasionally send an e-mail indicating he would be away for a while and would get in touch when he returned. It would be months before Jake surfaced again, and each time he seemed different. It wasn't his outward appearance that changed, but his demeanor. After his father was killed in the line of duty and his mother remarried a widower with four young children, Jake's visits to Miami dwindled until they stopped completely.

However, Diego's friendship with Harry Ellis began in

grade school and, unlike his relationship with Rosario Collier, grew stronger over the years. Harry brokered the deal between ColeDiz and the Ugandan cotton grower, and he'd given him the idea of setting up a tea garden after his wife returned from Wadmalaw Island. She couldn't stop talking about a trip to the Charleston Tea Plantation she'd arranged for her fifth-grade class.

"Do you have any Southern relatives?" Diego asked Vivienne, breaking the comfortable silence.

"Not that I know. None of my relatives on either side have ever talked about having family in the South."

"So, you're a Yankee through and through?"

"I suppose so. Does that bother you?"

Diego dropped a kiss on her hair. "Not in the least, *m'ija*."

Tilting her chin, Vivienne smiled up at him. "That's good to know."

He met her gaze under hooded lids. "Why?"

"Because I like you, Diego Cole-Thomas, and it would be a shame if you held my Northern roots against me."

"You like me?"

"You know I do."

"I know nothing of the sort, Ms. Neal. Maybe you need to show me how much you like me."

Her hand slipped lower, resting on his hard, flat belly. "I am feeling you up. Isn't that enough?"

Diego kissed her again. "It's a start."

Vivienne nodded. It was a start—the start of something she knew would change her forever. She'd resolved to have an affair with Diego, and when it ended she knew she wouldn't have any regrets.

It was as if her life had been on hold for years, while she waited for a man who would remind her why she'd been born a woman. She'd thought Sean was that man, but unfortunately she'd made a mistake. All of the signs were there even before they were married. Focused on his pursuit of power, he'd campaigned to the point of exhaustion. He was diagnosed with a fever of 102 degrees the day he was to be sworn in as a Member of the House, but he refused to remain in bed and miss the swearing-in ceremony. He returned home, collapsed into bed and spent the next two weeks recuperating from pneumonia.

Sean was her past.

Diego was her present.

What Vivienne refused to think about was her own future.

PART TWO
Vivienne Kay Neal

Chapter 13

Vivienne felt as if she'd known Harry and Anissa Ellis for years instead of two hours. She sat on the screened-in back porch with the grade-school teacher, drinking herbal sweet tea while listening to her relate the history of the Sea Islands.

Anissa rested a hand over her slightly rounded belly. "I know it was culture shock for Harry to leave Florida, but after twelve years he's now more Gullah than I am."

Vivienne smiled at the tall, raw-boned woman with strong African features that validated her claim to a heritage that spanned centuries. Tiny twists framed a round face with high cheekbones, slanting dark eyes and a wide mouth that tilted in the most beguiling smile.

"I've heard that the Gullahs have their own language."

Anissa nodded. "That's true. There's an ongoing movement to not only preserve the language, but also the culture."

She rubbed her belly. "I'm going to make certain my son or daughter will understand both languages."

"You don't know what you're having?" Vivienne asked.

"Unlike Harry, I'd rather not know."

Vivienne stared out the screen at an ancient oak tree draped in Spanish moss. The Ellises lived in a Lowcountry-styled plantation house on an island with a less than idyllic history. Anissa had explained that Sullivan's Island was the point of debarkation for thousands of imported slaves between 1700 and 1775. The island was famous for Fort Moultrie, which was a significant and strategic location during the Revolutionary and Civil Wars.

"Harry and I had almost given up having a child of our own, because we'd been trying for the past ten years."

"Had you considered adopting?"

"Not seriously. I have my students at school, the dogs who believe they're human and this house. It's taken me almost a decade to restore and furnish it."

"It's beautiful," Vivienne said truthfully.

When she'd walked into the entryway she felt as if she'd stepped back in time. If it hadn't been for electricity and indoor plumbing Vivienne would've believed she was transported back to the eighteenth century. What she hadn't expected was sharing the Ellises' guesthouse with Diego.

It was a smaller version of the grand house, but instead of six bedrooms it had one bedroom, an adjoining bathroom, kitchen and parlor. She'd briefly met Diego's gaze, praying he'd brought protection with him.

"When's the big day?"

Anissa went completely still when she felt the baby move. "I've been given a due date of October third."

Vivienne calculated quickly. Anissa was six months into

her term. The conversation she'd had with Diego came to mind. He'd taken the responsibility of protecting her against an unplanned pregnancy, but he'd also said that if she did become pregnant he would insist on marriage. He claimed he'd been raised to accept responsibility for his actions, and she'd been raised to fall in love, marry and start a family. She'd done exactly that in that order, but having a child had eluded her.

Whenever she thought about what had gone wrong in her marriage to Sean she hadn't been able to come up with a plausible answer. She knew couples fell out of love with each other, but Sean professed to still be in love with her.

There were occasions when women or men let themselves go and they were no longer attractive to their spouse, but that wasn't the case with her and Sean. Then there was sex—or the lack thereof. Vivienne had never rebuffed her husband or pleaded a headache, which left her baffled as to why he created diversions so as not to sleep with her.

Even when they did share a bed, he either claimed exhaustion or he was coming down with something. After a while she no longer cared if he'd lost interest in sex or he'd taken a lover. After four years of a lackluster union, she'd had enough.

Anissa set down her glass of water, pushing to her feet. "It's time I get up and start dinner."

Vivienne rose with her. "Can I help you?"

"No, no. You're a guest."

"And you're carrying a child," Vivienne countered. She'd taken note of the slight swelling in Anissa's ankles, and knew if she stood on her feet for any length of time it was certain to exacerbate the swelling. "Either you let me help you or Diego and I will take you and your husband out for dinner."

Anissa cradled her belly. "I've sworn off eating out because I ate something that didn't agree with me. To this day I haven't figured out what it was."

"What do you plan on preparing tonight?" Vivienne asked, following her hostess off the porch.

"I'd decided on fried chicken, roasted corn, a tomato salad and red velvet cake."

"What if I fry the chicken and roast the corn, while you make the salad and cake?"

"Now I know why you and Diego are a couple."

"Why would you say something like that?" Vivienne didn't know why she sounded so defensive.

"Aside from my husband, Diego is the most stubborn, determined, single-minded man I've ever known. He's like a dog with a bone, and you're no different."

She stared at the other woman, wondering if what she'd said was true. Had Anissa seen what she couldn't or hadn't wanted to acknowledge? She'd admit to being strong-willed as was Diego, but that's where the similarities ended. He was intimidating and tyrannical—something she wasn't.

"If you say so," she drawled.

A wide grin split Anissa's smooth, dark face. "Because you didn't deny that you and Diego are two of a kind, then I'm going to let you help me in my own kitchen."

Vivienne's grin matched that of her hostess. "Do I detect a little possessiveness, Mrs. Ellis?"

"Yes, you do. I worked very hard to get my man and the house I always dreamed about."

"How did you meet Harry?"

Looping her arm through Vivienne's as if they'd been friends for years instead of meeting only hours before,

Anissa led her down a wide hallway and into a large ultra-modern kitchen. "We'll talk and cook at the same time. And if I'm going to spill my guts about Harry, then you're going to have to do the same about Diego. I must admit I was very surprised when Harry told me that Diego was bringing a woman with him."

"Has he ever brought a woman with him?"

"This is the first time Diego has come to Sullivan's Island for a visit. I usually see him whenever Harry and I go to Florida to visit his folks. Every time I extend an invitation, he claims he's too busy to get away."

"Diego does have an incredibly busy schedule. I've taken on the responsibility of trying to keep his personal social calendar from conflicting with his business obligations."

"Once word gets out that Sean Gregory's widow is dating Diego Cole-Thomas, the tabloids are going to have a field day."

Vivienne felt her heart stop and then start up again. "You know who I am?"

"I know because I'm a teacher who likes to keep up with what's going on in Washington for my students. Every morning we set aside fifteen minutes to discuss the national news. I recognized your face from a picture that was taken on your wedding day."

Major news stations had run photographs of her and Sean dating from their engagement and up, including several D.C. social gatherings. "Diego and I will deal with that when it happens." Vivienne didn't tell Anissa that she and Diego were friends. However, she didn't know how friendly they'd be after sharing the guest-house.

"Good for you, Vivienne. You're a young woman, and

there's no reason why you'd have to spend the rest of your life in mourning."

Let's hope everyone else thinks like you, she mused. "Do you soak your chicken in buttermilk?" she asked Anissa."

"No. But, I did soak it in saltwater overnight."

"Would you mind if we try my fried chicken recipe?"

Anissa shook her head. "No, Vivienne, I wouldn't mind. Let me know what seasonings you need and I'll get them for you."

Reaching for the pad and pen on a countertop, Vivienne wrote down what she needed for her unique Southern-fried chicken recipe while Anissa gathered the ingredients she needed for a red velvet cake.

James McGhie felt as if he'd hit a brick wall. He'd called Vivienne Gregory, pretending to be a friend of her husband, but she told him what he already knew. He tapped in a number on his cell, praying the person on the other end wouldn't answer. But this night his prayers would go unanswered when the voice he'd come to detest came through the earpiece.

"You better have good news for me, Jimmie boy."

"I don't."

"Then, why the hell are you calling me, Jimmie boy?"

"The name is James, not Jimmy. And I'll forget that you called me boy."

"I'll call you whatever the hell I want to call you, McGhie. I've given you enough money to own you and the children you'll never have if you don't come up with that book."

James made a tight fist. "Jaffe's not talking."

"What about the hooker who got close to him?"

"She's in jail for stealing a credit card from one of her johns, who just happened to be a very influential lobbyist."

"Where's Gregory's wife?"

"I don't know."

"I don't know," the man with the gravelly voice mimicked. "You found nothing in the D.C. town house, Jaffe's not talking and the pretty little widow knows nothing. In baseball that means you've just struck out! Find the Gregory woman and make her talk. I'm giving you to Labor Day to come up with what I need. After that all bets are off, and if I have to get someone else to get what I want, then don't say you haven't been warned."

Rage made it almost impossible for James to think clearly. "Don't threaten me."

"I already did. Get the damn book."

Without warning, the line went dead, and James was tempted to throw the tiny phone against the wall. He'd been paid well to find a book which may not even exist, but he'd taken the case because he'd made plans to take his mother and leave the country for good. All of his adult life he'd worked to keep his country safe, and now he was still working, not for his government, but for a group of men who'd circumvented the laws they took an oath to uphold.

Well, if the frog thought he was going to threaten Mrs. McGhie's only child, then he didn't know who he was dealing with. James was aware of the consequence if he didn't find the book, but he wouldn't be the only one taking a fall.

He had no wife or children to mourn his passing. He didn't even own property. What James McGhie had was an offshore joint bank account. When he'd taken his mother to the Caribbean on vacation and took her to a bank to sign a signature card for the joint account she'd questioned why he wanted to open an account so far from home. He gave her an answer that seemed to assuage her curiosity, but only after he promised to take her to a casino.

Mrs. McGhie loved casinos, but didn't like losing money. James didn't plan on dying for a long time, yet if perchance an accident befell him, then Mrs. McGhie would find herself a very wealthy woman and the frog would lose everything.

Anissa peered through the glass of the oven door to check on her cake. "Do you think we need biscuits?"

Vivienne carefully dropped pieces of chicken coated in a seasoned flour mixture of garlic and onion powder, paprika and cayenne pepper. "Biscuits sound wonderful. But, you'll have to make them because mine usually don't come out flaky enough."

She enjoyed cooking with Anissa, who sang along with the songs coming from a radio on the countertop. A few times she stopped to cut a dance step, Vivienne joining her. Anissa had married Harry within days of graduating college. They'd lived in West Palm Beach for a year before buying a small cottage in Charleston. Harry, who'd quit his teaching position to dabble in real estate had found his niche. Within a year he'd earned enough in commissions to buy their dream house on Sullivan's Island.

"Okay, I'll make the biscuits," Anissa volunteered, peering over the deep pot with the frying chicken. "Lawdy, lawdy! That smells wonderful."

"It's the thyme, rosemary, garlic and sage." She'd added the fresh herbs to the hot peanut oil to give it additional flavor.

Anissa pointed to the fried herbs on a paper towel. "What are you going to do with them, Vivienne?"

"Once the chicken's done, I'm going to break them into tiny pieces and sprinkle them over the chicken."

"I hope Diego realizes how lucky he is. You're perfect for him," Anissa added when Vivienne looked at her in confusion.

"I don't know about us being perfect for each other, but I can admit that he's a great guy."

"He's a great catch—for any woman. I'd hinted in the past that I wanted to hook him up with a few of my girlfriends. But, he was always so nice when he told me thanks, but no thanks. I think that's why he hadn't wanted to come for a visit."

Vivienne wanted to tell Anissa that men like Diego didn't need help getting a woman. All he had to do was walk into a room and he would garner more female attention than he needed. And whenever they were out together she was made to feel that she held his complete attention, unlike some men who had to check out every woman within their line of vision.

Anissa was right that he was a great catch, but not for her. She'd promised to give Diego the next six months of her life, and no more. The year had begun with her initiating divorce proceedings and would end with her walking away from a man for whom she was beginning to have feelings. What she had to do was be careful—very, very careful that she wouldn't find herself in over her head, because Diego was too masculine, too virile, to ignore for any length of time.

"Good gravy, something smells good," Harry Ellis announced, walking into the kitchen.

Anissa smiled at her husband. "That's Vivienne's fried chicken."

"Can't be," Harry said.

Vivienne smiled at the shocked expression on her host's

face. He was only an inch taller than his wife, but his girth made him appear shorter. His redbone complexion was sprinkled with freckles that looked like tiny specks from a distance. He'd shaved his head, but his eyebrows and lashes were a brownish-red.

"It is," Anissa confirmed.

Harry turned to grin at Diego who'd come into the kitchen. "Hot damn, Diego. Your woman's all right."

Crossing his arms over his chest, Diego angled his head as he stared at Vivienne at the stove. He didn't know why, but something told him she wouldn't sit by and let Anissa wait on her. She'd jumped right in to help their hosts prepare dinner.

"She's more than all right, Harry. She's incredible."

Harry winked at his childhood friend. "I'm glad you said it or else Anissa would be frying pan me for looking at another woman."

Anissa rolled her eyes at Harry. "Stop lying!"

"But you would, baby. Didn't you tell me that you were going to hit me with a cast-iron skillet if you caught me talking to Dulcina Roberts?"

"That's because whenever the heifer's around you she starts with the moon eyes. And nothing you say is so funny that she has to fall all over you."

Harry walked over to Anissa and hugged her. "You know you're sexy when you're jealous."

She pushed him away. "Get out of here, Harry Ellis. A jealous woman ain't hardly sexy."

Harry looked at Diego. "Aren't jealous women sexy?"

A hint of a smile touched Diego's firm mouth. "Don't start me lying, brother. Jealous women can be dangerous, and you know it."

Vivienne and Anissa exchanged smiles and fist bumps as Harry's face turned a deep red shade. "See what you did, Diego. I thought you were my boy."

"I am your boy, but I'm not crazy enough to go toe-to-toe with two hormonal women." He'd remembered what Vivienne told him about her being in the most fertile phase of her cycle.

Harry bobbed his head. "I forgot about that."

"And, you can forget about eating if you keep running off at the mouth, Harry Leroy Ellis." He pantomimed zipping his mouth, eliciting laughter from everyone.

Anissa kissed Harry's cheek. "We'll sit down to eat in about twenty minutes. Can you please set the table in the dining room?"

"Of course, baby."

The two couples sat in the formal dining room enjoying a traditional Southern dinner. The fried chicken had turned out better than Vivienne had expected, the roasted corn with chili lime butter was sweet and tender, Anissa's cherry tomatoes with buttermilk blue cheese dressing was explosive on the palate and the biscuits were so light they literally melted on the tongue. Harry had brewed coffee, while his wife passed around slices of red velvet cake.

Light from the massive chandelier sparkled off the china, silver and delicate stemware. Vivienne met Diego's knowing gaze across the expanse of the table, nodding agreement when he pantomimed walking with two fingers on the pristine linen tablecloth. It would take a very long walk to aid in the digestion of all of the food she'd eaten.

Anissa pushed back her chair to stand, but Harry stopped her. "Sit down, baby. I'll take care of the dishes."

Diego stood up. "I'll help you."

Harry dismissed him with a wave of his hand. "No. Now that it's stopped raining I suggest you and Vivienne take a walk along the beach."

Needing no further prompting, Vivienne stood and waited for Diego to come around the table. "You may have to carry me," she whispered for his ears only.

"That's easy enough to do. You weigh next to nothing."

"I weigh enough, thank you."

Reaching for her hand, he cradled it gently. "I bet I have a hundred pounds on you."

"How much do you weigh?"

"Two-twenty."

"I weigh more than one-twenty, but I'm willing to bet that I'll weigh close to two hundred by the end of the year if I keep eating the way I have this past week."

Diego led Vivienne out a side door and headed in the direction of the beach. "This is the first time I've actually seen you eat. Usually you pick at your food or there's not enough food on your plate to make a bird full."

Vivienne didn't come back at him. She was experiencing a feeling of calm for the first time in a very long time. Her visiting the sea island made her feel as if time moved so slowly that it appeared to stand still. The wind had swept away the storm clouds, leaving the sky a vibrant indigo as the sun began its descent.

When they made their way to the beach, Vivienne sat and removed her sandals and dug her toes in the sand that still held the heat of the day. Diego dropped down beside her and wound his arm around her body. They watched in awe as the sun dipped lower and lower before slipping below the horizon.

"Do you think you can find your way back in the dark?" she asked Diego. Anissa told her that the island was only three miles long and less than a quarter mile wide.

"Their house isn't far from the lighthouse, so we'll use that as a landmark. Are you ready to go back?"

Vivienne nodded before realizing Diego couldn't see her. "Yes." Sitting on the beach conjured up images of tens or maybe hundreds of thousands of African slaves who'd stood on the same beach so many years ago, unaware of their fate.

Diego stood, then reached down to pull Vivienne to her feet, supporting her body while she slipped her feet into her sandals. "Ready, *m'ija?*"

"*Sí, m'ijo.*"

And she was.

She was ready for any and everything.

Chapter 14

Diego unlocked the door to the guesthouse, but didn't go in. "I'm going to sit out here for a while."

Vivienne knew he wanted to give her time to ready herself for bed before coming in. Tiptoeing, she kissed his cheek. "I'll see you later."

She walked through the parlor and into the bedroom. Opening her overnight bag, she took out a small quilted bag with her personal items and a nightgown, then made her way to the bathroom. A large claw-foot bathtub, ceiling fan and a countertop lined with candles beckoned her in.

Vivienne turned on the faucets and added a capful of lavender bath salts, leaving the water to trickle into the tub. In the time it took to brush her teeth and clean the makeup from her face the bathtub was half-filled and the space was redolent of the smell of herbs.

It'd been a while since she'd treated herself to a leisurely bath, but she knew she couldn't linger because Diego was waiting to use the bathroom. She didn't want him to wander in before she got into bed.

Fifteen minutes later, she slipped into bed. The only illumination came from a trio of candles under hurricane chimneys resting on a marble-topped table. The furnishings in the bedroom, like the others in the guesthouse, were reproductions from a bygone era. Vivienne lay, staring up at the shadows on the ceiling, and tried slowing down her runaway heartbeat. Counting slowly, she managed to calm herself enough to relax. Her final thoughts were of Diego before sleep overtook her.

Diego waited more than an hour before going inside and locking the door behind him. Sleeping with Vivienne was something he'd wanted to do within minutes of meeting her, but now it was to become a reality. He was more than experienced when it came to women and sex, but this was different.

When Harry told him that he and Vivienne would share his guesthouse, he hadn't bothered to tell his friend that he wasn't sexually involved with Vivienne, or he could've asked for separate bedrooms. But he knew the day of reckoning couldn't be put off forever. He'd taken all of the steps to alleviate the guilt that would've ensued if she were still his employee.

Although he wasn't cynical by nature, Diego always found it hard to believe that people fell in love at first sight. He hadn't known Vivienne Neal well enough to say that, but he knew he was falling in love with her.

Ironically, he wouldn't be the first Cole man to admit when he'd met the woman whom he would eventually marry, he'd known she was the one. It'd happened with Samuel and M.J., and his uncles. Joshua had married Vanessa Blanchard eight days after they first met, and confirmed bachelor Martin had taken one glance at Parris Simmons and fallen hard.

He walked into the bedroom and stopped short. There was enough light coming from the candles to make out the shape in the bed. The soft sound of Vivienne's breathing indicated she'd fallen asleep while waiting for him. Gathering his grooming kit off the triple dresser, he headed for the bathroom.

Vivienne woke immediately when she felt heat, then the weight of Diego's arm, on her waist. "I tried waiting up for you."

"It's okay, *m'ija,*" he whispered in her ear. "Go back to sleep."

Now she was fully awake. "It's too late for that." Shifting slightly, she turned to face him. "Where are your pajamas?"

Diego smiled. "I don't own a pair."

"Now I know what to give you for Christmas."

He sobered. "Will you still be around for Christmas?"

"If I'm not, then I'll mail you a pair."

"Does my not wearing pajamas bother you?"

"What would you do if it did, Diego?" she asked, answering his question with one of her own.

"I'd sleep out on the sofa."

Her eyebrows shot up. "You'd do that for me?"

His arm tightened around her waist, bringing her closer to his chest. "Don't you know by now that I'd do anything for you, Vivienne Neal?"

Diego's passionate entreaty left her speechless. "No…I didn't know," she stammered.

"All you have to do is ask and I'll get it for you," he whispered against her moist, parted lips.

A shiver shook Vivienne and suddenly she felt cold despite the heat coming from Diego's large body. "What if I ask you to make love to me?"

"That's the easiest thing you'll ever have to ask me."

Vivienne closed her eyes, letting her senses take over when she felt him draw back the sheet. Everything was magnified, from the smell of soap on Diego's skin to the smell of clean linen and the soft, subtle scent of burning candles. Never were the differences in their bodies more evident than when she felt the hair on his legs against her smooth legs.

A warming settled in her middle as she opened her mouth to his rapacious kiss when he moved over her. Anchoring her arms under his shoulders, Vivienne held on to Diego, not wanting to let him go. He kissed her mouth before moving to her throat and still lower to her breasts. The stubble on his chin grazed the nipples and she arched off the bed. She always knew when she was ovulating because her breasts were tender to the touch.

"Yes, yes, yes," she chanted when he suckled her breasts, then alternated pulling the hardened nipples between his teeth.

Kissing Diego, holding him and feeling his growing hardness rising up against her belly confirmed that her passion had been dormant. She'd spent four years in a passionless marriage, not taking a lover because she hadn't known she was waiting for Diego Cole-Thomas.

Her legs curled around his, holding him captive when his

tongue moved in and out of her mouth, simulating his making love to her, and eliciting a throbbing between her thighs.

Diego was shocked at Vivienne's passionate response to his lovemaking. He'd wanted to take her quickly, yet he wanted it to last throughout the night. He knew he had to be gentle with her. Not only was she more fragile than any other woman he'd slept with, but she was also fragile emotionally.

Rising slightly, he reached between their bodies and found the source of her feminine heat. Slowly, gently, he slipped a finger between the moist folds and penetrated her, nearly ejaculating when her flesh closed around him. She was so tight that he feared hurting her.

Breathing heavily, Diego pressed his mouth to her ear. "I don't know if we're going to be able to do this."

"Why, Diego?" Vivienne's query was a sob.

"You're too small. I don't want to hurt you."

Biting down on her lower lip, she struggled not to cry. "Please, *m'ijo,* don't leave me like this."

Diego felt his heart turn over. "I don't want to tear you."

"I'm not a virgin, Diego." She pounded his back with her fist. "Do it!"

"Vivienne."

"Just do it!" she screamed.

Diego released her and reached for the condom on the bedside table. He watched Vivienne as she watched him slip it on. If he had to penetrate her, then he had to make certain she was fully aroused.

Moving over her again, he began the ritual of tasting every inch of her body. He started with her hair, then moved down to her face. By the time his tongue dipped into the opening between her legs, Vivienne was moaning and writhing as if under a powerful spell.

A moan of ecstasy slipped from Vivienne's lips, followed rapidly by another, then another. The next sound was a gasp when Diego eased his penis into her body, filling her with his hardness until there was no room. His labored breathing echoed loudly in the stillness of the room.

"Are you all right, baby?"

She smiled. "I've never been better."

It was Diego's turn to smile. "But it's going to get better."

And it did. He moved slowly, pushing and withdrawing until she followed his lead. She felt the heat of Diego's body sweep down the length of hers, felt his penis grow longer, harder, while her head thrashed wildly back and forth on the pillow.

The pleasure Diego offered Vivienne escalated and spiraled out of control, sending her hurtling into a fiery blaze of an awesome, shuddering ecstasy. She screamed his name at the same time as he groaned out hers. She climaxed over and over until she felt herself slipping away from reality.

Diego buried his face against the column of her neck and waited for his heart to return to a normal rhythm. Not only had he fallen in love with Vivienne, but he also loved her.

Reluctantly, he withdrew from her hot, moist body and left the bed to discard the condom. Standing in the bathroom, he stared at his reflection in the mirror over the vanity. The face that stared back at him was that of a stranger. Vivienne had changed him so much that he didn't recognize who he was or what he'd become.

And for the first time in his life he was afraid, afraid of the power Vivienne had over him and what she would do if she ever became aware of it. He found it laughable that a woman would become his Achilles' heel.

He'd become the consummate deal maker when he sought to make his mark as CEO of ColeDiz, but he realized that he could also give it all up if it meant losing the woman whose smell was stamped on him like a permanent tattoo.

Vivienne woke to find Diego's chest pressed to her back. His body generated so much heat that she felt as if she were running a temperature. She tried moving, then stopped short. The slight ache between her legs was a reminder of what had occurred the night before.

Heat burned her face, but this time it wasn't because of Diego but shame when she remembered begging and demanding that he make love to her. And he had made love to her in a way that made her believe she was losing her mind. She did remember climaxing, but not much after that.

"Good morning," Diego mumbled in a deep voice that seemed to come from his belly.

"Good morning," she said, smiling. "How are you?"

Diego rested his hand over her naked hip. "That's what I should be asking you."

"It's all good."

He chuckled softly. "Are you sure?"

"Very sure."

"Can you walk?"

"Of course I can walk."

"We'll see later," he said cryptically.

Turning over on her side, Vivienne looked at Diego for the first time, her breath catching in her throat. It wasn't the only time she'd seen him unshaven, and the stubble on his lean face enhanced rather than detracted from his sensuality.

"What's that supposed to mean?"

Diego stared at Vivienne under hooded lids, wondering

if she could see what he was feeling. Did she know by looking at him that he was in love with her, that he wanted to marry her?

"Last night you asked me to make love to you, and I did. Now it's my turn. I want you to make love to me, Vivienne Neal."

She blinked once. "You're kidding."

"Do I look as if I'm kidding?"

Vivienne gave him a long, penetrating stare. "I guess not."

She didn't know what to make of the enigmatic man with whom she shared a bed. Was their relationship going to be a tit for tat? But she intended to find out. "Can I do anything I want?"

A slow smile spread across Diego's dark brown face. "Yes."

Whipping back the sheet, she mounted him. Her gaze never left his when she pressed her breasts to his chest. Lowering her head, she trailed light kisses over his hirsute pectorals and down his flat belly, smiling when his stomach muscles contracted.

"Are you okay, darling?" she crooned seductively. His breathing had deepened.

"It's all good," he said, repeating what she'd said.

Vivienne picked up the flaccid penis resting against his thigh and squeezed it gently. Her eyes grew wide when it quickly filled with blood. "Are you still good?" she asked, beginning a slow up-and-down stroking motion.

"Yeah! I think so."

Diego had asked her to make love to him, and she would, but not in the traditional sense. Holding him firmly in her fist, Vivienne lowered her head and took him into her mouth. Diego sat up as if she'd branded him with a hot poker.

"No!"

Ignoring his protest, her tongue and teeth worked their magic, while at the same time Diego bellowed like a wounded bull. She kissed, suckled and nipped gently until she felt his penis increase in girth.

Diego's arms flailed like a bird in flight, and he knew if he didn't extricate himself from Vivienne's mouth he would embarrass himself. Reaching out, he caught her hair and forcibly pulled her head back. It took seconds for him to get a condom and slip it down his tumescence, put Vivienne on her back and push into her warmth.

This coming together wasn't for her or for him—it was for both of them. He took her hard, fast, she arching with every thrust of his hips. His mouth was busy, kissing her eyelids, mouth and throat. His passion rose quickly and when he felt the rush of his climax he fastened his mouth to the hollow of her throat and surrendered to the sweetest agony he'd ever known.

Vivienne gasped when she felt the waves of ecstasy crash over her, the pleasure so explosive she felt her heart stop for several seconds. A deep feeling of peace entered her and all she wanted to do was sleep, but Diego had collapsed heavily on her, not permitting her to breathe.

"Diego, you have to get off me."

He rolled over, pressing his face to the pillow. "Don't ever do that again," he mumbled.

Vivienne opened her eyes and glared at him. "You did ask me to make love to you."

"But not like that, baby."

"You can't have it both ways, Diego. You give me pleasure and I give you pleasure. Why can't you accept that?"

Diego wanted to tell Vivienne he always wanted to be

in control. "You're right," he said instead. Reaching for her, he pulled her into his arms.

"What's on the agenda for today?"

"Not much."

Vivienne sat up, but Diego eased her back down. "I thought we're going to Wadmalaw Island."

"We're going tomorrow."

"What about seeing the property you just bought?"

"We'll do that tomorrow, too. Today we're going to kick back and relax."

"When are we going back to Florida?"

Diego ruffled her hair. "Why are you so full of questions this morning?"

Vivienne glared at him. "I just like to know how to plan my day."

"Today's plans include, relax, relax and relax some more. I've made arrangements for us to fly back late Wednesday evening. Does that meet with your approval, boss lady?"

"Real funny, Diego."

He winked at her. "Do you think I can convince my girl-friend to take a shower with me."

"Only if you don't try feeling me up."

"I don't know if I can do that."

"Try hard, *m'ijo.*"

Vivienne and Diego lay in bed talking about everything but themselves. What they'd shared was too new to talk about openly and honestly. What they were aware of was an invisible thread binding them together where they'd become one, even their bodies were joined.

Then, as if on cue, they left the bed and walked to the bathroom. They shared a shower, splashing and laughing like children. Diego wrapped Vivienne in a bath sheet and carried her back to the bedroom. He dried her body, covered her with the sheet and joined her in the bed. The sun was high in the sky when they woke for the second time, hunger driving them to seek food.

Diego was greeted by the last person he'd expected to see when he walked into his office early Thursday morning. "What are you doing here? I thought you were still on vacation."

A scowl distorted his cousin's delicate features.

"I ended it."

"Ended what, Joseph?"

The young lawyer folded his arms over his chest. "Kiara and I broke up."

Diego shook his head in amazement. "You take some woman halfway around the world to break up with her?"

Joseph ran a hand over his close-cropped curly hair. "She wouldn't let it go, Diego. She kept asking when we were getting married until I couldn't take it anymore."

Taking a seat opposite his cousin, Diego glared at him. "What the hell do you expect? You've been dating the woman for years, so she has a right to expect some sort of commitment."

"You're a fine one to talk, *primo*. How many women have you dated and not proposed to?"

"I've never dated one for four years, *primo*," he shot back. "How is she?"

"Mad as hell. Even if I thought about making up with her I couldn't now."

"Why not?"

"She said things that can't be repeated in polite company."

"People say a lot of things when they're angry."

Joseph closed his eyes and exhaled. "That's true." He opened his eyes. "But this time she went too far."

Diego had come to work after spending three glorious days with Vivienne, and he didn't want to step into the role as therapist to his cousin when he'd warned Joseph that the ups and downs of his personal life were adversely affecting his job performance.

"Let me know now if you want time off to get your private life in order, or if you're here to work."

"I'm here, because I'm ready to work."

Diego leaned closer. "If you jerk me around again, I'll fire your ass."

A deep flush suffused the younger man's face. There was a look in Joseph's eyes that hadn't been there before. "What do you want me to do?"

"I need you to contact Harry Ellis and draw up the documents to transfer the title of the property he paid for the tea garden to ColeDiz. By the way, I paid him from my personal account because he had a cash flow problem."

Joseph nodded. "Once I get the deed for the property I'll have accounting repay you."

"I went to see the property and it's perfect for a tea garden but only after we get rid of the mosquitoes, snakes and gators."

"You're kidding?"

"I wish I was. Once the engineers drain a nearby swamp it'll be ready for a fall planting."

Joseph whistled softly. "You're serious about this, aren't you?"

The seconds ticked off as Diego stared at his cousin. "As serious as you are about breaking it off with Kiara."

"It's true what they say around here."

"And that is," Diego drawled.

"You're a real sonofabitch."

Diego went completely still, though there was a lethal calmness in his eyes. "I'll let you say that to my face just this one time, only because we share blood," he warned softly in Spanish. "Remember, there will not be a second time. Now, I want you to leave my office and never come here again unless I tell you to come." Joseph stood up and walked out, not seeing the stunned expression on his cousin's face. The day that had begun with Diego waking up to find Vivienne beside him had suddenly soured because Joseph Cole-Wilson couldn't control his love life.

What Joseph didn't know was that his older cousin's involvement with Vivienne Neal had changed and mellowed him. A week before, if Joseph had said what he'd just told him he would have fired him—and family be damned. He'd been voted in as CEO, and if the board members didn't like his style for taking the company in a new direction then they could ask him to resign.

Sonofabitch! If that was how his employees saw him, then he would make certain not to disappoint them. He walked to the area where his executive assistant sat and left a note on her desk. One thing he could count on, and that was Lourdes following his directives without question.

Chapter 15

Diego stood at one end of the U-shaped table in the conference room, waiting for the employees of ColeDiz to file into the room. "Let's go, people, please find a seat." It wasn't often that he called an impromptu staff meeting, but he felt it necessary to air a few differences and/or grievances.

"Please close the door, Lourdes."

Lourdes Wallace closed the door and sat down. She'd seen the expression on her boss's face enough to know he wasn't in a good mood. Her tenure with ColeDiz spanned some twenty years and there was a fragile period of adjustment when she had to transfer her loyalty from father to son. Timothy Cole-Thomas was a pussycat, while Diego was a man-eating tiger. Each man had his own style, but she'd come to respect and admire Diego for taking risks his father never would've considered. The result was higher profits and year-end bonuses.

Diego's eyes narrowed when he stared at a bruise on the cheek of a newly hired accounting clerk. It was the second time he'd noticed the woman had come to work with bruises. The first time it'd been a black eye. He made a mental note to have Caitlin talk to her.

Taking a chair, he turned his attentions to the others sitting around the table. "I called this meeting to clear up a few things. First, I'd like a show of hands from those who believe I'm a sonofabitch." Gasps reverberated throughout the room. "Come now, people, don't be shy." Joseph's gaze was directed at the opposite wall. "Well, since no one is willing to man up I don't ever want to hear the word bandied about again.

"I didn't call this meeting to intimidate anyone or put them on the spot, but to give you an update about a new venture."

Diego knew he had everyone's rapt attention when he told them about ColeDiz going into the business of growing and selling tea. Most seemed genuinely interested when they asked questions to which he had the answers.

"We will sell tea in bags that will revolutionize the outdated bag with the string that isn't secure enough to support a wet tea bag."

"Will the tag have the ColeDiz logo?" a paralegal asked.

Diego hesitated. "I'm not certain. I'm certain our production department will come up with something that's eye-catching. Depending upon the weather, tea can be harvested year-round, which translates in higher profits that will be reflected in year-end bonuses." The announcement elicited thunderous applause. "I suppose the sonofabitch ain't too bad, is he?"

"No comment," called out a legal secretary.

Diego gave her a withering look until she dropped her

gaze. "I hope everyone will enjoy the weekend and have a safe Fourth of July."

He stood up and walked out of the room amid hushed voices. Lourdes had rescheduled his meeting with the community center board for later that afternoon, then he'd be free to spend the next four days with Vivienne, while introducing her to his family. Relatives would begin arriving on Friday and hang out in Palm Beach and West Palm Beach for a week. Diego was prepared to offer his Jupiter Island retreat for the overflow.

James McGhie watched Pamela Neal as she got out of her car and went into her home through the attached garage. He'd spent the past two days watching her leave and return to her home without her husband. One could tell a lot about a person if they didn't know they were under surveillance.

Pamela left every morning at seven to jog and returned at eight. Then, she didn't emerge again until ten when she drove a quarter of a mile to pick up a friend. From there she drove to a golf course where the two met up with another woman. They played nine holes, had lunch, then went home. James planned to get the information he needed as to Vivienne Gregory's whereabouts, but not from her mother. He would question one of Pamela's friends— the flirtatious one who seemed more inclined to flirt than swing a golf club.

Starting up his rental, he executed a U-turn and drove to the house with a white picket fence and matching shutters. Getting out, he walked to the front door and rang the bell. The inner door opened and he flashed his winning smile.

"Good afternoon. I was driving by and noticed the For

Sale sign in the house at the end of the block. I was wondering whether you could tell me something about the neighborhood." The woman didn't unlock the screen door, and he hadn't expected her to, because after all he was a stranger. Reaching into his pocket he removed a case with a badge and photo ID. "I'm a federal police officer and..." The door opened as if the badge was the magic key.

Twenty minutes later James got into his vehicle with the information he needed to track down Vivienne Gregory. A hypodermic filled with a truth serum had become the magic elixir.

Vivienne felt her heart rate kick into a higher gear when Diego led her across a manicured lawn to where a crowd had gathered under a large white tent at the Cole family West Palm Beach compound.

Anissa's prediction had come to fruition when Diego had taken her out to dinner at a popular Palm Beach restaurant and a photographer had taken their picture when they'd walked out of the restaurant holding hands. His long-range lens had captured their image at the exact moment Diego had lowered his head to whisper in her ear. The gesture was innocent enough, but the caption was enough to make readers draw their own conclusions as to their relationship.

He gave her hand a gentle squeeze. "I'm going to test you when we get home. I expect you to remember everyone's name."

"Yeah, right," she drawled.

Diego had delayed their spending the summer on Jupiter Island for a week because he'd offered it to his New Mexico relatives. She'd found his cousins friendly and outgoing and their children intelligent and absolutely adorable. Diego kept them entertained when he raced them across the inground pool, grilled hamburgers and franks on the outdoor grill and set up a mock disco in the outdoor living room replete with a basketball he'd sprayed with silver paint and suspended from the ceiling.

She'd stepped in as his hostess when the children were put to bed and the adults were engaged in more grown-up activities. Vivienne thought Emily Delgado stunningly beautiful with her black hair, brown skin and brilliant green eyes. Her eldest son, Alejandro, had inherited his grandfather's platinum hair and green eyes and he stood out among his other raven-haired siblings and cousins.

"Why is the pool covered, Diego?"

"That's to keep the kids from jumping in fully clothed. Unfortunately, it's something that has been going on for years."

"Whatever happened to swimsuits?"

"They wear them under their clothing. I suppose it's a form of rebellion or independence, depending how you view it."

"What do you think it is?" she asked.

"Rebellion, of course."

"Did you do it?"

Diego smiled. "Hell, yeah. Come, let me introduce you to the family's patriarch. Martin is Samuel's oldest son."

Vivienne stared at a tall, white-haired man with deeply tanned skin and a devastatingly sexy, dimpled smile. She extended her hand, returning his smile. "Hello, I'm—"

"Vivienne Gregory. I followed your husband's career. Please accept my condolences for your loss."

Vivienne's smile faded. Each time someone mentioned Sean's untimely death it reopened the wound that refused to heal. In fact, they wouldn't even allow it to close enough to scab over.

"Thank you, Martin."

He patted her hand in a comforting gesture. "I might sound a little biased, but if you're involved with my nephew, then you've picked a winner."

She shared a knowing glance with Diego. "I know that."

Martin's expressive black eyebrows lifted slightly. "Then, I wish you both the best."

"Why did it sound like he was giving us his blessing?" Vivienne asked Diego when he led her under the tent.

"That's because he was. There's one more person I want you to meet before you meet the others."

"Who?"

"My great-grandmother."

"M.J.?"

"Yes, M.J."

"How old is she?"

"One hundred and five."

Diego escorted Vivienne into the twenty-four-room mansion filled with priceless furnishings and artifacts. He led her to a room on the first floor that had been set up as M.J.'s bedroom, because she could no longer navigate the stairs.

Vivienne walked into the bedroom to see a frail woman with a long silver braid resting over her shoulder. Her delicate skin was smooth and if it hadn't been for the tiny lines around her eyes she could've passed for a woman twenty years younger. Dressed in a pristine white blouse and dark slacks, she was seated on a silk-and-velvet-striped chaise.

Diego went down on one knee. "*Abuelita,* I have someone I'd like you to meet." He'd spoken to her in Spanish.

M.J. opened her eyes and stared at her great-grandson. "Sammy?"

"No, *abuelita*, it's Diego."

Her black eyes focused on the face so close to her own. "But you look so much like my Sammy."

"That's what everyone says." He motioned for Vivienne to come closer. "This is someone who is very special to me, *abuelita*."

"Do you love her?"

Diego stared, complete surprise freezing his features. "I like her."

"That's not what I asked you," M.J. snapped in rapid Spanish. "I asked you if you love her."

He didn't want to lie to his great-grandmother, but he also didn't want Vivienne to know how he actually felt about her. *"Sí, abuelita. La quiero."*

M.J. smiled for the first time, flashing deep dimples in her tissue-paper-thin cheeks. *"Bueno."* Her hands shook slightly as she attempted to pull a ring off her left ring finger. "Help with this," she ordered Diego. She managed to take off the ring with his assistance. "Take it for your *novia*."

"She's not my *novia*."

"She will be." M.J. waved her hand, dismissing him. "Now go and let me sleep."

Diego kissed her cheek before he stood up. "Let's go," he said softly to Vivienne.

Waiting until they left the bedroom, he opened his hand to stare at the ring Samuel had given M.J. for their engagement. The Old Mine Cut center diamond was at least three carats. It was flanked by two large marquis diamonds and a latticework of forty-two additional diamonds. It was the first time M.J. had taken off the ring in eighty-five years.

Why me? he thought. Why did his great-grandmother give him the ring when she could've given it to her sons for their wives.

"She believes you're Sammy," Vivienne said, reading his mind.

"That's because I'm the only one who looks like him."

"I'm glad you humored her, Diego."

"Who said I was humoring her?"

"Weren't you?"

He shook his head. "No. I meant every word I said."

It was Vivienne's turn to shake her head. "You can't."

Diego leaned closer. "Who says I can't."

"It's not going to work."

He heard the panic in Vivienne's voice, but he was past caring. "Because you say it isn't, or you don't want it to work?"

"Both!" she spat out.

Pushing his face inches from hers, he glared at her. "Don't ever tell me what to say or think."

"Have you forgotten that you can't intimidate me?"

"No."

"Then, change your tone, Diego."

He clamped his jaw so tight his teeth ached. "Let's go back outside."

Diego couldn't understand why Vivienne didn't want him to love her. Had she been with Sean Gregory so long that she felt undeserving of the gift. She'd stayed with a man who professed to love her, but didn't or couldn't show her that love.

Meanwhile, each and every time he made love to Vivienne he told her without words that he loved her, would protect her with risk to his own life, and he didn't want what they had to end.

The Cole family matriarch, Marguerite-Josefina Isabel Diaz Cole, had forced him to reach inside of himself to bare his soul in front of the woman who had the power to emotionally bring him to his knees.

No one noticed his strained expression or tone when he introduced Vivienne to his family. His mother had given him a quizzical look, but hadn't said anything when he revealed that he and Vivienne were living together. It was his grandmother who had a lot to say.

"Please come with me." Nancy Cole-Thomas took his hand at the same time as she flashed a dimpled smile that appeared more a grimace than a smile. Her curly hair was completely silver and was the perfect complement to her olive coloring. She and her sister Josephine were younger versions of their mother.

"What's up, *abuela?*"

Nancy waved at him. "Don't you dare *abuela* me, Diego Samuel Cole-Thomas."

Diego knew something wasn't right whenever his grandmother called him by his full name. "What now?"

"Don't you dare take that tone with me, Diego. What's up with you shacking up with a woman? You were raised better than that. After all—"

"I know," he drawled facetiously, "we're Coles and Cole men don't disrespect women by living with them."

Black eyes flashing fire, Nancy sucked in her breath in an attempt to control her temper. "Then, why haven't you put a ring on her finger?"

"Maybe it's because she doesn't want to get married." He told his grandmother everything—how he'd hired Vivienne to be his social secretary, her being Sean Gregory's widow and about M.J. giving him her engagement ring. Taking the ring from the pocket of his jeans he cradled it in the palm of his hand. "*Abuelita* has to be senile if she believes I'm Sammy."

Nancy waved a hand. "There's nothing senile about my mother and you know it. She has everyone fooled into thinking she is. What she is, is a manipulative old woman who must have things go her way."

Diego gave his grandmother a skeptical look. "And you don't?"

"The only reason I put up with your smart-ass mouth is because you're my first grandchild. But one of these days even that's going to wear thin."

Diego winked at her. "What are you going to do, *abuela*, put me over your knee and spank me?"

"Maybe I should've spanked Timothy, then he would've been inclined to spank you."

"Remember, Coles don't spank their children."

Nancy expelled a breath. "It's not easy being a Cole."

"You don't say," Diego quipped.

"What if I talk to Vivienne about your current situation?"

"Stay out of it, *abuela*. I don't have a problem living with a woman."

"But what if people outside the family get wind of it. I will not be made to look like a fool among the women in my social circle."

"They're all a bunch of phonies and fakes. Everything about them is fake from their affected accents to their body parts."

"Diego!"

"*Es verdadero* and you know it. My friends could care less about someone living together or having a baby without benefit of marriage."

"Ay, don't say that," Nancy said, crossing herself. "Having babies without being married is not acceptable."

"Surely you jest, *abuela*. Have you forgotten how many women in our family were either pregnant or had a child before they became Cole women—Parris, Regina, Serena, Jolene, and Alexandra who was swole up when she married Merrick last year."

Nancy wrinkled her nose as if she'd caught a whiff of something malodorous. "I'd like to change the subject, because my grandson has forgotten that he's Cuban aristocracy."

"There is no Cuban aristocracy."

"There was and my mother was from that class."

"*Abuela*, please, let's not regress."

"Speaking of regressing, I hear that you're now the twenty-first century Samuel Claridge Cole. Joseph told us about your tea project in the Sea Islands. I haven't seen him this excited since he got into law school."

Diego hoped he was able to sustain his excitement to see the project completed. Taking Nancy's arm, he led her back to where generations of Coles had come together to reunite and bond.

"It's nice that you let Regina and Sara and their kids stay at your place on Jupiter."

"I couldn't see them coming in and spending a week in a hotel. The children would go crazy. Besides, there's more than enough room for them to have the run of the place."

Diego spied Vivienne with Alexandra Grayslake, holding Alex's daughter, who'd celebrated her first birthday in April. For someone who professed to not wanting a child she was always holding or playing with them.

She looked and saw him staring at her. Their gazes

fused, but the spell was broken when Vivienne turned to listen to something Merrick was saying. Throwing back her head, she laughed, baring her smooth throat. The image stayed with Diego throughout the afternoon and into the evening until he told her it was time to go home.

Vivienne walked ahead of Diego as soon as he opened the door. She'd moved into his bedroom since returning from South Carolina, but tonight she decided it was time to put some space between them.

She'd begun to see glimpses of Sean in Diego, and she didn't like it. This was not to say she didn't enjoy sleeping with him, but she did not intend to fall into the same trap where all she was good for was to do a man's bidding.

He'd told M.J. that he loved her, not that he was in love with her. She'd lost count of the number of times he claimed he loved her passion, her fashion sense, her social graces and etc., etc., etc.

Sean had waited a year before he used her for an accessory, and it'd only taken two weeks for Diego to make her his paid consort. Well, she'd had enough! She'd permitted a man to use her for the last time.

"Vivienne, wait!"

Racing up the staircase, she managed to make it to her old bedroom, close and lock the door before Diego could reach her. Closing her eyes, she braced her back against the door.

"Open the door, Vivienne. We have to talk."

"Go away, Diego. We have nothing to talk about."

"Hiding behind the door isn't going to solve anything."

She opened her eyes. "It'll keep me out of your bed."

"Open the door."

"No!"

Vivienne felt the vibration and within seconds it dawned on her what was happening. Diego was pounding on the door. It was with the second vibration that the lock gave. He'd kicked opened the door.

Eyes wide, she backpedaled. The look in Diego's eyes was frightening as he stalked her. Turning on her heels she raced for the bedroom, he a step behind her. She screamed when he lifted her high off the floor and carried her to the bed.

Diego dropped Vivienne on the bed, his body following hers down. "Why didn't you open the door?" he said between clenched teeth.

She pounded his shoulder. "Let me go, Diego."

"Why? So you can run away."

Her eyes filled with tears. "Where am I going? I don't have a home to go to."

Cradling her face between his hands, he kissed her eyelids. "You have a home, baby. You have me."

She opened her eyes, trying to make out his face in the darkened room. The drapes were open and the only light came from the streetlights along the private roads. "I don't want to leave you, Diego, but I will if you pressure me into doing something I don't want to do. I had enough of that with Sean."

"I'm not your late husband."

"I know that, but there're times when you do or say something and it's like I'm still married to him."

"I want you to tell me when I start acting crazy."

Vivienne smiled. "You're always crazy, Diego."

"I know, because I'm crazy about you."

His hand moved from her face to her blouse. Slowly, methodically, he undid the buttons, baring her chest. The seconds ticked off as he undressed her, then himself. The banked fire flared to life when he anchored her hips in one hand and used the other to guide his erection into her body. They groaned in unison as flesh met flesh.

Diego knew this coming together would be over soon after it'd begun as he quickened his thrusts, his penis sliding in and out of her body as heat shot through him like an electric current.

Vivienne opened her legs and her mouth to the man holding her to his heart and surrendered all she was and would be to him. Love flowed through her, the pleasure pure and explosive. Diego changed tempo, slowing then quickening, then slowing down again. He touched her womb and she screamed and continued screaming as the orgasms kept coming, overlapping each other.

Anchoring her arms under his shoulders, she held on to him, shaking and weeping with the joy that took her beyond herself and reality. She felt Diego go still, then quicken his thrusts as he released his passion inside her. It hadn't mattered that he hadn't protected her because she was expecting her menses.

They lay together, limbs entwined, until Diego pulled out, scooped her off the bed and carried her across the hall to his bedroom. They made love a second time, and when Vivienne walked into the bathroom the following morning she breathed an audible sigh when the evidence verified that she'd picked the right time of the month to have unprotected sex. Her menses, as usual, had come on time.

Chapter 16

Diego was facedown on the bed when Vivienne returned to the bedroom. Running, she jumped onto the bed, her body covering his. "Do you plan to spend the day in bed?" she whispered in his ear. "What's the matter?" she asked when he emitted an unintelligible grunt.

"The matter is that I'm trying to get some sleep so that I'll have enough energy to make love to the woman who has me as randy as a billy goat."

She smiled. "Sorry, Mister Billy Goat, but we're not going to be doing anything for a few days."

Diego shifted on the bed, bringing Vivienne to lie beside him. "What's the matter?"

"I'm on my menses."

His expressive eyebrows lifted. "Okay, so that means we'll have to devise another plan to have fun."

A slight frown appeared between Vivienne's eyes. "What?"

Diego stared at the delicate features of the woman in his bed with a mane of tousled hair falling over her forehead in sensual disarray. Reaching over, he pushed strands off her cheek. "I want to take you away for a few days."

"Why?"

"I want to apologize for my caveman behavior last night."

A smile replaced Vivienne's frown. "You were rather beastly and thuggish."

"I'm sorry about that. Did I frighten you?"

She waved a hand, while at the same time rolled her eyes upward. "Please, Diego. You take yourself a bit too seriously. You should save the theatrics for your employees at the ColeDiz office. You're a big dog with no bite."

A hint of a smile tugged at the corners of his mouth. "You're doing a lot of trash talking now that you're not on the payroll."

"Even if I was on the payroll you still wouldn't fire me, Diego Cole-Thomas. You need me and you know it."

Diego sobered. "You're wrong, Vivienne Kay Neal. I don't need you as much as I want you."

Vivienne ran her forefinger down the length of his nose. "Careful, boss. Remember, we're actors in a role that'll end in mid-December."

"Do you want it to end, Vivienne?"

She shrugged a shoulder under the tank top she'd put on over a pair of shorts after showering. "It's not what I want, Diego. I have to do what's best for my future, and performing as companion to a wealthy man isn't something I want."

Diego went completely still. Before last night's outburst, he'd thought Vivienne enjoyed going out with him. Or was she so accomplished that she'd fooled him? After all, she'd had four years in which to become the consummate actress.

"Do I make you feel like a kept woman?"

Vivienne's eyelids fluttered wildly as she processed his query. She wanted to say yes, but then it would be a half lie. Part of her felt as if she'd prostituted herself when she agreed to become his consort, but then she couldn't openly admit that she hadn't enjoyed being with Diego.

"There are times when I do," she said truthfully. "I was ticked off yesterday because you'd lied to your great-grandmother about us."

Resting his head on his folded arm, Diego closed his eyes for a second. "What did I lie about?"

"You told her, under duress of course, that you love me."

"I told M.J. the truth."

"You love me?"

Diego nodded. "You don't believe me?"

He loved her beauty, femininity and intelligence. He loved Vivienne's spirited temperament, her willingness to get in his face without fear of reprisal, her all-encompassing passion and that she held nothing back. He wanted to give her what Sean Gregory hadn't or couldn't. The late politician hadn't deserved her any more than Vivienne deserved to be treated so shabbily.

"No, Diego, I don't believe you."

"Sean Gregory really did a number on you, didn't he?"

"You're damn skippy he did, Diego. You're no different than Sean. He'd professed to love me, but he didn't know how to show it."

Diego sat up, pulling Vivienne into the circle of his embrace. "Will you allow me to prove to you I'm not lying?"

"No."

"No?" he repeated, giving her an incredulous look.

"Which part of no don't you understand, Diego? I don't want you to ask. I need you to show me. Show, not tell, that I mean more to you than an accessory, more than a willing warm body whenever you feel like a randy billy goat, and more than someone you've bought and paid for."

Diego buried his face against the column of her scented neck. He'd believed himself in love with Lisa Turner, but what he felt for Vivienne Neal was different. If he were completely honest with himself then he would have to admit that he'd never been in love.

"Come away with me for a few days," Diego whispered.

"Why?"

"So I can begin to show you what you've come to mean to me."

Vivienne squeezed her eyes tightly shut. She wanted so much to believe Diego, but she couldn't. Although they hadn't been together a month she felt as if she'd known Diego for years. They were so attuned that there were times when she knew what he was feeling, could complete his sentences. The world and everyone in it ceased to exist whenever she lay in his arms, whenever he joined his body to hers. Everything around them could come to a crashing halt, but it wasn't important because of how he made her feel.

Don't you know by now that I'd do anything for you, Vivienne Neal? All you have to do is ask and I'll get it for you.

Vivienne didn't know why, but she could recall Diego's impassioned words as if they'd been tattooed on her body. She wanted to love him yet she was so frightened, frightened for herself and the time when she would have to leave Diego.

"Where do you want to go, *m'ijo?*"

"Let's go to New York. We can check into a hotel, order room service and tour the city."

"What about your family, Diego?"

"What about them, *m'ija?*"

"We can't go away when they've come thousands of miles to see you."

"They didn't come to see me, Vivienne, and it's not the only time I'll get together this year. Alexandra and Merrick have offered to host Thanksgiving at their place."

Vivienne thought about Thanksgiving, knowing she would have to go to Connecticut to celebrate the holiday with her parents. By that time it would be too cold for her father to golf every day. "Is Merrick and Alex's house large enough to accommodate everyone?"

"No. Second- and third-generation Coles have established a tradition to get together on Thanksgiving. It gives their children a chance to interact with one another without their grandparents smothering them with hugs and kisses."

Vivienne smiled. "I loved visiting my grandmother. During the Christmas shopping season we'd take the train to New York City where we'd spend the day in FAO Schwartz, then get on the subway to Brooklyn to eat at Junior's. We'd return to Connecticut with shopping bags filled with toys and cheesecake."

Diego traced her hairline with his forefinger. "It sounds as if you had a wonderful childhood."

"It was okay."

"Just okay, Vivienne? You grew up privileged."

"And you didn't, Mr. Cole-Thomas?"

"No."

"Please, Diego. My grandparents raised their three children in a two-bedroom apartment in a less than desirable Stamford neighborhood. My grandfather worked two jobs to save enough money to send his children to college. I'm sure that wasn't a concern for your grandmother who grew up in a twenty-four-room mansion. My father was awarded a partial scholarship to attend Yale, but even with student loans and working part-time he wasn't able to make the tuition."

"Where did he go?"

"He went to a state college. Daddy finally became a Yale man when he went to law school. The first thing he did when his firm won a landmark case was to set up a scholarship fund for college-bound high school students from impoverished families."

A bright smile lit up Diego's face like rays from the rising sun. He cradled Vivienne's head in his hands and pressed a kiss to her forehead. "You've just given me an incredible idea."

"What?"

"I'll tell you on the way to New York."

"Why can't you tell me now?"

"Because I need to think about it first, and I think better in the shower. Speaking of showers, I think it's time I get out of bed."

Vivienne moved off the bed. "What time are we leaving?"

Diego glanced at the clock on the fireplace mantel. "I'd like to leave before noon. I'll call and have the jet readied, then I need to make a hotel reservation."

"Where are we staying?" she asked, averting her gaze away from Diego's magnificent nude body.

"I'll let you choose."

Her head came around as she stared at his solemn expression. "Why should I choose, Diego?"

"You said you wanted me to show you how much I care about you. And that means doing whatever makes you happy. Choose the hotel, Vivienne, so I can make the reservation."

"Do you prefer the East Side or the West Side?"

Diego successfully concealed a smile. Vivienne was permitting him a choice where he probably wouldn't have asked her. He would've chosen the hotel without soliciting her input. "It doesn't matter. I like both."

"What if we compromise?"

He smiled. "That'll work."

"My first choice would be an inn on East Forty-Ninth called the Box Tree. The rooms are small, but the turn-of-the-century European ambience makes up for the size."

"Call them and see if you can get a room. If there's none available then you should have a second choice in mind."

"I also like the Parker Meridien."

"Isn't it near Central Park?"

Vivienne nodded. "Yes."

"If you can't get a room at the Box Tree, then reserve a suite at the Parker Meridien. You have my credit card information," Diego said over his shoulder as he walked out of the bedroom and into the adjoining bath.

Vivienne stripped the bed of linen, putting it into a laundry bag. Twice each week the bags were placed outside the door for pickup by a laundry service. She'd continued to check Diego's socks to make certain they were a match.

Since she no longer officially worked for Diego she'd come to feel more like a wife. What she shared with the enigmatic man was what she'd wanted for her and Sean. They went to bed together, made love and woke up in the same bed. She continued to prepare breakfast and they always shared the evening meal.

Diego Cole-Thomas claimed he loved her, and Vivienne knew that she was falling in love with him. However, he wasn't the first and only man to profess to love her. When, she asked herself, had she become a pessimist, a cynic, someone who'd demanded proof before she was able to believe?

She'd challenged Diego to show her and he'd accepted the challenge. He'd scheduled a week's vacation to spend with his out-of-town relatives, but then modified his plans to spend time with her. Covering her face with her hands, Vivienne bit her lip. She wasn't married to Diego, yet she'd made more demands on him than she'd done with Sean. The one time she'd tried to pressure Sean into doing what she wanted, he'd walked out on her and returned to Washington. It was another week before she heard from him again.

It took years before she realized why she hadn't challenged Sean: she was in love with him and hadn't wanted to do or say anything to jeopardize their marriage. However, in the end it had been she who knew she couldn't continue living a lie. Her marriage to Sean Gregory was over before they'd celebrated their first wedding anniversary.

The decision to divorce Sean had become a well-thought-out plan, and when she called to have her attorney draw up the documents, Vivienne knew she'd embarked on a plan of action that would not only change her life but could possibly destroy Sean Gregory's political career. The charge of alienation of affection would've certainly led to the suspicion that Sean was having an affair. This information would've given his political opponents cause to have him investigated in order to uncover some immoral impropriety.

The first and only time Vivienne had asked Sean whether he was sleeping with another woman his reply was that if he wasn't sleeping with her then he wasn't sleeping with any woman. His flippant reply made her ask him if perhaps he was sleeping with a man or other men. The tension between them was smothering, and when Sean finally spoke it was to tell her that he wasn't attracted to men, and at that moment she believed him.

But now she didn't know what to believe because even though she'd dated, married and slept with Sean Bailey Gregory she hadn't known him. He'd been as much a mystery in life as he was in death.

Lowering her hands, Vivienne stared at her fingers. She'd taken off the wedding band Sean had placed on her finger, giving it to Diego when he accused her of not letting go of her past. She had let go of her past the day she'd come to Washington to let Sean know she was divorcing him. Her past was behind her and now she had to plan for her future.

Diego winked at Vivienne when they sat together in the rear of a Town Car on their way into Manhattan. Their flight plan was changed from touching down at LaGuardia to Long Island because of a security problem at that airport. A call from the car service indicated they would be picked up from the smaller airport.

"Do you want water?" he asked, reaching for a bottle.

"No, thank you. I'm good."

He gave her a sidelong glance. "You didn't eat anything during the flight." The flight attendant had served grilled rib eye steak sandwiches with a mixed green salad and sweet tea.

Shifting on her seat, Vivienne rested her head on Diego's

shoulder. "That's because I ate too much at breakfast." She'd eaten grits, eggs, bacon and drank two cups of coffee, while Diego ate half a grapefruit and coffee.

"You look as if you've put on some weight since you began hanging out with me," Diego teased.

"I have."

"I suppose you'll need a new wardrobe."

Vivienne shook her head. "I don't think so."

"I'll pay for the clothes."

"It's not about you paying for my clothes, Diego. It's about getting more exercise. I've done more eating and sitting in the past two weeks than I have in a very long time. Even when I was working I used to walk during my lunch break."

"Was it because you don't want to get fat?" Diego asked.

Vivienne rolled her eyes at him. "No. I'm not that vain. I didn't have time to go to a health club, so walking was my way of exercising."

"You know there's a health club at the condo."

"I have to check it out when I get a break."

Diego straightened. "What do you mean when you get a break? Are you saying I'm working you that hard?"

"I'm not saying that," Vivienne said defensively. "I still haven't established a regimen for how I want to set up my day."

"What is there to set up, *m'ija?* You get up, shower, make breakfast, then you have the rest of the day to yourself. And if you tell me that you're cleaning or vacuuming I'm going to go apeshit, Vivienne."

"I make the bed."

"Okay. You make the bed. What else do you do?"

"I clean around the bathroom."

Diego's deep-set eyes narrowed. "Clean how?"

Vivienne's temper flared. "What's with the interrogation?"

"I pay a cleaning service top dollar to keep my house clean. And if you're spending your time cleaning then why do I need them? As of today you will no longer clean around the bathroom."

"But I can't stand seeing hair in the sink, floor or counters."

"Get used to it, Vivienne."

"You're nothing more than a bully, Diego."

He flashed a smile. "I've been called worse."

"I'm sure you have," she retorted, "and I'm certain you don't want to hear my personal laundry list."

"Stand in line," Diego said sardonically. Reaching for his BlackBerry, he scrolled through the directory, then punched a button. "This is Diego Cole-Thomas and I'd like to increase the number of days for service. I'd like someone to come in Monday through Friday." He shot Vivienne a pointed look when she rolled her eyes at him. "Yes. It can go into effect at the beginning of next week. Thank you very much."

"You don't have to look so smug, Diego," Vivienne drawled when he ended the call.

"I just solved your problem of superfluous hair."

"You're throwing away money."

"My money," he countered.

"That's wasteful and sinful."

Diego's expressive eyebrows lifted. "Maybe I should show you my tax returns so you can see how much I donate to my favorite charities."

"That's what I call guilt tribute."

"Nothing I do or say is out of guilt, *m'ija*. Speaking of money, something you said about your father setting up a scholarship fund for needy students."

"What about it?"

"I'd like your assistance in setting up a foundation for high school students who are planning on business careers."

"That's a wonderful idea, Diego. Has anyone in your family done something like this?"

"My cousin Tyler solicited the family and their well-heeled friends to donate a hundred million dollars for a hospital in Hillsboro, Mississippi. The hospital was named for his deceased father-in-law and grandfather. Tyler, who'd moved to Mississippi to study infant mortality rates, set up a clinic, fell in love and married a local girl. We all have our favorite charities, but it's time the Coles concentrate on a single cause, making it easier for our brightest to realize their potential."

Vivienne took a breath of surprise. "That's an incredible proposal, because the students can intern at ColeDiz."

"There you go," Diego crooned.

"You'll have a lot of work ahead of you contacting colleges and recruiting students."

"That's where I need your help, *m'ija*." He pressed a kiss to her hair. "Will you help me?"

Tilting her chin, Vivienne met his gaze. The cynic in her said Diego would do or say anything to keep her with him, but an emotion she couldn't fathom said differently. "Yes, Diego, I'll help you."

"Thank you, darling."

His calling her darling was Vivienne's undoing. Closing her eyes, she melted into his warmth and strength. What Diego had proposed wouldn't take six months or even a year. It would take several years to set up the scholarship program and even more before the internships would prove a success.

Diego wasn't asking for a small piece of her life.

He was asking for her future.

Chapter 17

Vivienne smiled at Diego across the table in a suite at the Parker Meridien a block from New York City's famed Central Park. They'd turned off the lamps and lit a quartet of candles on a side table and one on the table where a waiter had served their dinner.

The sun had set, the streetlights had come on and light coming through high-rise apartment and office buildings lit up the night like stars. They'd arrived at the hotel mid-afternoon, checked in, shared a shower and then gotten into bed together where they talked for hours before falling asleep in each other's arms.

"I'm glad you suggested coming to New York. I love this city."

Diego put a flute to his mouth, taking a deep swallow of premium champagne. "We're close enough to Connecticut, so if you want you can call your folks and I'll arrange for you to see them."

"That would've been possible if we'd come up last week. My parents always spend the first two weeks in July on Martha's Vineyard."

"Do they have a place there?" Diego asked.

"No. But my aunt does. She used to rent a small cottage not far from Oak Bluffs every summer. Once she retired she bought a larger house, renovated it and now lives there year-round."

"Do you like Cape Cod?"

Vivienne touched a napkin to the corners of her mouth. "I love it. I've been there during the summer and winter, and I can't decide which season I like best."

"I find it rather desolate once the tourists leave."

"You've been to the Cape?"

"They didn't come down this time, but my cousin Gabriel and his wife live in Cotuit. Summer is expected to deliver their third child before the end of the month. She and Gabriel are really excited because after two boys they're finally going to have a daughter."

Vivienne traced the rim of her flute with a finger. "The Coles are very prolific. How do you keep up with the names of all the children?"

"I have a family tree template and whenever I get a birth announcement I add the name to the corresponding parents. Emily and Chris Delgado's kids are Alejandro, Esperanza and Mateo. Chris's sister is married to Salem Lassiter and their kids are Isaiah, Eve and Nona, who happened to be identical twins."

"That's not fair, Diego. Your family tree is a cheat sheet."

"No one ever asks how I remember their names."

"It's still cheating, darling."

The seconds ticked off as Diego stared at Vivienne. He much preferred looking at her to engaging in a verbal interchange. They'd shared a shower, touching and kissing when what he'd wanted to do was be inside her. Making love to her the night before without a condom had become an exhilarating experience. He wanted Vivienne in the same way an addict craved a drug, because she'd become his personal drug of choice.

His parents—his mother in particular—had accused him of being driven, driven to achieve the best grades, driven to come out a winner in any competition and driven to distinguish himself, while continuing the success of his predecessors as CEO of ColeDiz.

Vivienne had pleaded with him not to wet her hair, but once he fastened his mouth to her breasts her protests ended. Their unrestrained water play ended when they lay on the tiles of the shower, breathing heavily from the passion that held them captive and made them one.

Diego nodded his head in time to the soulful voice of Seal coming from the hotel radio. He extended his hand. "Will you dance with me, Miss Neal?"

Pushing back her chair, Vivienne rose to her feet, waiting for Diego to round the table. "Yes, I will, Mr. Cole-Thomas."

Smiling, she went into his embrace, the curves of her body molded to his length. She reached her arms under his shoulders when Diego tightened his hold around her body. "You smell pretty."

Diego chuckled softly. "That's because I smell like you."

Vivienne smiled and closed her eyes. When she'd offered to wash Diego's back she'd used her shower gel and sponge. Taking a shower together had become an adventure when they splashed each other like children.

I love this man, she mused. She hadn't known how it'd happened so quickly, but she'd fallen in love with an enigma—a man who was as intoxicatingly sensual as he was intimidating.

Pulling back slightly, Diego stared down at the woman cradled to his heart. "What was that sigh all about?"

Vivienne tilted her chin, smiling up at Diego. "I just resigned myself to the fact that I like you, *m'ijo*."

A smile crinkled the skin around his eyes. "Thank you."

She pressed the pad of her thumb to the cleft in his strong chin. "No, Diego, thank you. Thank you for being you."

"You're thanking me for being a bully?"

Standing on tiptoe, Vivienne brushed a kiss over his mouth. "You are my bully."

"I'm sorry if I raised my voice to you."

"It's not about you raising your voice, Diego. It's the way in which you say things. Your tone can be as sharp as a Samurai sword. I don't know if you realize it, but just your presence is intimidating. There're times when you have this look on your face that says I'm not to be played with or not today. I suppose you don't want to change because it has worked for you, but there are times when you don't have to be so serious."

The song ended but Diego still held on to Vivienne. "Running ColeDiz is serious."

"It's not so serious that you have to affect a screwed-up face."

"I don't go to work to skin and grin."

"I'm not talking about skinning and grinning, Diego.

I'm talking about catching more flies with honey than with vinegar. Your employees are afraid of you."

"How would you know that? You were only in the office one time."

Vivienne nodded. "That's true. But your personnel director practically genuflected before she left your office."

Diego thought about what Vivienne had observed. He knew most of the employees, with the exception of Lourdes and Joseph, avoided him like the plague. Then there was his cousin's comment that everyone thought of him as an SOB.

"What do you suggest I do to soften my image?"

Vivienne kissed him again. "Do you have staff meetings?"

"Yes."

"How often?" Vivienne asked.

"They're usually every other month. Why?"

"Hold your next one at a restaurant with a very relaxed setting. Have the restaurant staff set up a buffet where everyone can select what they want to eat and drink. Not only will you find them more receptive but also a lot more forthcoming with ideas and suggestions about how to grow the company."

"Is that what you did at your company?"

She nodded. "At first it was just upper management until one of the vice presidents realized it was the employees who did the so-called grunt work that really knew what was and wasn't working."

Tightening his grip on Vivienne's waist, Diego spun her around and around until she pleaded with him to stop. "You are incredible."

"No, I'm not. Think of me as an outsider looking in."

"You're hardly an outsider," he argued softly. "You

know more about me than most people—and that includes
family members."

"You can learn a lot about a person when you sleep
with them."

The flickering candles threw long and short shadows on
the walls, making it difficult for Diego to make out
Vivienne's features. He wanted to rebut her statement, and
then changed his mind. She'd slept with Sean Gregory yet
knew very little about the man she'd married.

"What do you want to do tomorrow?" he asked instead.

"I'd like to take a tour of the Village, Chinatown and
Little Italy."

"Don't you want to get your hair styled?"

Vivienne ran her fingers through her hair that was still
slightly damp. "No. I'll put it up in a ponytail. Why did you
ask?"

"I'd like to take you out to dinner before we go back,
and I didn't want you to say that you had to go to a salon."

"I just went two days ago. That's why I asked you not
to wet my hair." Diego had taken off her shower cap and
filled it with water, fashioning it into a water balloon.
"There's no way I'm going to sit under a dryer for an hour,
then endure having my hair blown out. We can either eat
in the hotel's restaurant or any of the eateries around
Lincoln Center."

"I thought you'd want to go to a fancy Big Apple restaurant."

"You thought wrong, Diego. We came here to relax and
take in the sights." Vivienne had packed one outfit that
would be appropriate for dining at a fancy restaurant, but
hoped that she wouldn't have to wear it.

Diego pressed a kiss to her forehead. "You're right."

Vivienne covered her mouth with her hand when she stifled a yawn. "Champagne always makes me sleepy."

"We should turn in now if we're going to have to get up early tomorrow."

She yawned again. "You're right."

Diego patted her behind over a pair of shorts. Both had put on shorts, T-shirts and sandals before the waiter had arrived with dinner. "I'm going to call housekeeping to have someone pick up the food." He didn't want to get up and have the suite smelling of leftover fish and chicken.

"Don't forget to put out the candles," Vivienne reminded him as she walked in the direction of the bedroom.

Smiling, Diego saluted her. "Yes, boss!"

The sound of her laughter floated back to him as he stood watching her retreating back. Vivienne had been forthcoming when she opened up about how she viewed him. Many times he'd overheard his uncles and male cousins talk about how their daughters had softened them.

Diego didn't have a daughter, but having Vivienne in his life had not only changed but also softened him.

Grinning, James McGhie was all teeth and gums when he tapped the numbers on his cell. "I located her," he said when his call was answered.

"Where is she?"

"She's in Florida. She was living with a former college roommate."

"Was, Jimmy boy?"

James decided not to respond to being called a variation of his name because he knew it gave the cretin on the other end of the line perverse pleasure in getting him rattled. Mrs. McGhie's precious baby boy was too close to completing his assignment to lose his composure. He'd decided locating the black book would become his last job. Once the balance of payment was deposited in his offshore account he was done. James had told his mother to put her affairs in order, because they were taking a trip. Mrs. McGhie didn't know the trip would become the last time she would sleep on American soil.

"She's now living with a man."

"I need a name, Jimmy."

"Diego Cole-Thomas. He's CEO of ColeDiz International Ltd."

"If you located her, then it should be a walk in the park to get to her."

"Not when she's living behind iron gates with 24/7 armed security."

"She has to leave sometime, Jimmy. Congress is in recess for the summer, but when it reconvenes I don't want this little problem in my face. Right now you have two choices—find the book or get rid of the little widow. Good night, Jimmy boy."

Nothing would please James more than snapping the condescending cretin's neck or diming him out. And if he continued to annoy him he would, from the luxurious comfort of his Caribbean condominium.

Diego took a step, pressing his chest to Vivienne's back. "Put your wallet back in your bag," he whispered harshly. "Now, Vivienne."

She dropped her wallet into the large tote and zipped it. "Can you please tell me what that was all about?"

"I'll tell you later." Reaching into the pocket of his

slacks, he removed a leather credit card case, handing the square of plastic to the smiling salesclerk.

He and Vivienne had gotten up early and were out of the hotel in time to mingle with pedestrians rushing to get to their jobs. The crush of yellow taxis, the rumble of subway cars under sidewalk grates and the incessant honking of automobile horns added to the cacophony of rush hour activity.

They'd walked down Fifth Avenue, stopping at a coffee shop to have breakfast. They continued down Fifth, flagging down a taxi at Twenty-Third Street to take them to the Lower East Side. Late-morning temperatures had reached the mideighties when Vivienne suggested they stop at a Little Italy café for iced lattes. However, it was Chinatown that held Diego in awe. He felt compelled to go into every gallery, antique and curio shop.

Vivienne's eyes lit up like a child's on Christmas Day when she pulled him into a jewelry store with displays of jade in colors ranging from white, lavender, green, red, brown to blackish. There was even yellow, but most of them were spotted. She'd decided to purchase a pale green jade and lavender jade bangle with end caps and hinge in twenty-one carat gold inscribed with Chinese characters representing health, wealth, good luck and happiness.

She watched the salesclerk rub the bangle with a soft felt cloth as the shopkeeper came over to take Diego's card to ring up her purchase. When Vivienne saw the bangle she knew it was the perfect gift to thank Alicia for her generosity.

Diego had pocketed his credit card, the gaily wrapped box with the bangle was in the bottom of her cavernous tote and they'd left the jewelry shop when he took her arm and steered her out onto the bustling avenue.

"What was that all about back there?" she asked, slipping on a pair of oversize sunglasses against the blinding summer sun.

"I noticed a man watching you and thought perhaps he was waiting to snatch your wallet."

"Where was he?"

"He was standing outside the shop, then followed us inside."

Vivienne gave Diego a sidelong glance behind the dark lenses. He wore a baseball cap that had seen better days. There was nothing about his appearance that indicated he was a multimillionaire.

"Maybe he was a worker taking a break."

"I doubt that, *m'ija*. He smelled as if he'd been dipped in a vat of booze and it's probably been a while since he had an encounter with soap and water. You have to be more vigilant, darling."

Vivienne moved closer to Diego. "Thank you for looking out for me."

"I will always look out for you, darling."

"And I you, darling," Vivienne intoned.

"I'm surprised you haven't bought anything for yourself," Diego said as they quickened their pace and jogged across Bayard Street.

"I have everything I want, Diego." She was financially set, in good health, in love and very, very happy.

Diego had to agree with Vivienne. He hadn't known what was missing in his life until the day she'd walked into his office at ColeDiz.

Vivienne knew something was wrong with Diego even before the jet touched down in West Palm Beach. He appeared listless and whenever she asked him a question his responses were monosyllabic.

Henri was there when they deplaned and when they arrived at the condo Diego mumbled something about not feeling well and that he was going to bed. Vivienne thought perhaps he was exhausted because they'd logged countless miles when they walked everywhere. One day they'd walked the length of Central Park and then back again. But then she dismissed the notion because at thirty-six Diego Cole-Thomas was physically in peak condition.

It was when she joined him in bed later that night she discovered his skin hot to the touch. She found a digital thermometer in a drawer under the bathroom countertop and took his temperature, panicking when it registered 102.6 degrees.

Reaching for his BlackBerry, she searched his directory for Celia's number. Vivienne knew she'd disturbed the doctor's sleep when she answered the call.

"Who is it?" Celia slurred.

"Celia, this is Vivienne. I'm sorry to call you, but Diego has a temperature over one hundred and two."

"Has he been complaining of a headache or stiff neck?" All semblance of sleep was missing from her voice.

"No. In fact, he hasn't said anything. He went to bed around four and is still asleep."

"I'll be there as soon as I can."

The line went dead before Vivienne could thank her. She returned to the kitchen to fill a plastic bag with ice, wrapping it in a towel. She had to attempt to cool down his body before his temperature spiked to dangerous levels.

Celia arrived, carrying a brown alligator medical bag stamped with her initials. She wore a pair of fitted jeans, an oversize T-shirt that probably belonged to her fiancé and a pair of running shoes. Her hair looked as if she'd used her fingers instead of a comb.

"How is he?" she asked when Vivienne opened the door.

"He's still asleep. He woke up briefly when I attempted to cool him down with an ice pack."

"Is he lucid?"

"He was when he told me what I could do with the ice."

Celia smiled, flashing dimples in both cheeks. "That sounds like my brother." She headed for the staircase. "You coming?" she asked when Vivienne hadn't moved.

"No. I'll wait down here."

Celia stared at Vivienne and then continued up the staircase to the second floor. When Vivienne called her and she'd heard the fear in her voice Celia knew there was more going on between her brother and his personal assistant than just business.

She walked into Diego's bedroom suite visibly shivering from the cool air. It was apparent Vivienne had adjusted the air-conditioning to keep him cool. Making her way over to the large bed she placed her hand on her brother's forehead. It was hot and dry to the touch.

Opening the bag, she sat on the side of the bed and took Diego's temperature. It now registered 101.8 degrees. He barely stirred when she checked his ears, throat and examined the lymph nodes in his neck and throat. As a precaution, Celia swabbed his throat and drew blood to rule out strep throat or a blood-borne infection. A very rainy spring had spawned an infestation of mosquitoes that had most municipalities spraying twice each day. She swabbed his hip with alcohol and injected him with a hypodermic filled with a potent antibiotic. Celia had brought sample packets of antibiotics Vivienne would have to give Diego every twelve hours for the next ten days.

Diego opened his eyes to find his sister standing over him. "What's up, Cee Cee?"

Smiling, she patted his cheek. "That's what I should be asking you, big brother."

Diego affected a grimace. "I think I ate something that didn't agree with me."

"I don't think so, Diego. If that were the case, then you would've been hurling up your guts. I took a throat culture and drew some blood. After they're sent to the lab I'll let you know if it's something more than a virus."

"You think it's just a virus?"

"Let's hope that's all it is, Superman." When all of the Cole-Thomases came down with a cold or the flu, Diego was the only one who seemed immune, thus he'd become known as Superman.

"I feel like—"

"Don't say it," Celia interrupted. "I gave you a shot and you should begin to feel better in a couple of days. You're lucky Vivienne called me, because if you'd been alone you could've lain here for days until someone came to look for you. And by that time it could've been too late."

Diego closed his eyes. "Damn, Cee Cee, you make it sound as if I was 'bout to check out."

Celia closed and locked her bag. "When Vivienne called me she said your body temperature was over one hundred and two, so slow your roll, Superman. I want you to take it easy for a couple of days. And when I say take it easy that means you will not leave the house. I'm leaving some antibiotics that I want you to take twice a day with food for the next ten days. I'll be back to check on you on Tuesday."

"I'll be okay."

"Sure you will. And if I find out that you took your butt into ColeDiz there will be hell to pay, Diego Samuel Cole-Thomas." Reaching for the cell phone attached to the pocket of her jeans, she dialed Joseph Cole-Wilson's number. She got his voice mail. "Hey, primo, this is Celia. I'm in Palm Beach with Diego and I'm playing doctor to my sick brother. This means that you have to step in and run ColeDiz until I give him medical clearance to return to work. Call me when you get this message. Adios."

Diego gritted his teeth and chided himself for the action because it sent sharp pains to his temple. He never could remember feeling so weak. "You had no right to tell him—"

"Don't tell me what I had a right to do, Diego!" Celia shouted. "ColeDiz will be here when you're six feet under, so do as I say and get well so you can get back to your mistress."

Diego opened his eyes. "ColeDiz is not my mistress."

"You could've fooled me. When was the last time you took time off and went somewhere?"

"That's none of your business." He didn't want to tell his sister that he and Vivienne had just spent the last four days in New York.

Celia knew arguing with her headstrong brother would end in a stalemate. "I'm going to let Vivienne know how often she should give you the medication. Feel better."

Pushing himself into a sitting position, Diego extended his arms. "Thank you, Celia."

Leaning over, she hugged Diego. "Please, just get well."

"I will follow your orders to the letter. Promise," he added when she gave him a skeptical look.

"I'm going to hold you to that promise."

"Hey, where's your ring?" Diego asked when he noticed her left hand.

"I don't wear it all the time. It gets in the way whenever I put on examining gloves."

"Is Yale taking care of you?"

Blushing, Celia lowered her gaze. "Yes. He's taking very good care of me."

"He better or I will hurt him."

Celia frowned. "When did my brothers turn into thugs?"

"What are you talking about?" Diego asked.

"First Nicky and now you. When I told Nicky that I was engaged he gave me the third degree about Yale. Then he said if Yale ever cheated on me he'd make a personal trip to Miami just to kick his ass. That's why I'm not going to tell either of you my business."

"Yale has nothing to worry about as long as he treats you right."

Celia waved a hand. "Enough about Yale and me. You get well."

"I will."

Diego waited for Celia to leave, then reached over and dimmed the table lamp. He hadn't remembered much after Henri drove him and Vivienne from the airport. The headache that had begun earlier that morning intensified during the flight until he managed to fall asleep.

He was just drifting off to sleep when Vivienne walked into the bedroom. Smiling, he stared up at her. "Thanks for being here."

Vivienne rested her hand on his stubbly cheek. It was much cooler to the touch. "I'll take care of you, Diego."

"I thought I was supposed to take care of you, *m'ija.*"

"You are, and I promised to take care of you, too." She

placed her fingertips over his parched lips. "I'm going to bring you some water, then I want you to rest. I'm going to sleep across the hall just in case whatever you have is contagious."

Diego tried smiling, but it looked like a grimace. "You're right." He closed his eyes. "I love you, *m'ija.*"

Vivienne stood at his bedside, watching as his features relaxed and his chest rose and fell in an even rhythm. "And I love you, too, *m'ijo.*" The admission had just passed her lips when his eyes opened and she met his knowing gaze. He hadn't fallen asleep.

"I love you and you love me, Vivienne. What are we going to do about it?"

Leaning over, she kissed his forehead. "We'll talk about it when you're better."

"I'm better now."

"No, you're not," she argued softly. Straightening, Vivienne gave him a sensual smile. "I'm going to get your water."

This time when Diego closed his eyes it was to sleep. He woke later to find a glass and pitcher of ice water on the bedside table. He filled a glass and drained it, then repeated the action. After the second glass he lay down to sleep again. When he woke the next day he vaguely remembered Vivienne telling him that she loved him.

But, then again maybe he'd imagined it because that was what he wanted—he wanted her to love him more than he'd wanted to become CEO of ColeDiz.

Chapter 18

Lourdes stuck her salt-and-pepper head inside Diego's office. He stood at the window, his back to the door. "Diego."

He turned to stare at her. "Yes."

"This letter is for Vivienne Neal, but it was addressed to the office."

Diego held out his hand. "Please give it to me." Walking into the office, Lourdes gave him the envelope. He glanced at it. Her name and the company name and address were typed. He turned it over. There was no return address. "Thanks."

Tapping the envelope against the palm of his hand, he wondered who would write to Vivienne at ColeDiz. She told him that she'd forwarded all of her mail to her friend's house, so whoever had sent the letter wasn't aware of that.

The summer had passed quickly, much too quickly for his comfort. He'd closed up the condo and moved to Jupiter

Island. The highlight of his day was driving home to find Vivienne waiting for him. Every once in a while he'd pretend they were married and he was going home to his wife. Somewhere in his subconscious he remembered Vivienne telling him that she loved him, but he hadn't said anything for fear that she would deny it.

It took three weeks for him to recover from what Celia said was a virus. Joseph had stepped in during his absence and executed the duties as acting CEO as if he were born to the position.

Walking over to a closet he slid back the door and slipped the envelope into the breast pocket of his jacket. His private line rang as he moved back over to the desk.

He picked up the receiver. "Diego."

"Diego…" Vivienne's words were swallowed up in a wave of sobbing.

"Vivienne. What's the matter?"

"Diego, I—I can't talk now."

His brow furrowed. "Talk to me, baby."

"Someone wants to kill me."

A spasm of fear gripped Diego, not permitting him to breathe. "Where are you?"

"I'm—I'm at the condo."

"Stay there!" he shouted. He couldn't understand why she'd left Jupiter Island to return to Palm Beach.

Everything seemed to move in slow motion as Diego grabbed his jacket. He was practically running when he passed Lourdes' desk. "Call Henri and tell him to bring the car around."

"Are you coming back, Diego?"

"Call him, Lourdes."

Henri was waiting in the parking lot when the elevator

opened. He straightened when he saw his boss's face. "Where to?"

"The condo."

Diego had barely sat down when Henri closed the door and raced around the car to take his position behind the wheel. The limo peeled out of the garage with a loud squealing of rubber on the roadway.

Questions bombarded Diego's mind like missiles during the ride. What was Vivienne doing at the condo when she should've been at the house on Jupiter Island? What had upset her so much that she'd called him in tears?

He was out of the car as soon as Henri maneuvered into the underground garage. Running to the elevator he punched the button with enough force to break his hand. The car arrived and he depressed the button for his floor, card key in hand. He slipped the key into the slot, waiting for the green light signal, then pushed open the door.

Diego found Vivienne in the kitchen, her eyes red and swollen. He pulled her up from the chair and cradled her to his chest. "What's the matter, baby?"

"I went to Alicia's to pick up my mail and I got that." She pointed to the single sheet of paper on the table. "Read it."

Still holding on to her, he picked up the paper at the same time as a chill invaded his body.

You have something I want. I gave your husband a book that he was to return to me. You have a week to find the book and if not then you're going to end up like Sean Gregory.

He glanced at the envelope. It was addressed to Vivienne at her former Connecticut address. The post office had forwarded it. "Do you know anything about this so-called book?"

Vivienne told Diego about the call from a James Kane. "He was certain that Sean had this book that belonged to him."

"Did he say what was in the book?"

"Yes. He said there were names, addresses and telephone numbers of political contributors."

Diego wanted to tell Vivienne that the names in the book were more than political contributors. "I'm going to make a telephone call to someone who might shed some light on this. You're not to leave here under any circumstances unless I'm with you. You're safer here than you'd be on Jupiter." He brushed a kiss over her mouth. "Now, go and wash that pretty face."

He walked out of the kitchen, into the home office and closed the door. As he dialed Jacob Jones's number he remembered the letter that had come to the office for Vivienne. Picking up a letter opener, he slid it under the flap and removed a single page of type. It was a copy of the letter.

"Thank you," he whispered when Jake answered the call. It took five minutes to tell Jake about the two letters.

"Don't you think it's a little odd that the forwarded letter would arrive at the same time as one addressed to ColeDiz?" Jake asked.

"I'd thought of that. What aren't you saying, Jake?"

"I'd say someone has a contact at the post office. Someone with enough security clearance to mess with the U.S. Mail. I'd suggest dusting the pages for prints, but whoever you're dealing with probably wore gloves. I'm going to let you in on a little secret."

"What's that?"

"The big boys know that Sean's accident was no accident, but a hit. Ask your lady if she or her husband has a safe-deposit box."

"Hold on, Jake."

Diego returned to the kitchen. Vivienne looked better. She'd washed her face and brushed her hair. "Do you or did your husband have a safe-deposit box?"

"I'm not sure. I remember Sean asking me to sign some bank cards because he said he had some valuable coins and he didn't want to keep them in the house."

"Where is the bank?"

"It's in D.C."

"Did he give you a key?"

Vivienne squeezed her eyes shut, trying to remember whether Sean had given her a key. "I don't remember, but I do have an envelope with some keys. Some belong to the locks at the warehouse where I've stored my furniture and there are a few others that I can't recall what they belong to."

"Is the envelope here?"

"Yes."

Diego smiled. "Please go and get it." He waited until Vivienne walked out of the kitchen to put the BlackBerry to his ear. "Did you hear that?"

"I got it," Jake confirmed. "If she does have a key, then all we have to do is find out what bank and which box."

"Can't you do that?" Diego asked.

"I'll have someone else do it."

Vivienne returned to the kitchen with a small kraft envelope, spilling its contents on the countertop. Diego picked up a key that looked as if it would fit a safe-deposit box. "I think I have the key."

"Give me a couple of hours to run the names through a database, then I'll get back to you with how you should proceed."

"Thanks, JJ."

"No problem."

Diego ended the call and pulled Vivienne to his chest. "This will be over before it can even begin."

Tilting her chin, Vivienne met his resolute stare. "How can you be so sure?"

"You're going to have to trust me, *m'ija.*"

She managed a half smile. "I suppose I don't have much of a choice, do I?"

"Yeah, you do," he drawled.

Her arms went around his slim waist inside his jacket. "He loves me, he loves me not."

"She loves me, she loves me not."

"She loves you, Diego."

Pulling back he stared at her. "Are you sure?"

Vivienne nodded. "Very, very sure."

"Show me, baby."

"Not now."

"When?"

"When this craziness is over."

Diego wanted the craziness gone, so that he and Vivienne could get on with their lives. "I'm going to cancel tonight's dinner party."

"Don't cancel because of me. Please go."

"Not without you, Vivienne."

She knew how important the dinner party was for Diego. A Mexican coffee producer wanted to sell off his remaining plantation to ColeDiz to cover a mountain of debts from ill-advised investments.

"Okay, I'll go."

"Are you sure you want to do this, *m'ija?*"

"Yes. After all, you did promise to protect me. And the jerk or jerks, whoever wrote that letter, gave me a week to come up with this phantom book."

Diego frowned. "It's not funny."

Her frown matched his. "Either I make jokes or cry, and joking is preferable to crying."

Cradling Vivienne's face, he pressed a kiss to her forehead. "Let's lie down and rest until it's time to leave."

"Okay."

Diego led her up the staircase and down the hallway and into his bedroom suite. He took his time undressing her, then himself. Carrying her as if she were a piece of fragile china, he placed her on the mattress and got into bed beside her.

Vivienne turned on her side, pressing her buttocks to Diego's groin. She'd become so accustomed to sleeping with him that she couldn't remember when she hadn't shared his bed. They'd become a couple in and out of bed. She knew it bothered his mother and grandmother that they were living together, but she wasn't bothered by it.

What they failed to realize was that she'd only been single for eight months, and she wanted to experience a modicum of independence before exchanging vows again. True, she lived with Diego, but he didn't monitor her comings and goings. She took time out to visit the salon, go shopping and visit Alicia. The week before, she and Alicia had driven down to South Beach to hang out at a popular club. They'd left the club at closing and when she called Diego to tell him she was on her way back to Jupiter Island he insisted she spend the night instead of attempting to make the drive in the dark.

When Alicia mentioned that Diego must really trust her, Vivienne's response was that he didn't have a choice. If she was going to cheat on him she didn't have to go all the way to Miami to sleep with a man. She loved Diego, loved everything about him. Once he'd understood that she wouldn't stand to be talked down to, then their relationship had changed. She closed her eyes and willed her mind blank.

Sleep wasn't as kind to Diego as he lay listening to Vivienne's even breathing. He hadn't wanted to believe that someone wanted Vivienne dead. The people who'd killed Sean Gregory had no compunction about killing Vivienne if she didn't come up with a book she never knew existed.

The phone he'd tucked under his leg vibrated and he slipped out of bed and into the sitting room to answer it. "Diego."

"I found the bank. It's in D.C. near the Dupont Circle Metro. Gregory opened a box in his and his wife's name. If she has the key, then she'll be able to open the box."

"I hope you're not suggesting she do that. What would stop these thugs from taking the book, then killing her?"

"When she goes to open the box, she won't be alone. We'll have agents in and around the bank, so she'll be protected."

"Hell no, Jake. You're not going to use Vivienne as a decoy."

"She's going to have to do it, Diego. She's the only one authorized to open that box."

"That's bull, and you know it. What happens when someone dies without a will? The vultures are waiting to punch the lock and see what's hiding inside."

"What if we get a female agent who resembles Vivienne?

They'll be dressed alike, so if anyone is watching when she comes out of the bank, they'll think it's her."

"That sounds like a better plan."

"I'll try to be on hand to make certain everything goes down okay."

"What do you want us to do now?" Diego asked.

"Wait for me to contact you as to when it's going down. Meanwhile keep her close to you. I'll have a few agents close by in case these guys decide to move before the week is up."

"Thanks again, JJ."

"I should be the one thanking you. If we catch a few big fish in this net, then I should be up for a nice promotion."

Diego wanted to ask who was going to promote him but knew Jake wouldn't tell him. "Good luck."

"Do me a favor, Diego?"

"What's that?"

"Make an honest woman out of her."

"I've tried, but she won't bite."

"You're losing your touch, Diego. I can remember a time when women were proposing to you."

"Those days are long gone. At my age I'm a lot more discriminating."

Jake snorted. "Have you thought that maybe you've met your match?"

"There's nothing to think about. I have."

"Later, Diego."

"Later JJ."

Vivienne walked into the mansion facing Biscayne Bay on Diego's arm, a frozen smile on her face. A fluted platinum-gray silk slip dress swirled around a pair of matching Manolo Blahnik stilettos whenever she took a step. She'd brushed her hair off her face into a chignon, adding a jeweled clip to the coil. Her makeup was dramatic: smoky eyes and carnelian-red lips.

It'd taken every ounce of courage for her to go through with her promise to attend the dinner party with Diego. She'd managed to quell an attack of nerves until she saw the small automatic handgun he'd tucked into a shoulder holster. Knowing the man she loved was carrying a weapon made the threat even more real.

Diego offered his hand to a tall, slender, middle-aged man with thinning black hair. "Señor Montalvo. It's a pleasure to meet you again."

The Mexican businessman took the proffered hand. "It is indeed my pleasure to see you again, Mr. Cole-Thomas." His sharp black gaze shifted to Vivienne. "What do we have here?"

"Ms. Vivienne Neal, *mi novia,*" Diego added, when he saw the spark of lust in the man's eyes.

Vivienne nodded. *"Estoy encantado,"* she said softly.

Jorge Montalvo leaned closer and smiled like a Cheshire cat. He hadn't expected her to speak Spanish. "I'm the one who is totally charmed, Señorita Neal. Mr. Cole-Thomas has exquisite taste in women."

I don't like you, Vivienne thought. The man had too many teeth and she didn't like the way he'd tried peering down the bodice of her dress. She gave Diego a saccharine smile. "Darling, could you please get me something to drink. I'm feeling a little light-headed."

Diego caught her meaning immediately. "Of course, *m'ija.* What do you think?" he asked when they were out of earshot of Montalvo.

"He's creepy."

"In other words, you don't like him?"

"On a scale of one to ten, ten being intensely dislike, then he's a ten."

"Thank you, *m'ija*. Now, if you don't mind I'd rather drink at home."

Vivienne had no choice but to follow Diego as he practically pulled her across the marble floor. "Where are we going?"

"Home. I only brought you here to meet Jorge Montalvo. If you would've said you liked him, then I would've stayed and done business with the man. But since you don't like him, we're going home."

Vivienne quickened her pace in order to keep up with Diego's longer legs. "You had me put on makeup, try to balance myself in a pair of stilettos all for a test."

"Don't forget, a very important test. The man wants me to buy his company. I don't need another coffee plantation, especially in Mexico. But you dressing up will not go to waste. We'll have our own private party at home."

"Are you going to dance with me?"

"Uh-huh. We're going to dance, kiss and anything else you want."

She moved closer to his side. "That sounds like a plan."

Henri held the rear door open as she slipped into the limo. She smiled at Diego when he sat beside her. He looked so incredibly handsome in a navy-blue suit and silk platinum tie. She'd continued to check his socks, making certain they were a match.

Diego pressed a button on the radio, then pulled Vivienne into his arms. He closed his eyes when he listened to Alicia Keys singing "Like You'll Never See Me Again."

"I love this song."

"The words are so sad."

"The sun doesn't shine every day."

A beat passed. "Do I make you happy, Diego?"

He opened his eyes. "Yes."

"But I could make you happier."

"How, baby?"

"I could marry you."

Diego froze as if he'd been impaled with a sharp instrument. "Yes you could, but you won't."

"You're wrong, *m'ijo*. I would marry you if you proposed properly."

Sitting up straight, he stared at her as if she were a stranger. "Don't play with me, Vivienne."

"I'm not playing, Diego. I love you and I know I want to spend the rest of my life with you."

"Do you want a child?"

"I want babies, lots of babies."

Diego felt as if he couldn't breathe. He thought he was dreaming and when he woke up everything would be a joke. He lifted her onto his lap. "We're going to get married and you're going to give me lots of beautiful, intelligent, feisty little babies."

He held her in his arms until they returned to the condo. Then he got down on one knee and proposed properly, slipping the engagement ring his great-grandmother had given him on her finger.

They had their own dinner party, cooking and dancing together. Then, when they slipped into bed together it was the first night of the rest of their lives together.

Chapter 19

"You're going to have to remove your ring, Mrs. Gregory."

Vivienne slipped off the diamond ring and handed it to Diego to hold for her. It was about to begin. James Kane had called her again to ask if she had the book. She told him that she had an idea of where it might be and that she was going to Washington to open a safe-deposit box. She'd been directed to give him the name of the bank.

A female agent who looked enough like Vivienne to be her sister had entered the bank wearing a tailored suit and heels, but once inside had changed into jeans, T-shirt and running shoes.

She and Diego had flown into D.C. the night before and were taken to a hotel where federal agents had been gathering to set a trap to catch the man or men threatening the widow of a murdered House Member.

"Pull your cap lower over your forehead," ordered the senior agent in charge.

"The taxi's here," called out another agent stationed by the door. "Are you ready, Mrs. Gregory?"

"Yes." Vivienne didn't mind them calling her Mrs. Gregory, because come the end of the year she would be known as Vivienne Cole-Thomas.

She was escorted down the stairwell instead of the elevator by federal police who were stationed outside the door on each floor. She curbed the urge to glance up at the snipers on the rooftops of buildings surrounding the hotel. The agent/taxi driver got out and held the rear door open for her. The ride was exactly three minutes door to door.

Vivienne got out in front of the bank and walked inside. She approached an officer on the platform and showed him her key. The nattily dressed elderly gentleman escorted her into the area for safe-deposit boxes. She signed the card, handing it to the bank officer who checked her signature against the one on file.

He took out a key and inserted it in one of the locks, then took hers and opened the door. She took out a long, slender metal box and placed it on a counter in another room. "I'll call you when I'm ready to put it back." He nodded and walked away.

Vivienne didn't know whether he was an actual bank employee or an agent. Her pulse was racing when she lifted the top and peered inside. It was there! A small black leather-bound book. It was the only item in the box.

Slipping the book in her waistband under the T-shirt, she closed the empty box and slipped it back into the space allotted for it.

"I'll take the book, Mrs. Gregory."

Vivienne turned and looked into the face of a woman so much like her own. She handed the book to the female agent, then sat down on a low stool to wait. The seconds ticked off as she waited as she'd been instructed to do. She'd almost given up hope when she heard footsteps. Rising to her feet, she saw Diego and another man coming toward her.

Launching herself against his chest, she clung to him as if he were her lifeline. *"M'ijo."*

He captured her mouth with his, stealing the breath from her lungs. "It's over, baby. They were waiting for her when she left the bank, but her men rounded them up."

"Thank goodness."

Reaching into his pocket, Diego took out the ring and slipped it on her finger. "This is where it belongs."

She snuggled closer to his body. "And this is where I belong." The agent cleared his throat and they sprang apart.

"The car is here that'll take you to the airport."

"Let's go, baby. Let's go home."

December 26

Vivienne Kay Neal stood in the garden of the house on Jupiter Island exchanging vows with Diego Samuel Cole-Thomas. It was only one event in a week of nonstop festivities that began when the Coles and Neals gathered in West Palm Beach for Christmas and would culminate with a New Year's Eve celebration rumored to be wilder than the previous year.

Diego had made an honest woman out of her before she'd begun showing. She was six weeks pregnant and she and Diego, on the advice of her obstetrician, delayed taking their honeymoon until she was past her first trimester.

Her voice carried easily in the hushed silence when she

promised to love her husband all the days of her life. Alicia, who stood in as her bridesmaid, handed her a platinum band. Smiling up at Diego, she slipped it on his finger. The exchange of rings and vows meant she was now Vivienne Cole-Thomas.

She stood in the receiving line, greeting those who'd come to witness her special day. Harry and Anissa had come with their baby daughter, who'd inherited her father's curly red hair.

Celia and Yale drove up from Miami, but had to leave by midnight to begin their two o'clock shift.

Peyton and Raquel came with the news they were expecting a baby. Brant and Bay stopped by and left a gift certificate for Waterford crystal. Nicholas Cole-Thomas left his horses long enough to congratulate his brother. Jacob Jones or JJ stopped by to witness the exchange of vows, then left as quietly as he'd come.

Elizabeth Gregory came down with the elder Neals. Sean's mother seemed in better spirits than Vivienne had seen her in a long time. She'd waited, but now she had closure.

The FBI arrested James McGhie, aka James Kane, for his involvement in Sean's murder. The former CIA-trained assassin didn't have to snitch on those who'd hired him because Sean's little black book contained enough facts to topple venerable politicians who were forced to resign in disgrace. Reporters were chomping at the bit, waiting for the new session of Congress to begin to see who would be subpoenaed and indicted and who would be sentenced to serve time in jail.

There were rumblings from some members that Sean had become supersnitch, informing on his peers, and he got what he deserved. To Vivienne he'd become a hero, but in the end he paid for it with his life.

The day she'd buried Sean, she put away her past. Now she had to look to the future with a new husband and a new baby on the way.

She danced with her husband, father, brother and then with every Cole male. Those not tall enough to reach her waist, hugged her legs. The sun set beyond the horizon and instead of winding down, the noise escalated.

Instead of tossing her bouquet, Vivienne handed it to Celia, who blushed furiously when she showed it to her fiancé.

Diego found his bride talking with his parents. "May I see you please?" he whispered in her ear.

Vivienne followed him to a secluded area of the garden. "What do you want?"

"I want to take my wife home."

"We're already home."

"Let's go back to the condo and hang out there for a while." She gave him a saucy smile. "And do what?"

"Nothing tonight, *m'ija*. You're exhausted and I don't want anything to happen to you or our baby."

"When are we going to tell everyone about the baby?"

Dipping his head, he brushed his mouth over hers. "New Year's Eve."

"Hey, get a room!" Joseph called out.

"That's what we intend to do," Diego countered.

Bending slightly, he swept Vivienne up in his arms and carried her around to where he'd parked his car. The roar of the Jaguar engine was drowned out by the voices raised in song as the lead singer for the live band launched into a popular song.

Her gown billowed around her as she slumped in the

seat and closed her eyes. She'd fought the pull of the sexy man who'd promised to go after what he wanted, and when he got it he didn't intend to let it go.

Vivienne felt the same, because she didn't intend to let him go.

It was as if both had their own secret agendas.

National bestselling author

ROCHELLE ALERS

Naughty

Parties, paparazzi, red-carpet catfights...

Wild child Breanna Parker's antics have
always been a ploy to gain attention from
her diva mother and record-producer father.
As her marriage implodes, Bree moves to
Rome. There she meets charismatic Reuben,
who becomes both her romantic and business
partner. But just as she's enjoying her
successful new life, Bree is confronted
with a devastating scandal that threatens
everything she's worked so hard for....

Coming the first week of March 2009
wherever books are sold.

KIMANI PRESS™

www.kimanipress.com
www.myspace.com/kimanipress

KPRA1280309

What if you met your future
soul mate, but were too busy
to give them the time of day?

ANGELA BASSETT&
COURTNEY B. VANCE

THE *NEW YORK TIMES* BESTSELLING REAL-LIFE STORY…

friends: a love story

They ran for years as friends in the same circles, had some
hits—but mostly misses—with other partners and shared one
dreadful first date together. Then, Courtney and Angela connected.

Experience the real-life love story of this inspirational African-
American celebrity couple. See how they've carved a meaningful
life together despite humble beginnings, family tragedy and the
ups and downs of stardom with love, faith and determination.

Available the first week of February 2009
wherever books are sold.

KIMANI PRESS™

From perennial bachelor to devoted groom…

For you *i Do*

Acclaimed Author
ANGIE DANIELS

Feisty Bianca Beaumont is engaged! She's blissful,
until friend London Brown proves she's marrying the
wrong guy. Now Bianca needs a husband to prevent
a scandal, so London proposes. Their marriage is
supposed to be in name only, but their sizzling
attraction may change everything.

"Each new Daniels romance is a true joy."
—*Romantic Times BOOKreviews*

Coming the first week of May 2009 wherever books are sold.

KIMANI™
ROMANCE

www.kimanipress.com
www.myspace.com/kimanipress

KPAD1130509

ESSENCE BESTSELLING AUTHOR

GWYNNE FORSTER

Swept Away

Veronica Overton was once one of the most respected women in Baltimore, but now her reputation is in ruins. With her confidence shattered, Veronica sets out to rebuild her life. Yet her search leads to family secrets— and ignites a smoldering attraction to Schyler Henderson. And not even their conflict and distrust of one another can cool the passion between them!

Coming the first week of May 2009 wherever books are sold.

ARABESQUE®

www.kimanipress.com
www.myspace.com/kimanipress

KPGF1590509

NATIONAL BESTSELLING AUTHOR

ROCHELLE ALERS

INVITES YOU TO MEET THE BEST MEN...

Close friends Kyle, Duncan and Ivan have become rich,
successful co-owners of a beautiful Harlem brownstone. But
they lack the perfect women to share their lives with—until
true love transforms them into grooms-to-be....

Man of Fate
June 2009

Man of Fortune
July 2009

Man of Fantasy
August 2009

ARABESQUE®